T0121934

MONOLITH

'Short stories for tall people de-boxing

An explosively beautiful walk through one man's lives - told
in six empirical, fact-fiction short stories. Life is different
than what you were 'taught.' Yes, brace yourself…

ROY WOODWARD

BALBOA.
PRESS

A DIVISION OF HAY HOUSE

Copyright © 2014 Roy Woodward.

All rights reserved. No part of this book may be used or reproduced by any means,
graphic, electronic, or mechanical, including photocopying, recording, taping or by any
information storage retrieval system without the written permission of the publisher
except in the case of brief quotations embodied in critical articles and reviews.

Balboa Press books may be ordered through booksellers or by contacting:

Balboa Press
A Division of Hay House
1663 Liberty Drive
Bloomington, IN 47403
www.balboapress.com
1 (877) 407-4847

Because of the dynamic nature of the Internet, any web addresses or links contained in
this book may have changed since publication and may no longer be valid. The views
expressed in this work are solely those of the author and do not necessarily reflect the views
of the publisher, and the publisher hereby disclaims any responsibility for them.

LEGAL DISCLAIMER: As a result of much dedicated prayer and fasting to VERIFY over 50
years researching ancient and modern subjects from all over the world - I found the subjects
you are about to read to be Truth personified. This means that my Source, your Source;
gave me a green light to help you. That Source, our Mutual Father; is who you can contact
if you find anything you don't agree with or that offends you. Ok? My First Amendment
Rights are herein declared as is my right to express my views under the obvious Laws of our
Constitution pertaining to Free Speech and a Free Press. Otherwise don't mess with what
might be a big blessing to you and millions - despite our differences of opinion or experience
with things far deeper in mental and spiritual concepts than you might not realize – yet...

The author of this book does not dispense medical advice or prescribe the use of any
technique as a form of treatment for physical, emotional, or medical problems without the
advice of a physician, either directly or indirectly. The intent of the author is only to offer
information of a general nature to help you in your quest for emotional and spiritual well-
being. In the event you use any of the information in this book for yourself, which is your
constitutional right, the author and the publisher assume no responsibility for your actions.

Any people depicted in stock imagery provided by Thinkstock are models,
and such images are being used for illustrative purposes only.
Certain stock imagery © Thinkstock.

Printed in the United States of America.

ISBN: 978-1-4525-1433-8 (sc)
ISBN: 978-1-4525-1435-2 (hc)
ISBN: 978-1-4525-1434-5 (e)

Library of Congress Control Number: 2014908465

Balboa Press rev. date: 5/28/2014

BOOK 1

MARVELOUS HOUSE OF INFINITE JOY

A true novel by Roy-David Woodward

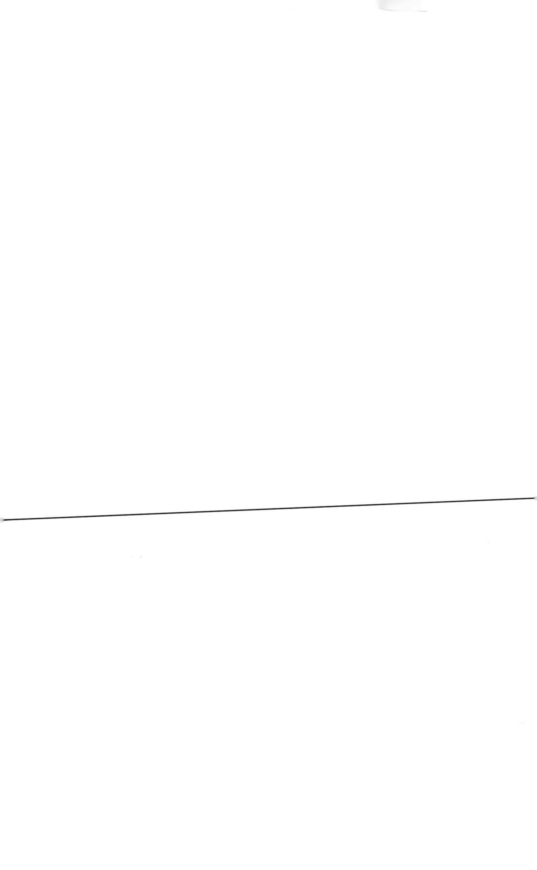

FOREWORD

WHAT IF LOVE IS.... You have it figured out yet?

- A good feeling to be with, on, or by someone,
- Better than being alone,
- Great sensual, sexual experience,
- A positive way to keep hate and hurt away,
- Makes cold nights warmer,
- Eating out in nice places,
- Traveling together, learning new things,

Well, the list could go on and it does with most of you. What IS Love, though? And is it the glue that holds the cosmos and you together? How do you 'do' love, keep it, feed it without boredom, resentment? Is good sex love? Does even 'really' good sex last...and then what? Is love in today's society old fashioned? Does it negate individualism...Is love of self enough and frequent sex partners just ice cream on the cake of life? Indirectly I'll be asking lots of questions you must have asked - forgive that, but they do get deeper thinking started –instead of you staying in dismal ruts. Does sex outside of marriage give guilt trips AND what is Marriage, Karezza, Kama Sutra, the Bridal Chamber besides ancient premises and rules, myths from old foggies...or 'Monolithly' covered up truths?

This treatise is for you, not my wallet, It's my duty because I found out...and I owe you.

Once I thought, (because society, schools, books taught it), that Love was a warm, fuzzy feeling, then sex, then marriage that kept the planet spinning with people, on-going creation basically. And like you, probably, I got caught up in "feel good" - the opposite sex. That led to a lot of problems Mom didn't tell me about and Dad was too macho to warn me of.

Later after most of the bruises, angers, resentments, failures had healed or been disinfected – I found it.

Simple logic, commonsense hit me (I was ready from the pain I had inflicted on myself.) Pain is simply a signal/warning that something's wrong, so don't ever try to DRUG that hollow, needing feeling out of the way, listen to it...

I realized my pain came from a source or The Source-Force - an automatic signal system – or Person-Power that had obviously 'made' me. All of me- If I could experience pain and others didn't - and things went well with them, there had to be positive-negative ways of doing things that caused definite results:

CAUSE AND EFFECT- Just related to Science labs? Nope.... Maybe, what you think, speak, do... you get?... Sooner or later... even if you don't realize it at the time? Right. Basic feel good or confusion. Complex when you resist deep stuff. Far deeper than Church, Sunday School or History 101

I began investigating Good and Evil, Right and Wrong , Destiny - all of the ups and downs in religion, science and societies failures. Most of it was a dead end search because groups, commercial power mongers who only cared for self - to be the head hid it. Big Brother or Big Daddy – or just plain Big Shot. (Ego, "Look at me, I'm important, pet me, pay me.") You get it. This disappointment led me to Eastern concepts and teachings much older by tens of thousands; than orthodox Christianity or any other religion. It became too obvious and quite a shock - that scoundrels way, way back in pre-Vatican days knew the Truth of Life and Love, but stole it, burned it in libraries after making copies from Memphis and Alexandria Egypt: Hundreds of thousands of papyri, scrolls, books, animal skin engravings, clay codices. A super macho, male, chauvinistic, patriarchal cult built the Holy Apostolic Military Catholic Church. What was bought, liked was copied by other groups, what was hated - was fought, hidden. Positive-Negative arose to baffle people like you and me – well meaning people. What is right, what is wrong? Too busy actually, to keep up with such questions it birthed a hierarchy of priests "Follow me, I am a full time God Man", they roared. "See my robes and our properties, our grandeur." Yes, all gained from your tithings, taxes, offerings: – your sweat and time -which if not given, reaped death, torture, prison. (Read Catholic inquisition, Cathar massacres, Assassinations), Apostalic mandates saying, doing things you knew or felt were haywire.

And what did you get? Intimidations, Guilt trips, Hell Fire, Damnation and Servitude - but you – you were too wrapped up in your society, church or job to stand up say anything. 'Go along with it, what does God expect?– the priests, the politicians have the clout, money, guns and tanks.' and you acquiesced, becoming Joe and Joan Average. Make a living, don't rock any boats, send your kids to a system that lies about history and religions – especially about Spirit ...and 'spirits' in their compartmentalized, earned - Heaven or Hell - Like your mom and dad, your husband or wife – or child, (Those people, humans who had passed on to Happy Hunting Grounds or Heavenly Sectors). If you were Amer-Indian you went there and arrowed super giant buffalo, lived safe of other tribes. If a Baptist, endless adorations of the Vatican figures of a Savior and his cannibalistic blood you got to drink in endless, futile communions. Another life later- a hard life of appeasing them all over again. Until you saw through it... Tossing your 'free' crown at a huge figure above you on an ornate throne. If a Cannibal, all of your enemies you could boil and digest for great strength, And if a Catholic, help from a pensive woman who birthed your Savior, not by the natural way - but by 'Holy Spirit impregnation.'

But worst of all...if an Atheist, or non-Christian, endless burnings in a lake of fire. Forever! No reprieve, no forgiveness, no helpful teachings to the contrary. All because they or YOU screwed up in a Garden, somewhere in time - or before? "Just Get OUT! We aren't going to bother with you punk rebels, we're out of patience, you have to obey Big Brothers', (That's plural, Gods' back there in that Garden) 'we don't want you copying our secrets...and living forever and knowing all we know.' That's a paraphrase, Friend and it tells it like it is according to your, 'Good Book.' Sure, it will hurt when you look deeply at what it says, what you were taught from paper and ink – and men - with an ax to grind: Your submission, your money.

Too bold? For most of you, Yes, but necessary also to add this: You have NO WAY OUT, no way according to them That's what most religions and counselors say… "Do it or else or go to Hell." Like the sound of that doctrine? Question: Would you as a parent do the same…? Stone your child for choosing a different path or God? (Read Old Testament) Hierarchy knows best. Shut up! Work, educate your kids our way to more futility and disappointments? Your sole 'authoritative' source – 'Them, 'they who make the rules you don't get to vote for, they take your money...and your life if you deny their power. Your governments, your shepherds, they who are supposed to be your servants-helpers. Authorities? WOW...Think Friend. This is all of your preliminary, your forced Pre-School you choose for finding Love – You did it, still do it the hard way. Because you refused to think or rock boats due to the consequences, (Read FEAR). Sorry, that's it… No wonder it was withheld from you… till maybe now?

ENTER LOVE: So listen well, I don't want to feed you more disappointments like this politico-religio-big pharma system: Love came from our Creator Source Force - Good Big Guy before Earth – way out there, somewhere. That love resulted from 'His' aloneness. (Lots of theories about that, the where, the background, whether he was 'the' God or Supreme we think we know – or was He a spin-off of other Creators, Sons. (BTW Mars, Venus ,Moon and other planets now more than hint that Earth wasn't the first human abode.) People and their creations do show out there while religionists whine about evolution versus creation Big Bangs! Yet know this: Out of 'Someone's need to create us, came love and our need likewise. We goofed it with lust - orgasm pre-occupation, programmed mental and physical masturbation and dissipation with quick-high drug cultures which governments foster – not fight as you believe. Billions in profit they dare not end. I could give more details but that would be usurping your right and need to research, fast and pray to get back on track: "Except you become as a little Child you shall in no wise, enter the Kingdom of Heaven!" Pretty corny? Hardly… You need the excitement-adventure now, of asking, QUESTIONING, searching at last, in your unknowingness - like an innocent child does with his Dad and Mother so you come through this disgusting impasse we each have allowed in our sold off freedoms.

So here are a few things simple things I did, do believe and have tried and proven - to study out if it hits you after all my yapping: Yes, your ability to 'receive' Love can be airlifted so hang on despite your doubts and cynicism: Organic Vegetarian diet, raw foods! Oats, Millet, Quinua, Sesame, Nuts, all Berries, Apples, NO wheat or soy of any kind and that means pastries, bread, etc. (GMO dangers) no form of dairy products unless they're raw, organically certified. (Goats milk is exceptional for you and infants), Distilled or highly filtered water, Sun every day without chemical sunscreen (use only Aloe Vera plant gel you raise), especially winter sun baths for your Vitamin D essentials, candle meditations, self massage, Apple Cider Vinegar hot baths, (two gallons to a tub), Dry brush your skin (before that vinegar bath). Do this bath before bed, wake renewed. No anti-biotics except natural onion and garlic, Acidophilus capsules or simmered broths with onions and garlic, (For parasite prevention and removal I use Black Walnut powder with lots of raw chopped Garlic swallowed with Pineapple juice), Fresh Parsley-Dandelion herb tea drink, Cayenne pepper capsules, Cat's Claw herb capsules or herb powder, Green Tea (plain), Cloves and Black Walnut Powder bitter tea rid the parasites you don't like to admit 90% of Americans have. Even the blatantly lying Depts. of Agriculture and Heart Research Foundations say parasites are the causes of the TWENTY MAJOR DISEASES of man and animals as they feed on your weakest body parts, heart and organs Yeah.

And most important –– FASTING and Gratitude. Took me many short and long (44 days) no food, just distilled water. My axiom about fasting is: 'You cannot have full discernment unless you do: The true Prophets fast of at least 40 days.

Love, attaining your mate, (Twin Flame) IS very difficult to achieve, unless you overcome anger, resentment, fear, appetite and obnoxious societal sex. I believe they used to call that 'self' control?

OK, this is the list above for minimum upkeep of the human body system to be clean, worthy of true Love – your ultimate achievement and gift to yourself ! Not your family docs way - he forgot to go natural. High tech and its profits got to him. His ancient Hippocratic Oath said. "DO NO HARM". Today the fully resistant strains of wonder drugs are scaring even them as they write your prescriptions. Simple commonsense is: You don't kill both good and bad bacteria by killing everything in your blood and liver with dead, inert, non enzymic poison chemistry! Really so simple it's stupid to let them convince you of their poisons. That's called thinking, compassion, commonsense and feeding life into yourself daily. All this detail to find and know LOVE? Yes – did you think it was going to be a rose garden?

Set back, smile. Here's how you learn Love and real Marriage. It might seem far too simple for most couples - of course one of you usually will rebel and refuse to try it. Which one? You guessed it, Husband, 'The Orgasm Machine'…

*Enter KAREZZA, KAMA SUTRA and THE BRIDAL CHAMBER on the internet pages. Most women will do a big Aha! Husbands scoff. Orgasm happy couples or individuals will have a long way to go unless they are very rare and very spiritual.

Last, the hardest of all: Getting a real handle on how the Vatican has fooled you about loved ones, their living spirits on the other side of mortality. That's one subject they didn't dare let you know about – allowing YOU a right and savvy to speak with them about anything, any question….and then finding out you were robbed of vital truths by false historians and religious zealots.

Of course there is a Caveat:

You must be cleaned up in body, bloodstream, lymph and thoughts. Mind you, not perfect - but down the road to handle deep stuff hidden from you, NOT by God or Source but by greedy Men who want you stupid living like re-acting subservient - un-thinking dutiful, patriotic slaves, blind militarists in creeds, oaths and bondage, feeding their wars, their divorce courts, their prisons because you didn't know, (or wouldn't try) this no cost wisdom .

DIGEST THIS Free Download "Antiquities Unveiled" By Jonathon Roberts in the 1800s. Good luck. This will be a big test of your surrender to Truth not spiritual ego trips. What you thought was from God, but was defiled by Man.

"Freely you have received, freely give." Yes, Share this explosive free Download by Professor Roberts. Bless all the honest men of our past for what you will find.

Now go ahead – read that after you read this book of mine. Read like your life depends on it...

CHAPTER 1

DAMMIT! I'M GOING BACK! She threw herself out of the huge arched doorway with all of the pent up fury in her lithe Olympic trained body. Jami Portchuka was mad, madder than she had ever known herself or anyone – Swinging down the glistening golden corridor she stopped at the Lagoon fountain –a mass of wetted color, phantasms of iridescent beauty spraying up a hundred feet, containing itself in but a circle the size of an umbrella from the deep bottom up to the fanning top.

And she wept. Great convulsing sobs jerked her platinum head. She fell on the counter of the Lagoon, low, wide, stone-like but soft, resilient to her splendid form of sinew, muscle and grace undisputed, never beaten down there – On Earth.

The two tall figures of The Counselor and his aid flowed out through the great arch, looking down through the sparkling, dancing sheen of the hall. Shaking their heads, lowering them on their large chests, they reentered. The Hall and everything seemed to dim, the colors fading into milky gloss.

I don't know what to do –for once in my life up here, I JUST don't know what to DO! He hit the marbled slab desk. It quivered. His Aid started to speak. The taller man waved – No, not now, let ME THINK! This is an epic condition. The Rules say...he drifted off, and our Hearts say... drifting still. The two men sat down in Lotus, their sheen robes wrapped tight around them. Quiet enveloped them like a blue fog. They wept.

Jami Portchuka? Yeah, that's her wallet, this is her. Any breath? She's gone, Mitch, what a waste... Do you know who this is?! Yep, I know.

His eye wetted. He brushed it away. The Gurney Sheet drew across her bloodied face, her hair a tangle of debris and water. The two paramedics drove silent down the rain slicked blacktop, blood dripping silently down to the ribbed aluminum floor.

Caring for, countering hostile or sorrowful situations for those in Heavenly compartments requires superior qualities, the best of good help. The two counselors knew their job, had certain leeway for unusual cases. Tonight in Sector 27 the lights dimmed and 'good help' went to bed with an ice bag on each head. Had they finally come to view the un-solvable problem?

Outside Complex A, Sector 27, a dim but eerie soft rose - violet hue, like gentle fog, spread slowly into the chasm of valleys and canyons that was known as the Green Belt where no being had ever been allowed or known to have visited. Miles high Redwoods, dwarfing those below on Earth, swayed and moaned in the light of three large Moons and their enfolding, spinning layers of specked swirls - few knew what housed their orbs for those specks were Worlds -entered occasionally by the black entrances that sucked and pulled as a mouth breathing from below the ceaseless canyons. Things here were large, infinite and mind challenging. One of the counselors gazed out of his bedroom window. Adjusting his ice bag he breathed slowly, 'We need YOUR help, these two are different and this is different, we mustn't disappoint them but precedent trys to rule my head, Father. My heart cries out for Jami and Clint.' At his last words the three Moons seemed to increase in light and rotation. He rubbed his eyes, the ice bag emitted a slight steam as its contents immediately melted. He fell back on his pillow, tears and a smile fashioning his face. He remembered Earth and the many times he had needed such signs that his prayers were heard... 'It will work out', and he drifted off to sleep and dreamed of weddings, laughter and a pair of 'twins' -a boy and a girl...named Jami and Clint, in a future long ago and far away...

CHAPTER 2

He had no idea she had felt what he was feeling, didn't even know for sure where she would be, how she would be. A form of Heavenly Rehab? A Ceremony of White Angels? Her parents there, crying for joy, while he was tearing his insides out in sorrow, hate, disbelief? Ohhh.. Why...? That was all that would come out or even make sense to speak – WHY?

So the nights came, the long, dark silent nights came. Did they go? He couldn't tell –all one night of wet pillows, a torn sheet or two, the clock no longer ticking it's cheap, creeping, click –click as it went on it's duty of grief bearer now a mass at the bottom of the wall across from the bed. How many nights, he couldn't tell, all alike. What was HE doing like this, no reason to just give in, feel sorry... for who? Everyone that knew Jami. Thinking her name, not even speaking it anymore made it's mark on his heart. He sat, now, at the kitchen table where once they had thrown oatmeal out of the circular box, at each other that New Years night. When they had kissed long, strong and he had scooped her up, taken her out under the million stars and kissed her – and kissed her, there on their awesome patio, in their awesome garden under that awesome Moon. That's how she had described it to her girlfriend, she said...Awesome! It wasss, Jami, it wasss...

He got dressed, first in a month. Then a knock at the door. Doorbells broke - he reminded himself. FIX it!

In front of the screen a slight, brown man, scarcely 5'4", maybe 110 soaked. He grinned as Clint opened the door puzzled. Jami send... Clint trembled as the man held his hand engulfed in Clint's. Whaatt? Clint san, Jami send!.. Jami! As if he didn't know who Jami was. What do you mean, Little Fella? You want Jami, come?... Clint San, listen to Little Fella... His jaw aside, Clint stood, one hip, knee bent, hand on the screen casing. Look...I don't know what you're here for, what you want or if this is some creepy joke, but...NoNo! No!, Clint San, Charlie tell true!, he took a breath, She want come back, love Clint San, need Clint San help! He raised on tip toe, grabbed Clint's shoulders, pulled him down. Whispered - me Angel..... No tell peoples!

CHAPTER 3

Look, Jami, Girl, we got's a problem - like you say down there. Big problem. You are supposed...to be happy, joyful, totally satisfied up here. You're miserable and, uhh, He's... blaming US! Do you realize Eternity, Infinity, Paradise – Well, yes, It/He/They have RULES! The tall man spread and un-spread his hands. And... uhh, you want us to change millions and millions of eons of rules –for you? It's unheard of, unreal, unreal, Jami! Have mercy, for cryin out loud. UNREAL? She glared, Why you…YOU, are unreal, you smug Rule Maker…you…Now wait, Jami, I don't make... Well, why are YOU talking to me? I WANT THE MANAGER –Big Guy! He faded out. Him, his robe, the room, everything –nothing around her – Then she heard…OK Jami, there is one thing we can do for you. Get you an audience…She looked around, straining her eyes at the sudden fog in the room, WHO? Yeah. Big Guy – Kind of... on the Net, ya know? Not here but... Well, it will be 'Personal Audience One.' That's what they call it and, uhh, He WILL listen. I won't promise anything, might be a waste, but you will never be the same after talking to Him – I promise. She squirmed in her lounge chair. OK, do that, When? Tomorrow morning EARLY, Four. Where? Our back room control pod. I'm there, Friend! She giggled as she slapped his robe, skipped out and down toward the Lagoon fountain. Wheee! It's working! Neck turned back toward the doorway she yelled, Hey! Thanks, thanks, I love you... and she FELL into the Lagoon. The Lagoon's under surface and side lights dimmed, then shot forth with extra brilliance, the tall spray fountain suddenly stopped dead in the air at ten feet, water bubbled furiously as Jami Portchuka got caught in the new whirlpool surrounding her. Spinning furiously for all of five minutes she was flipped out like leaf – into the arms of - the tallest most impressive woman she had ever seen.

15

CHAPTER 4

Clint O'Connell picked up Charlie, the self-proclaimed Angel. He sat him down on the Pool Table eye to eye with the grinning man. OK, Shoot!

The little brown man looked up at Clint's face, the jaw thrust forward, the eyes blinking, the big hands up alongside his shoulders. Head cocked, he looked at Clint. Charlie know Clint not believe, think tlick, rotten tlick. No tlick, Clint San. Now Charlie tell whole deal, OK? You better, Little Guy, you better! He levitated a foot taller than Clint, then speaking slowly, drifting back down to the table, his voice deeper. Strange place up there, Clint San - not like peoples think, Better! Nice people, good people. Know love there better than here. He pointed down to the floor. Charlie live there long, long time since he do good tings for peoples in old time China. Then - he King Lao tse. Big guy, big gold, big love, throne, everyting. When die, go to that place Clint San call Heaven –like Earth place, better all ways, people Charlie know when King. Help Charlie understand China, good, bad. One day, Heaven time, Tall Man call Charlie, sit Charlie down by arms, look sad, tear in eye. Tell bout Jami die, come Heaven. Jami want go back! Most people want stay! Man train Charlie all bout Jami –everyting. And Charlie know Jami's Clint San like Jami do… Two people –One Love, he say, like before, long time go, at Beginning. Two but one, one but two. See? Clint smiled, it was beginning to sound real, fantastic but real.

Alright, Fella - for suddenly Charlie seemed bigger and it didn't seem right to call him Little Fellow anymore. Go on. Well, Charlie watch all movie Jami, Clint San, two-one peoples. Tall Man…Who's this Tall Man? Not know –just know Counselor. Go on, what were you about to say? Uh, He tell Charlie, wait few days, then go tell Clint San Jami do big trouble Heaven! Want Clint San. Hey! Dead or alive, Charlie? Clint laughed. Charlie blinked, then threw his head back and laughed hard with Clint. She want come back, you. Come back!? She say Heaven, Big Guys, can do anyting. And then, what? She get mad when Tall Man, Charlie call C. not say true! Why that, Charlie? Clint San, Charlie not get all Tall Man say to Jami and Charlie- but C. tell Charlie wait more… Charlie do. Then he tell Charlie, Come talk Clint San - say, Working on someting for Jami, Clint San. WHAT? He say not ask –yet. Charlie go back, tonight, come back maybe tom… MAYBE?! Why you little codger, after all this you'd better come back!… Clint put his hands up, Hey, I'm sorry! Charlie cowered. It's not you, it's that C. isn't it?… Charlie just do errands, not spill guts, Tall Man C. say, No more yet, Clint San.

OK. Clint set the Man-Angel down off the pool table. Charlie straightened his flimsy saffron robe, smiled at Clint … and… disappeared . Clint sat down, obviously shaken.

CHAPTER 5

Standing in the whirling tube, Jami shook violently, feeling strange, far different than before the Lagoon experience and being taken back to her apartment in the arms of the Amazon woman with the red hair and the blue shoes. What a lecture she got. History of Heaven, Tall Guy and his buddy, the layout all on a screen beyond words and WHY she couldn't go back –yet, maybe never. So she cried as the woman with red hair faded out of sight. But...she WAS going to have THE interview, a chance, Red said.

Without any notice her skin tingled, she saw her arms disappear, her feet turn to smog and she remembered nothing more – until. How'd she get here? She didn't remember going to the Counselor this morning.

Whhaa?...

He wasn't as tall as C. that Tall Guy, but he sure was handsome! She waited as He walked around the oak, gold trimmed desk. WHAT a Man, what a desk! She gulped as He came over, sat her down on a love seat... carefully, slowly He reached out, hand on her hair. At that moment at that smile, every whit of anger, rebellion, apprehension –it all just went –how she didn't know. It was as if she had been baptized up to the heart with pure Love back at that fountain. Her breasts leaped,

That's where she felt it –in her heart. Wow! She said, jerking upright. He sat down next to her. Jami...He took her hand, You are quite a special person, aren't you? She blushed, Well, if YOU say so, I guess I am, but, I'm sorry I have been...No No! Don't be sorry –it's so natural when you truly love and love someone like you and Clint do...She interrupted, Do? But I thought that... Jami, things can always change when YOU do. Haven't you found that out? Well, I... Yes, guess I have like just now, What did you DO? To ME? Jami, I am Love. He rose. Began long strides with His long legs, bulging beneath His blue robe, his shawl whipping about him. I was just a Man, Jami. Was. Can you believe that despite all you heard about me? I guess so if you say so, but I was taught... Yes, it is evident what is said about me. I changed like you can change. He smiled that... she started to think – That ungodly smile. And she stopped grinning. Yes Jami, Father allowed me to become what I am inside. Beauty, Peace, Patience –all of the things you are inside when you practice it daily. DAILY, Jami! His look became stern, commanding and then that smile came again. Pardon, but I have seen so many of you fluctuate like leaves in the wind...He looked off as if seeing below. What shall I call you, Sir? Well, certainly not Sir! I am no Knight. I am the Day Star rather. But what would you like to call me? What you are, what you really are, to me, to them, she pointed at the floor. Jami? Well are you, uuhh..., Jesus? He shook his head. I could be - if my detractors ever got together on their histories and their records. No, Dear Heart, I am not, never was Jesus. Though I have been close to that many times. How? He placed his head in his hands. I lived many lives in the spiritual form of what I am now –and was not then, Yes, once I lived in Galilee and Qumron, and once as fabled Krishna, Buddha and in the Greek man Apollonius. Many embodiments. She cringed at her questions, Stupe!! No, you are most welcome to ask ALL things, my little Sister. She reached out to Him, as He had arisen and was now across the room, striding back and forth, His left arm raised slightly to the ceiling –as if reaching for something unseen. Why... has it all been so complicated, Si...? Nay, nay! Well, the... Let me set you at ease, Jami. Your request to me is not futile. To common Men, Yes. Not to me and our Father of Lights. Lights? He is Light, Jami. I dwell among that Light in his dimension. Well, are you...Ch...? He coughed. Who then? I won't burden you with that which your Clint has already surmised about me. He is correct. What do you mean? Jami, the excited Chronology and Empire Builders took me from many sources, had to compress me into their favorite or memorized things and personalities. Their Gods, Demons, Angels – even, Jami - into their Old Testament God – A false god, no more resembling my Father, your Father - than... he paused for a word. The Man in the Moon! They both laughed. He stepped over and ruffled her hair like a big Brother. She loved this Guy! Good, Jami, and I love you! NOW, to business...

CHAPTER 6

The wall to her left became a sky of beautiful blue, matching his robe. Watch this, Jami! It's just great! He seemed really enthralled with what was forming on the scene. Watch yourself a few minutes. I WANT YOU TO SEE YOU, as you were, as you became. It won't pain you, I'll go easy. He did a slight bow and waved His left hand in a circle. She saw and the minutes went too slow even though He was... going easy...Hmmnn. She winced! The wall went blank. He sat down at His desk, put His tongue in His tanned cheek and ...amazingly...whistled. A long low whistle.

What? She asked, startled. Oh, I was just remembering, Jami, things your reflections brought to mind before He indwelt me. Indwelt? Who? How?... It happens once you make up your mind to overcome something – or someone...his eyes actually misted and a heavy tear fell to the floor, plopping like a raindrop. YOU? What happened? I was in love, so in love - before I was married to The Magdalene, greatly in love -even a bit of lust, if I'm honest. But 'they' saved me with counsel. Strong counsel. About what? But, Hey... maybe this is in the Box and I'm...No, Dear, no boxes here, I want you to know, Jami. It's important to me because of my past, my decisions. It was, as I say, a lot of pure love, a bit of youthful lust all mixed up with duty –I thought. We were supposed to marry then, there, those people, their laws and mores...He smiled that great smile, I overcame my self and my cells –if I may call them that. That's all, let's go on, but know - I was NOT always perfect as you tend to type me!

CHAPTER 7

She woke up in Big Girl's lap. The Amazon Lady. Cradled like a baby. Oh, you're awake. Quite an experience, Mmmn? Jami Porchuka, the Heavenly trouble maker, once Polish Super Girl Olympian, looked up into those unbelievable eyes –like pools, like the Lagoon with lights on, she thought. Whew! Things are sure different up here, She thought. Yes they are, Dear. You read minds? Why not? This place is unlimited in possibilities, Jami. Try me. Wow, it's true –you just asked me if I'm hungry! Are you? The conversation continued via thought for a few moments. Impressed? Sure am. Your name is? Skyla. I was an Amazon, Jami, down there in North Africa. We girls went hunting for husband/mates in your Fatherland, Poland. Mmm Mmm! Clear over there in Europe. Those Polish men were exceptional Warriors, hardy, fearless. But... lets eat! She stood Jami on her feet like a childweight, smoothed the new blue-white robe she was now clothed in. Touched her hair and an Orchid pinned itself over her ear. Hey, that's neat! Normal, friend... Normal.

The Dining Hall was something else! she thought. Isn't it? We girls never had anything like this down there in Africa –and we really had some spreads after every New Moon! As she was thinking of it, the tall strawberry Malt appeared before her on the table that floated over their laps. Heyy! Like it? That's pretty sly! And then the open faced Avacodo sandwich, dark spinach leaves protruding temptingly. Good enough, for this Pole Vaulter! Jami grinned, as she picked up the repast. Pole Vaulter? Asked Skyla – Yeah, being a Pole I grabbed a pole –She laughed at her joke. Skyla chuckled as she picked up her spoon and dipped into the soup.

Around them, for that 200 feet or more, sat every type, color and nationality imaginable. People, some VERY strange looking, never seen by Jami, even in children's fantasy books. Her eyebrows up, she munched on her sandwich. Gee, Skyla...Yes, not just from Earth Honey, from different places all over the starry spaces and... then some.

She wiggled in her chair, brushed her hair back. Ok, then, Indwelt? He resumed: The Father's one Son, the only, as you would say, and as has been written. Just one, not like His Earthly wards. Just one. But, loving desperately, all of the others - You. But if...? Wait, let me clarify, Jami. A great Being, The All, exists out there, here, everywhere - when He needs to He can travel, grow, diminish down to a microcosmic speck! I'm like that now. He indwelt me down there, finally. After I got it straight. Well – She was shaking hard, her feet tapping the floor, you? I became a partner with Him, that simple. Two minds, two hearts, One Love in one body, Sound familiar? See? Huh? Where did the rest of Him go? He grinned at her question: Everywhere in space, time, to all the hearts that wanted Him in them too some day. See, Jami? He, Me, Father, Love, Concern, Compassion... are not something that can be pieced out and then wither or be no more. But Infinite. Never limited! She shuddered and wrapped her arms around her chest. Jami, I always wanted that, felt those things, the Quickening we call it –gradual, growing, pulling at us inwardly. Like a small Tornado. Never stopping unless we do. But I kept procrastinating. Thinking I would lose me like the eastern people think, going into a puff of light, just disappearing – the drop of water lost in the Ocean. She frowned. Yes, they do, mostly - the Hindus, Buddhists, Janns and Sikhs –many still DO. Then Jami I wanted, as you might say, Nobody messing with my individuality! Felt that once in a while, Jami? Oh, YES, especially all my life down there and then when I got up here – Well, it seemed like I had no choice even here, ESPECIALLY here! She stood up trembling. DO I? You certainly do, Dear. You certainly do... You ARE going back! As all can if they elect to, if they need to, if they lack in some necessity. Especially you, Jami - he beamed, IF THEY LOVE LIKE YOU AND CLINT. He threw his tousled head back, the waves of semi long hair rippling light in the liquidness of the chandelier. And he laughed the laugh so often heard in Heaven or His Father's realms when The Christ was moved to Infinite Joy.

She fainted then, again - at the exact time that Charlie left Clint there by the screen door. When Charlie walked over to it, pool cue chalk all over his flimsy robe...and vanished in a puff of golden-violet sparkles.

CHAPTER 8

The Cathedral ceiling, also a hundred feet tall, reacted to the dozens of candles at the ornate Greek Orthodox altar, scintillating, shadows and brilliances intertwining above Clint O'Connell as he sat next to Sam, hands on the pew in front. Sam, the same, watched the ceiling. Both men now dressed in their Running Gear, waiting till after their weekly Wednesday trek to the Cathedral had ended in a small form of naïve ecstasy —helping now but little the agony of just the two of them. She had been checked, finally told them, for the Cancer. Came out positive. Six months maybe. They couldn't get their breath. That announcement had riddled their composure for the whole week. Jami, dying? No! Stupid examination, lots of times wrong, mixed up, couldn't be! But then, the blood, the infrequent pain, the fainting spells when they all three ran in the woods. That was real, too damned real! And so they planned an attack. Prayer times every Wednesday morning before the run. And the Reflexology on her hands, feet and spine. Alternatives maybe too late… The prayer Clint did, his broad hands spread across her head, blessing her, pleading with... And then suddenly she got better. They rejoiced, went to Vegas, had a ball, the three of them and Sam's fill in for Jami's perfection...

They never knew till that rainy day when she was found near her Harley - but they talked, guessed many times, that first few days. Did she know something she didn't tell them? Did the bleeding start again, the searing pains? Did the rain, the slick road near the woods cause it? Did she choose that way out? Alone, no mess, just the curve, the lake edge. Harley flattened out at 60. On purpose? Accident? Did she even know herself what was happening? Did she prefer drowning instead of drawn out sympathies, Clint's tears and pleadings with her in his arms, sobbing? And they sat there, a few worshippers moving past them, looking at the two virile men with tears running down their tanned cheeks, their bony cheekbones gritting teeth, trying not to cry out loud.

Later in the Rectory the two sat across from the Priest, now adorned, not in rich robes and miter. He pushed the sleeves of his sweat shirt up above his muscular elbows, forearms as large as Clint's, legs out in front, ankles crossed. Hands now holding a tall glass of something they knew not...Saki, Men, Saki. Got used to it when we did the Japanese occupation. Moderate though – He winked, looked up, cocking his head. What can I do for you Men?

CHAPTER 9

JAMI! JAMI! Time to get up, the Tours ready to leave. She rubbed her eyes, next thing she knew she was in her robe, this one Magenta with white sparkles and a caftan of White over her shoulder, tucked into a fold of her robe. Silver and rust sandals, each with a small white flower atop. I'd almost forgotten, Skye. Is it compulsory? Nope, but you don't want to miss this! You might decide after seeing it, that your Clint can't quite compete with all you'll be seeing. It's something else, as you would say, Jami.

Sitting on the broad platform of roiling vapor which backed them for comfort, the six fellow passengers watched, eyes blinking, mouths agape. Jami, pinching at the Vapor which was soft-solid underneath them and behind their backs was – vapor, nothing but color, undulating color and fragrance. Vapor, mist like – like pine forests after a rain, she remembered. She sighed, leaned back into the comfort and watched with the others. Impressed? Skye winked, Ya ain't seen nothing yet, Baby!

A 'Heaven hour' later the six were levitated onto a gigantic Barge Type structure, placed near a shore of what appeared to be an endless Lake of mirror still water. Silver water, touched up against lush green grass of also seemingly endless distance. Moving slightly forward motion, the Barge containing hundreds of 'people' floated out, out, out –until the green shore disappeared and all about them was water, now turning blue-green. Porpoises by the literal thousands, began appearing, diving, leaping, frolicking like happy children. Several bringing sea flowers, she guessed, over to Jami's side of the twin decked Barge. Her fingers trailed in the water- A bluish Porpoise surfaced and placed a flower in her palm. She stroked it's head. It SPOKE! Hello, Jami, How you doing? The flower went into Mary Poppins bursts of sparkles and metallic color in Jami's hand. Ohh, my God...Skye! Yeah, something aren't they - in their 'natural' habitat, hmmnn?

In the distance a bronze Light House glistened, its day beam shining amid the haze of the lake water. A voice came over the Barge. KEEP YOUR EYES ON THE LIGHT, FOLKS, DON'T GET LOST! The company wondered... Lost?, Jami said out loud. What's that mean, Skye? That's mostly for those Dear, who are scheduled to go back down tomorrow. Easy to forget what you are supposed to BE... She winked her wink. Tomorrow? No, not you, not yet, Dear. The passengers looked at Jami wondering...

Jami turned more to Skye next to her, Do you know when I...No, Jami, but I don't think it will be too long after today. That's IF you don't change your mind... Skye looked into the distant horizon, past the Light House. The platinum haired girl, shook her head as she remembered Clint's arms, his smile, his tenderness and strength. Their talks especially. No, nothing, Skye, could...and at that instant she and all of the group saw... it. And a near swoon hit the occupants of the Barge. The full sight, of that Ship, must wait for those who... well, maybe you get the idea...

CHAPTER 10

Sure, you're right. The Priest, unconcernedly reached over, gripping both men by a shoulder. It's there: Bibles, Zohar,Koran, Nag Hamadi, Gita and how do they miss it? It's called fear, it's called traditional unteaching. Most of all it is not wanting to change precepts or favorite religious upbringing. We all —he paused for effect, ALL have been here before, had that old hat of forgetfulness placed on us as we came back down. As a favor, Men, so we wouldn't have remorse over WHAT MIGHT HAVE BEEN —if we had hung in there and 'accentuated the positive' —he hummed the tune from the 40s. A few bars to associate. Clint spoke first, then Sam followed with the same words: Why don't the authorities like you Guys tell...We could, we have, thousands of times and ways. Conventionality always wins above Priests or Truth. Always, men, sorry, but it's true. We tell, they deny. We tell, they kill us. We show them all the places and books, scriptures and scrolls where the GREAT LAW is expounded and they want someone to die for them, someone to take responsibility for them. Always the same —except for a few, very few who get it... So for the others we stand in pulpits, swing Incense Censers - and pray...Others take their money...He sighed and stood, rubbing his chest. But as for your last question about Charlie: I don't know. Tricks get played, Astral tricksters. Sounds like something I'd like to believe if I was a Clint —but I guess we will have to wait and see. And, Yes, I do believe in the Walk-In theory or fact, whichever you choose to believe it is. If your Jami —he looked at both men, is coming back... that's one way she can get here. But I'd leave room for something else that goes with what we have been discussing. He hesitated...A way you might not necessarily jump up and down about...He picked up his shower towel, engulfed their hands and was gone into the Rectory locker room.

CHAPTER 11

Soaping his cropped gray beard Stanislaus Demetripopolus mused on the last few minutes of their conversation. Turning the water up hotter, he gritted his jaw tight, turning slowly as the steam rose in the circular enclosure. Did I say too much? Not enough? A minute later after the icy blast of cold water had turned him redder still than the hot water, he held the thick towel over his heavy power lifter chest...Maybe I should... and at that moment as was not uncommon, Stanislaus Demet, as he was known for short among his fellow priests, heard it: Son, pray for Clint O'Connell in the Holy Rosary of St. Michael. He is going to need discernment and the patience of Job... And that was it. He shrugged, Yes, I go now to the altar.

Outside the first snow of the season wafted down upon the sleeping city as Stanislaus, now in his regalia knelt down before the tall, ornate Greek structure of antiquity.

CHAPTER 12

Jami's orange stripped cat woke him up, sitting on his chest. Clint cursed, remembering he hadn't put Charlie out –too damned many Charlie's to keep track of...he mumbled, as he held the cat and slipped on his Moccasins. The cat looked up into Clint's sleep puffy eyes. Clint stopped. The cat reached up, one paw on his cheek, head tucked against Clint's shoulder. Like he had done so often to Jamie...Hey, cut it out, Charlie, you...and he gave the cat a hug as he tossed him out the door into the back yard. As he was closing the door he saw a small sandaled foot blocking the opening. Clint San!... Good Morning! Charlie back.

Clint sat across from Charlie on the sectional lounge, Charlie's feet hovering a few inches off the floor on the tweed foot stool that Jamie had made that last June. He remembered...She had stapled her thumb. She was brave as a Marine as he pulled it out. Memories...will they...OK, Charlie, what's happening? Charlie talk, Clint San listen. Charlie hurry fast, go. Well, you've got the floor. Charlie looked at the floor, puzzled. Never mind it's just an expression, Charlie. Go on.

Clint San, Jamie come soon! Four days time! All say go, up Heaven. Happy time! Well, how is it...No say more, Clint San, big hurry, China people big flood, Charlie go - Chow! The sparkles stayed on the footstool for a few seconds. Clint took a deep breath. What would people say? Sam? Would this make all the papers, big thing on T-V? He walked back and forth for a few minutes wiggling his fingers as if they had just unthawed. He grinned, Is this happening to me? Jamie? Back to life? Come on, Clint, pinch yourself. And he did and it left a mark...

How'd he take it? Well, how would he take it, Slim? The Counselor, hands on hips looked down through the wall, smiling a little ruefully. I'm glad that's him that's going to go through this. Look at that smile on his face...ugh! The shock when he realizes...But now Jamie...She walked in, glided rather, looking radiant in her white and pink robe. Slim looked at the Counselor, Pink? Yeah, that's it. Only way, he said, but she won't know...Their conversation by thought ended as Jamie hugged each of them. Today? Yes, Jamie, back you go at One O'clock! Excited? Huh, you kidding?!

Uhh, Jami will you lay down on the couch for a few minutes, I want to ask you a few pertinent questions...She flopped down happily, Sure, shoot! Well, umm, first: Did you know you were going 60 when you hit that curve by the lakeside? I...guess so. Didn't you think that was an inordinate speed for a Harley even with good rubber? No, not really... Not really? Well...Jami, did you want to DIE? She jerked up. Why are you asking that?! Did you? She paused before answering. Maybe. I don't really know. She gulped. Are you sure you don't know? Pretty sure... He strode closer, knelt by her side – Jami, a lot depends on you being utterly truthful to yourself, not just to us here. Talk to me.

Look! Have YO ever been dying – a day at a time? The kneeling Counselor looked at his Aid. Really dying, and you knew it? And your friends thought you were getting well, and...she sobbed uncontrollably. C. put his hand on her head. She calmed. Go on. I couldn't think right. Clint, Sam, my Folks, my Girlfriend, it...all just bunched up on me that morning. I pressed the pedal a little deeper...Jami, it was raining…I don't know, Sir, I just don't know for sure...She turned her head into the pillowed couch sobbing…

She next found herself on the Lagoon ledge. Alone. What do you think, Mac? The tall counselor, shook his head. Maybe she really doesn't know. Thin line stuff, this. But one thing for sure she will have time to figure it out. They zoomed in on Jamie at the Lagoon fountain as Skye materialized at the girl's side.

Skye! Yes, how are you, Dear? Oh, so excited! I'll bet. Is that what you are going to wear down...? I guess. Why? He'll think you look cute in pink. Think? I'll bet he will just be enthralled with you in pink! Jami, smoothed the fabric that wasn't - over her long thighs. Oh, Skye...

CHAPTER 13

Sitting at the kitchen table, finishing his oatmeal and bananas, Clint gazed out the window, snowflakes, a slight blue showing in the western sky. A car pulled in over at the neighbor's house. A Sheriffs four wheeler, star on the side barely seeable through the snowfall. He was stapling a paper, something on the door. He got back in the 4 X and pulled into Clint's wide front drive. Clint got up, walked through the living room, opened the door. Waiting. It wasn't Sam. Hal! What's up over there? The short Deputy pursed his lips. Accident last night near Vegas. All of them killed except one, Clint. Horrible mess they said. Freak wind shear hit and...God! Clint grabbed the door casings with both hands, swayed. Again? What were you tacking on...A notice. Legality. No next of kin, property is under probate immediately. The Law, Clint. Yeah, I know...he remembered the...Well, who was it that didn't...? He found it hard to say die anymore. Their new baby. Born four days before in a Vegas emergency clinic.

It was bruised up a little, cut on her forehead.

Seven days later Sam knocked as Clint was doing the laundry. Hey! Ya OK, Clint? Yeah, getting used to lonesome - but maybe...he grinned. The secret they both were ruminating around in their heads... Yeah. Sam grinned then frowned as he took a paper out of his tan plastic brief. Umn, Clint. Yeah? The neighbors. You guys got along well? Oh, sure, Sam, Why? This paper was in the stuff their lawyer went through. What is it? Sam's jaw went to the side. Welll, it's somewhat of a shock to a lot of people. Probably more to you, than me. Well...He handed it. Clint sat down. Sit, Sam, let me...

MONOLITH

Laying the paper down after reading it slowly twice, Clint O'Connell blanched white, then again twice more. I...Yeah, I know, me too, Clint. Me??! Looks like it. Legal guardian by the James' and the State? That's what they wanted, she did. She? Before she died. Who? Mrs. James. Me? Why ME?! You read it. She thought her little girl would like to be raised as a future Olympic Star, Clint. See there, the appendage... Oh, God! Sam, how can I...? Got me, Bro. I'm about out of answers. Got to go on another call. Get a hold of the department by tomorrow noon. They'll need an answer or the kid will go to foster care. Good luck, Clint. The tan uniformed man walked out to the Jeep, his head shaking side to side.

My God, My God! My God, What next?! He kneeled down on the rug, not in prayer, but in fatigue. And then he heard Charlie Cat, pawing the screen outside in the snow. He was cold...Where's love? So was he.

CHAPTER 14

Clint's Mom and Dad, Sam and the State people stood outside the glass as Clint, inside the incubation section held the infant. As Clint eyed the little girl, he noticed the small cut over the baby's right eyebrow. Hmnn, Jamie had a cut there too, the only one on her... He thought. There's that old synchronicity thing, and he shrugged it off. 'Upstairs' the Tall Man, his Aid and Skye looked at each other, half smiling, half frowning. Do you think, Skye asked, that he gets it? Not a chance, the Aid said – We put a block on him. Too much too soon and he crumbles.

Sign here Mr. O'Connell. Yes, here and over here also. Just initial this third place. Fine. You are a Daddy! The woman with the pen back in her hand, placed the copy in her brief case. Sat it down on the desk, reached out and grabbed Clint, kissing him on the mouth. You might be an Olympian but you are even more of one great Man, Mr. O'Connell! Tears coursing down her face, she fled down the hall with the two State attendants. Mrs. O'Connell beaming, held the child now. Mr. O'Connell sighed and patted his Son's back. Clint stood motionless, arms hanging limp at his side. Well, uh, better get going... The baby cooed, looking over at Clint. Clint looked at her. Cute little fart, isn't she, Mom? CLINT!

CHAPTER 15

Sam and Clint waddled through the doorway with the Baby Bed, trying not to scratch it. Ok? Yeah, little bit more. Tight squeeze, Clint, There! Over here? Yep. They stood back eyeing their labor. Now the stuff... several trips and the small bassinet, the chest – pink to match the bed and the bassinet were all aligned in the guest room that had never been used in the short three years Clint and Jamie had been married. Nice, huh? Yeah, Ok for two Machos, I guess. Later that day Mr. And Mrs. O'Connell showed up, Sam gone, Clint sitting at the Kitchen table, chin in his hands. A bowl of Shredded Wheat, soggy, untouched before him. Son! What's wrong? Oh, nothing really, Mom –just thinking a little. She bent down over him. Mom... What would Jamie want me to do? Do? Well, the baby and me working. YOU can't keep taking care of her, your job won't let you take anymore time off...Now. Hey, stop that, Son –We have someone outside waiting to meet you. Glenn O'Connell went to the door, opened it and waved. Ok, come on in Francis. And she did, all 300 pounds of her. Clint, Francis Skylar. Francis, our Son, Clint. They shook, Fran's hand engulfing Clint's and fingers lapping over. Clint winced. What a grip! He thought.

Looking Francis over - feet to the top of her red hair, he smiled as she flexed an arm. Clint, Francis was available at the Agency we talked to. She has a lot in common with you. Yeah? Yes, she was a Gold Medallist ten years ago in Serbia at that game you didn't get to go to with your shoulder messed up!

Ohh? Well, uh, Francis, how much time can you spend with my new Daughter? How much do you get for this kind of deal?... She was one big woman!... Probably, he thought, as he couldn't help himself, staring - all

6' 9" of her. No problem, Son, Clint's Dad spoke up. The agency had a call after we chose Francis and said they had been contacted by the local T-V stations and the Masons and several other organizations. Fact is, Son. You got it made. Francis is free for sixteen years if you want her! Room, board, salary –the works. It's all paid for in an annuity, guaranteed. The whole town and state chipped in when they heard about little Jenny - and Francis is willing if you are. Clint sank down from where he had arisen to shake Francis' hand. I ... don't know what to say –Fran...Is this what you want to do, aren't you married or something? No, not even something, she laughed. I am most available, and Mr. O'Connell, I wouldn't miss this for all the World! Really!! Can I bring my stuff in? Well, sure, uh, I'll move my King into little Jenny's room and you can have that Bath there and plenty of privacy, and...he was flustered and it showed. I'll sleep out in the Cabin loft, it's warm and I have my computer out there anyway and my...Hey, Mr. O'Connell, don't spoil me right away! Let me spoil you. You've been through too much to be worrying about this old hunk! Well, is that Ok, Francis, the room, the King size, the bath? Perfect, but you let me do what needs to be done on all levels, Alright Mr. O'...Hey, just Clint, please. He reached out for that right. This time he was ready. They squeezed. Both grinned. Yeah, like Jamie had said –Quite a Man. She eyed him up and down. Guess Jamie...she thought, didn't trade off too much Heaven after all.

CHAPTER 16

You might not think such things can happen like this? Well, I'm beginning to be convinced. He reached out and gripped the Counselor's hand. Are we a team or not?! Feels good, doesn't it? Wait till you see next weeks schedule! Why? Well, we won't be bored, Pal...The China Syndrome, let's call it. Little Charlie brought back quite a few cases just for us. The rest of them? Station II, all ten thousand of them. They've got the staff – Guess they see us as the specialists that can handle the screamers and rebels, huh? Yeah –and then some. They drifted out toward the glass like Ocean with a touch of the desk pad. The Ship loomed above them and the figures, small, doll-like, looking down at them as they boarded the pads, waved happily, All thousand of them. The Aid gulped...

Inside the craft, rather, City! The two men moved to the top level of what was indeed a City in the bluest of skies. Reaching miles in the air, it's pyramidal shape, circular at the topmost pinnacle glowed in the bright Sunlight. The Aid rolled up the sleeves of his shimmering robe, Ok, lets get busy...The taller man smiled. Good feeling, Huh? Sure is... The small silver blue discs billowed out of the cap of the immense craft, while others spewed out from the base near the water.

CHAPTER 17

This gal is something else! Clint watched her running the lake beach. At the least 300 she is a cotton pickin' Gazelle, Jenny! Look at that stride! Jenny, playing with her toes was unconcerned. Clint laid back. How long now and no word from Charlie. Well, guess they want me patient. Somehow he felt better than he would have thought. Sure, the tears after he shut the Cabin door and drapes so Francis couldn't hear, but it was somehow different and he couldn't place it. Francie, as he had started calling her flopped own on the oversize quilt, she brought with her, lots of strange stuff in her room. He'd peeked in while she was at the Health Store and he was sitting Jenny. Good little Jenny, hardly a peep out of her at night, Francie had said and eats like a little pony! Well, there had been one other appetite like that in the house and she matched Clint – His eyes drifted out of the large window onto the patio with the equipment. Jamie, Girl, I miss you so much, hurry up, please, what's going on… Jenny let out a squeal, crying like a banshee for ten minutes. When Clint picked her up she went down to semi silent, gooing, reaching up, grasping his nose, patting his face. Actually patting me, Jenny... where did you learn that?

Hey!... In here Francie, with Jenny. She's patting my face!! Do tellll? Well, how about that? Francis packed the double Fridge, then packed the upright freezer, then the pantries, then went out to the garage shelves and packed them. Things ARE plentiful, she crooned. What? Oh, just thankful for all this great food we have. She raised her eyebrows remembering North Africa and the famines and the feasts, the unbelievable hardships, the raids by the Spaniards, their losses, her best friend, her Mother and Sister. She sighed, No past Skyla, no more past! You gots a girl child to raise. And maybe a man child to

a body good to see them appreciate us Girls. Damn them, she smiled good naturedly – They used to burn us at the stake and spear us on the battlefield. There you go again, Skyla. No more PAST! Your turn, Clint. He lowered to the bench after pulling Francie up with some effort. What an enigma! All that beauty and humor and she...Skyla forgot again - Hey, Clint and Sammy, I love you two, try to relax around me. I'm not going to poison you or seduce you. I'm here for you and Ja...She almost said it, caught herself...Jenny. Wow!

She held the other end of the Olympic Set with just one hand, Sam with two hands. Clint stiffened his arms. Ok, Baby, do your thing!, She said, rubbing his head with her free hand. Sam using both of his to spot Clint's bench presses. That's 20 Clint, don't overdo it, Sam yelled out –you haven't had a weight in your hands for weeks. Clint let them have the bar, got up puffing and sweating, hand on his right shoulder. Aaaahh, you're right, Sam, did it again, STUP!! He winced. Francie felt his bare shoulder. Rotor Cuff, Huh? Yeah, thought the auxiliary fibers had done their job on the healing. Guess I'm just Macho Man, sorry Guys! Hey, Clint, you're gonna be Ok. She felt his sweaty shoulder, screwed her mouth up. You watch Mama Francis... And that was it. Until Sam did his thing, making 18 reps and getting sidetracked by looking up under Franci's sweatshirt. That's it, I'm pooped. She grinned...Keep your eyes on the bar, Sammy! She thought. Sam leaving, hugged her, best he could with her girth and kissed her cheek. She reciprocated, kissing him on the forehead. Love you, Sam, really do. Thanks for everything you're doing for us, Francie. Yeah. He left. She went over to Clint sitting at the patio now, eating a small bowl of ice cream. She pushed it aside. That shoulder... You can't live with one like that and be your man. I know. Well lick that up and let's see what happens... What do you mean? Be still...She clapped three times,, mumbled some strange words,, rubbed her hands together so fast Clint just saw a blur of pink nails. Hold still now! She placed her hands on his shoulder. A blast of pain as bones seemed to leap inside, then peace, what peace, all over him...Francie, what did you...Be quiet, I'm not through, Hush! Lay back there, Clint.

She motioned to the lounge at his back. Close your eyes. No, don't talk. Close your eyes.

And from the other room he swore he heard 'JAMI' crying. She spoke up again, Just Jenny, Clint, just Jenny. Listen to me: That baby in there IS Jamie! Clint jerked upright. No! Stay, Boy, Stay! Let me talk now. She had to come down that way, like all other folks when they Reincarnate, rather Embody, truer way of putting it, Clint. And YOU have to raise her, WE, have to raise her. Got that? Clint groaned deep within his Soul. Oh, God, Francie I thought all along some kind of miracle was going to h...It did, Clint San. Clint jerked again, looked around the room, looked into Skye's golden flecked violet eyes. WHO are YOU? My name is Skye, Clint, and that's where I come from. Clint fainted.

CHAPTER 19

Standing next to Clint O'Connell, now towering over Skyla's head, the figure of the Christ, that which Jamie had been so daringly privileged to know, smiled, radiant teeth and eyes, forehead glistening with a spot of light like an arc welding tip. He placed a hand on Clint, unseen, unknown to Skyla. Then vanished and in his place stood Charlie, radiant, beaming smile, arms waving rapturously. Clint San, Skyla – Charlie back. He was robed, sandaled, crowned in Lao tse's finest. The two 'Earthlings' stood tall before the ancient one, heads tilted. Charlie! The robe, loose, too long by two feet, the Crown, down over his eyes. And then everything changed. Charlie left. Lao tse filled out the Robe, the Crown lifted up to where it once fit the owner.

Clint stirred in his heart. He understood miracles. Skyla wept, holding Lao tse against her. Jenny wailed. The three of them went in, light emanating from the Crib. Jenny stilled and then Clint and Skyla were there alone looking down at Jenny. A small delicate star was there where the cut had been. They hugged and Jenny chortled, tossing her bottle at the foot of her bed. Thank you, thank you, Franc... Skyla, thank you...

CHAPTER 20

So. Aah, that's it? I uhh, raise this baby, till she's grown –then I get my Jamie back? Clint sat across from Francis, who he would now know as Skyla. Yep, that's it as far as I know, Clint, but I haven't heard it all yet, may be more and better, even worse things, but...She raised those beautiful eyebrows, the wavy red bangs shading the most exotic eyes he had ever seen and a horrible thought hit him right between his baby blues – Am I falling out of love with my Jamie and into something with this 300 pound giant Miss Universe? God, Clint, stop it. It's just hormones –and don't you forget it! At his last exclamation Skyla stood up, walked over to where Clint sat across from her - reached down, picked him up by one arm, WITH one arm...Now what were you thinking, Friend?! Dangling like a child Clint blushed, tried to think of some retort. No words? Well you had plenty of THOUGHTS, my Boy, plenty of thoughts! Now when you get through undressing me and wondering what it...she blushed now. Hey, hey, Skyla, I'm sorry, I truly am, let me down...She dropped him on the shag rug like a sack of rice. Ok, but no more of that, I don't want your thoughts in my head if they come out like that Playboy Magazine Centerfold I just saw materializing. Got it? Look, Skyla, do you realize what you are? What you do to men's eye's? We ARE Human, you know.

Yeah, I could tell, Clint and I didn't really have to read your mind to know just how Human. You think I don't have a few thoughts about you? You do? Of course, I'm pretty pure stock, my Boy, and my hormones click a lot faster than yours by double – BUT- I've been places you haven't, seen things you saw one day and forgot when you came back down again. We have to cool it. I might blush just like you and...Sam. Oh, she's noticed Sam too? Read his mind? Yes, I have! she revealed with her ESP. Well, how can we handle this then? He stood now, close to her. I have an idea that just might work, Clint. You might go bananas if I decide to tell you, even try it out, but...What? Well sit down. If you stay standing you might fall down. Oh, by the way, notice a big grown man like you have those fainting spells lately? Yeah, what's with that? They do that to you when you can't take the trauma of the moment. That simple, or when they want to block off something. Well, I thought it might have to do with all of the shocks I've been getting lately. No. you're Ok, just fine, no worry. But back to the subject I was musing on...What is it? He leaned back against the large ornate sofa pillow, hands clasped behind his neck, confident, thinking he could take anything she could dish out. She grinned. Don't be too sure.

With that she began undressing, casually till she was down to her violet Bra and Pants. Ever heard of Kama Sutra, Clint? He gulped a reply –Sure. Know much about it? Not more than it's a --- he was getting redder and redder as her breasts stretched with each breath under the semi transparent material. A what? Oh, aah, it's a form of highly evolved love making the Hindus and other Easterners have mastered over thousands of years. They, uhh, don't do orgasms, no climaxes. Pretty good definition, Clint. What else? Well, they say us Westerners are missing a lot of health and longevity by not checking into it. She paused...and a lot less Divorces! Yeah?. Right, go on, Clint. Well that it's a way of coming up Higher spiritually and experiencing a form of ecstasy far beyond orgasm. Now you gots it. But more, Clint... This: That Male seed and the Woman's eggs are holy objects. No, you won't find many believing or doing this and the argument goes that God, click, God - made the sex organs for baby making and funtimes. Mostly today it's funtimes, Right? That's about it, I guess. He swallowed a little easier as he got used to her near nakedness. You Ok, Clint? I'm trying… Good!

If you and me are on a kind of 'neutralized battlefield' and we don't want to kill each other off or get into big time trouble with our

Commanders —then we have to work around this sex thing between us – Almost... She paused again, almost as if Jamie is here watching our every word and move – especially our thoughts? She grinned, one eyebrow up. You're so right, Skyla. I must admit, when I look at you from a distance and the size factor isn't so direct, like you look - can I use normal- well, I want your body. THERE! I said it, dammit!. Me too, Clint. I want your body, like crazy! You do? Sure do! But, why? I thought you were from 'up there' and you were uhh, perfect. Yes, to the first –Too perfect to the second. Hey, I was an Amazon warrior –female. We only sexed when we wanted girl children to raise like us. CLINT, we actually killed our male seed bearers after the coitus! I'd heard that. Am I safe? She threw her lovely head back and laughed till the china closet rattled. Safe? Clint, I love you, Dammit, don't you know that? You do? Yes! And she scooped him up off of the sofa and kissed him like he had never been kissed –even in his dreams. The warmth of her feminine body engulfed him The smell of her hair, like lavender and roses encircled his face, Good Great God, Skyla!

CHAPTER 21

The two men in the glowing robes sat on the Fountain's edge, munching cheese and apple slices. I heard. You did? Didn't know you were aware of what was being said down there. Yes, it's getting serious, but she's handling it better than I'd hoped. There's a lot of hormones spinning down there in that marvelous house...he shook his head slowly. Well... can we interfere? Not unless little Jamie is threatened. Can't have her in trauma. So, uhh what do we do? Wait...He pushed the knob, the screen glowed, the two on Earth on rugs across from each other, near nude. The screen shorted out...

Now look, Clint...YES? She punched his arm, Nooo!, Kama Sutra and Karezza is a way we can handle this attraction we have for each other... He interrupted, Grasping straws, Skye? Yeah, she flexed her jaw, took a breath and ran her hands down her breasts and over her rock hard stomach – continuing down her tubular tanned thighs. Listen, Sexy Man! Me, this Girl, you're drooling over, I never was in love before down there in North Africa, hardly saw naked men close. Never made a baby, warred on Locals, Spaniards, Portuguese, never did even watch a sex act. I was a Virgin – still am. I was a warrior and a guard over the captured males from Poland and Russia. That's it? That's it, Clint!

So what's your plan? Take your clothes off, Clint. Leave your Shorts on. Yeah? Now sit down on that Hassock there, you're too tight to sit in Hindu Lotus,? No, I've had Yoga, two years of it. Ok, then pull that large throw rug over here, you use the other one. Put them about 8 feet apart. Sit facing me, Clint, Lotus. She dropped to the rug and faced him, legs locked in Lotus like him. Ok? Now what? Clint was breathing hard, blinking... Breathe from your navel, slow deep, let your belly pooch out as you breathe from the floor of your being there. Floor? An expression, Clint. Breathe low, slow, all the way in and hold it till you see me let the breath out. Good. Relax! It's just me Skyla, Sky, to you, Clint, she winked. Hey! I'm trying to relax, Girl! Look at me wherever you want to. That's Ok, there too. Sure? Yes, I'm sure. And? Now my breasts. Hmnn. I know! MAN, SKYLA!! He reddened, gulped twice.

And she looked at Clint. How long do we do this? Be quiet, I'll tell you when! Okkk...

An hour went by. She slipped a strap down an inch. He took a deeper breath. Now you. What? An edge of your shorts. Just an inch down one side. He gulped again. Umhuh...And? Sh...! Another thirty minutes the other bra strap, shorts down another inch.

That's enough. Clint collapsed on the rug. She rolled over to him. We did good, Man! You were great. Anybody else and I'd be getting raped. You, raped, on this planet? Hey! They rolled, laughing, Clint trying to pin her to the rug. Like this, Clint. She pressed him off of her, rolled over and pinned him like a lightweight. Looking down at him, legs spread over his stomach, her amber hair dangling down over his face, her semi nude breasts glowing with obvious passion –she lowered down and they kissed. Long, delicately, joyfully in that marvelous living room, in that marvelous house.

Above the two Counselors and Skyla and a third male figure stood next to Skye embracing her... See it all worked out, I knew it would. Oh Yeah...

THE BEGINNING

BOOK 2

MARTINE SALVATORE

Global Private Investigator

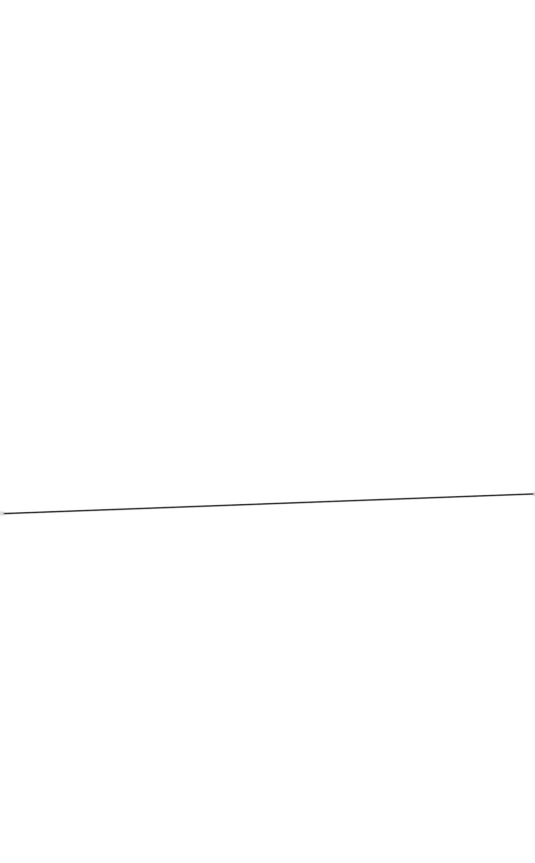

FOREWORD

"I never thought I would lower myself to write a story like MARTINE SALVATORE. Mundane, sexy, vulgar at times - yet common stuff to you who live such things, watch such violent, bloody and streetwise stories being spelled out in your life or someone you know. A real paradox for a guy who has turned from such a life and tried hard to be what his Creator-Father-Source wants. Well, here it is, a handful of what can be a windfall of movie wealth in the right hands. I'm tossing this book out, one of a six-pak - MARTINE and the others with it, Jami, Clint, Charlie, Sam – to see...First, if I'm still as good as Cecil said, second to see if one man can really change things as big and preposterous as America has facing it. Yeah, me....

(Yes, I do have plans for BIG money. What? Greedy? No, but to to augment America's Non-Existing Civilian Defense needs. We are sitting ducks. I plan small villages across our threatened nation – with fully equipped large Quonsets holding everything FEMA, Red Cross and White House forgot to do. Forgot? You know better than that...)

The following explanation may hit a nerve, cause something to happen as you read you never expected. Once one of my early books, (when I was a punk, fledgling Writer-Researcher) was presented to Cecil B. De Mille of Ten Commandments fame... He got quite excited over it: (American Safari) – story of the Invasion of America by China's hordes of poor manipulated people) like we now see in the current re-make movie Red Dawn...We got acquainted, amazed -he agreed to produce it "as an epic movie, bigger than my Ten Commandments", he said. Then, he died a few months before starting production. Bad shock to a young writer. Yet Cecil, Burt Lancaster and Playhouse 90 said I was 'A' writer! And that praised and polished my ego back then when I needed it – (Wife, nine kids). Now years later, China is ready to do her thing under new management, made ready by various problems and defaults, needing more grain and farm land free of flooding and earthquakes. Her population has no conscience when it's belly thins....Nor do leaders hesitate to do what seems necessary. The means to the end....also to collect what we borrowed and mortgaged as our economy dropped.

That American Safari script got produced, 'stolen' in the Cecil chaos by a famous major studio and became a Z movie called Nightmare Alley with George Peppard and Jan-Michael Vincent – a real dog of a movie recently copied with two Red Dawn shockers. I got not a cent for the 'borrowed' epic Cecil version… Inferior job horribly butchered. Seemed no one then except Cecil believed anyone would have the audacity to invade us…. Nevertheless it coincides almost perfectly with General George Washington's vision at Valley Forge, mine and Mother Shipton's prophecies hundreds of years ago. As well as Titus' invasion and sack of Jerusalem. Washington's vision is in our Congressional Record Archives. Someone thought it that important. Mother Shipton, burned at the stake, still ridiculed and rarely read, has a similar story to tell as me and the General. I have hesitated to revive, redo American Safari because it is not fun stuff to see with my present eyes: What was once just a 'possibility' of happening is right now, (tomorrow?) on our doorstep. I have mentioned American Safari so you might one day find that I had something to lay on you that isn't just good, exciting writing ability but THE MESSAGE it carries. The other stories might seem more important to those who abhor 'trying times'. Me too...

These six Booklets making up the total Book, have a slew of messages for about every type or brain size person . As said, MARTINE SALVATORE; - is a Redneck Version of overcoming the worst possible life can hand you…and more. It will probably get raves because it is very sexy. New York Times loves such endeavors. Having been there, done that, I understand. A current, delightful disease to be morally free of. Yet, good reading it is… Good luck … 'getting it'

CHAPTER 1

MARTINE SALVATORE
Global Private Investigator

Martine Goodenough stood before Third Circuit Court judge, Maxwell Johnson in upper state New York. Ms. Goodenough will you please step forward a bit, I have a hearing aid.? Thank you. You wish to change your last name, Correct? Yes...And your request here says you have decided on an Italian derivative though you are obviously Nordic or British extraction....He paused, looking over his small glasses. Does that matter, Judge? Well not to the court but perhaps to you – What is your employment, Dear? I'm a prostitute, high end. He blinked as she smiled. He became stone-faced. Uhhh, and are you licensed in the State of New York? No, I free lance, no pimps, They're Bastards! She gritted her jaws.

He sat back in his high backed ornate chair, pulling his black sheen robe closer around him as if protecting himself from what he could only hesitatingly feel creeping through his elderly but fit body. Ah, MARTINE, may I call you MARTINE? Of course, please relax, Sir, I understand. You didn't want me to lie did you? Oh, no, it's just a shock that someone as lovely as you can be here as candid as you are.... Yes. Well, tell me, I have to inquire. Why are you changing your name? And are you in any trouble you should reveal to the court? Well, Sir, first, Because of my profession my name gets a lot of slurs. Like: Am I good enough? My price is $1,000. I see. Do you type yourself an Escort or a Call Girl? A prostitute – it can't be dressed up. I screw men and I am good at it, I'm a straight out Whore, Sir. Martine!!... He couldn't help himself. Maxwell Johnson, dignitary thought he'd heard everything. He nodded. Right, more of your candid nature, I suppose. She fumbled at her blouse neckline. He blushed.

About any troubles, Ms?....She looked down, hesitating, thinking he had not noticed on his spec sheet. Two nights in jail for assault and battery, intent to kill with a deadly weapon. He started to stand and gathered himself, looking down at the papers, shuffling them. YOU? What did you do? Nothing. He tried to rape me at knife point in the back of that dress shop...She looked far into the distance....Did you have a gun? a... ? I'm Martial Arts, Judge - three Black Belts, Tai Quando, others. What did you do to him, Martine? I broke the bastard's arm and a leg, shoved his knife up his butt while he was howling....He could have asked me to coffee, he was cute....Martine! He coughed uncontrollably. I'm sorry, Sir, I...

He sat back wiping his mouth, his sweating forehead. He began....I've never....I know Sir, I'm too bold. BOLD? Dear you are the exception! How did you escape heavy prosecution? Three clerks witnessed him dragging me back there... she looked off again.. They watched him tear my dress off, rip my bra and pants. Just stood there, shitless, mouths hanging open. I did my thing. Did he live? Almost bled to death. He made it. They called it Self Defense, finally let me out of that hole. She bit her lip, remembering the filth of the county jail. And your future, what will you do after your name change, keep seducing men? Yes, I can't stop, I'm a sex addict, I love to orgasm - she blushed... Often as possible and prostitution gives me the chance. It's like I'm getting even for something. DEAR GOD! Martine! What's happened to you!

That's too long a story, Sir.

She stepped closer to the podium. I've tried treatment, medication, hypnotism. I... something happened when I was 14, don't know but it made me...She looked down, bitter, a Man Hater, but that's debatable with my hang ups – no one can get through to it. I tried but I.... The

Court Reporter, a squat, round faced matron was weeping, searching for a tissue with one hand, typing with the other. The court guard blinking. Martine looked over at the two of them...then back to the judge. He reached for his gavel, struck it half-heartedly. You are now officially, by the statutes of the State of New York, Martine Salvatore, 27 year old natural born citizen, free of all legal infringements. You are a remarkable woman Ms. Salvatore, may God bless and ...he stalled, I...also bless you, Dear.

She turned and with long, high-heeled strides lifted her head, paused, turned and winked back at the judge. He smiled and winked back as she felt the Glock 9 mm pistol tucked into her waist at her back She took a deep breath, gripped her fists, exited through the carved door. She pressed one hand to her groin. Yes, she was wet – again....God!... and by a Judge!

CHAPTER 2

Outside she noticed a red pickup across the street, two men looking at her far too intently. An uneasy feeling engulfed her. She unconsciously pulled her coat tighter. The Driver nodded cockily. Same old stares she thought. No class.

As she prepared to head to the Hotel she decided she was hungry - and cold...and very alone in a grubby world.

Fast forward – one year later, North Dakota, cheap P.I. Training course completed, clandestine, but legal, an irony for what she planned to charge. Same old $1,000 but this time an hour, not a night! She smiled broadly as she walked across the wide boulevard to the restaurant with the neon flashing sign. Inside a stout fifty-ish man handed her a menu, the slim girl escorted her to a booth. Coffee? With real cream and honey, no sweeteners, please… Sitting casually she looked in her purses wallet – It was still there, the check from The Ed Parker Kenpo Nationals last month – Her hands were still sore. One hundred thousand dollars for her Kenpo Karate win. Three wipeouts of America's best. The tall guy, lean faced across from her booth smiled. She looked away. Handsome. She looked back, his legs were out in the aisle. Yes, tall...His hair was crisp, wavy, longer than most pros. Dark everything. Hmmm. He didn't look back. A rustle of motion at the entrance doors. Both looked...Two men, obviously drunk or on drugs lurched against each other, grunted and sat down across from Martine near the tall hunks side in the next booth.

Martine got a pen and paper out of her heavy leather purse, The Glock, deep in the side section. She patted it, Good Baby, I'm tired of using my knuckles. She began printing words and numbers in itemized sequence. The hunk curious, she didn't notice. She was intent, face glowing... Hey, Honey, one of the drunks was leaning into her, Care if I sit with you. I'm lonesome as Hell today - he grinned, toothless at 30. Martine scooted back a ways... Why you creep, get out of my face! Hey! she motioned to the manager. He shook his head. The tall handsome man slid out of his booth silently, a glass of water in his hand. Pardon me, Bud - would you like a drink? The water flew into his face. Handsome picked him up like a doll, the partner on his feet now. Tall turned and grabbed the man by his crotch, hoisting him up to his face. Let's go, Guys, you need to go get some manners – ever heard of them? In four strides, the two men, off the ground – he strode through the double doors tossing the men safely into the new snow banks.

Get lost! Martine, now in the doorway, smiled, You do quite well don't you? Meaning? You didn't hesitate. How could I, you're lovely and you looked so vulnerable. She grinned. If he only knew what I was getting ready to...She put out her lightly gloved hand. Martine Salvatore'...she rolled it around in her mouth...sounded good... Ranch Meadows – You serious? Yep, Dad had a sense of humor, Mom fought it, Dad laughed and held his ground. Stubborn. I'm his boy. His eyes wetted momentarily. She started to question but - Well, thanks, Mr. Meadows but...she almost blew it, deciding not to infer she was quite sufficient...Are you afoot, MARTINE? Yes, I had a Taxi to my hotel and courthouse appointment from the airport.

CHAPTER 3

The warming Sun had melted the late snow, a few piles left around the streets. Can I call you Martine? Guess you earned it, Mister. He grunted, took her hand. Nice meeting you. Where you headed? Doesn't matter today, I just started a new life and...You did? Yes, let's walk, Ranch Meadows - looks like a park down that way...lots of trees, I like trees. He looked over at her puzzled by something...

She took a deep breath, thinking, God I wish I was sufficient... all the way. She took his arm. His jaw dropped a little. The wetness, she flinched - every time, Dammit! Worse here...she looked over at him. God, what a man...

The long slope of the park grounds faded behind them as they passed several couples and a man with a Collie. Martine stopped, Beautiful animal! Yes, she's more of a girlfriend really. We have a love affair, her and my wife. Ranch nodded, felt the dog's ears. No ticks like my Lab had he mumbled, problem here in Dakota. They moved on. Soon no more parksters showed, the wind had picked up, they pulled their collars up, Ranch opened his large coat and wrapped it around her. She looked up, smiling. God... From the distance further down, a roar as two Kamakazi 450s skidded into the opening. A tan pickup, pulled in alongside the two tan cycles. The truck had a magnetic sign on the door as did the two cycles in decals – Botticelli Graphite Inc. Ranch tensed – The two cafe 'drunks' weren't drunk after all -here they were, sober after 20 minutes! He spread his legs wide, knees slightly bent. Hi, Guys. The pickup driver and his buddy were out now – A shotgun in the passengers hands. Meadows? Yes, that's me, Why?

You just buried your parents we hear, today? Right? We knew your folks. A very stubborn couple...Ranches knees bent lower, his fingers spread. She noticed the two flat, rough knuckles on each hand, Hmm.

CHAPTER 4

What do you Gents want besides trouble? Your wallet and her purse for one...Well, guess you won't have much trouble with that Shotgun in our bellies. He raised his arms, opened his fingers as if giving in... Then Martine moved, her heavy purse slamming into the Shotgun, her spiked heel in the man's groin. He screamed as the gun blast shattered the downwind away from the small city complex. The other three men shocked at Martine's act, headed for Ranch who was roaring into them. ....Over in seconds, Martine fumbled for the Glock. Dropping her purse she leveled it, hands sideways at the Driver. The Glock, cool in her hands. She pulled the trigger as he started at Ranch with a knife, the other men down bleeding and moaning. No sound from the gun. Ranch slapped the man down like a fly, the large knife flying. He lurched out manipulating the gun from Martine's hands. She winced. Where did he learn that! A real pro move, she thought.

No more noise Martine! We have enough trouble without the police. He handed the gun back to her startled hands. That wasn't something you learned in gym class. He grunted. No. But wait, Let me see the gun... She handed it to him butt first. He turned it up, slammed his hand onto the base of the clip. Clip wasn't in all the way. Is it new? Yesterday. Hockshop? Yes. Well, it needs work. He retrieved the Shotgun and the knife, tossed them into the cab. Help me here. What? He had opened the Pickup's camper shell, lowered the tailgate. Come on!. He had the arms of one of the unconscious men, she took his ankles Wha...Just do it...Finally all four bodies were in the truck. Ranch had the roll of Duct Tape he saw on the trucks dash.. He had taped the men's mouths, ankles. Wrists behind their backs, WHAT..?. Martine, bewildered stood aside as he slammed the tailgate. Get in! He went to the two motorcycles, rolled them into the tall bushes.

Starting the truck he mumbled, A river down there... A few hundred feet and there it was, roaring water midstream, dark water at their tall bank.

Get out, give me your coat. Wh...? Give me the Glock! Wrapping the gun with her coat several times he went around to the tailgate, opened it, lifted his arm, shot each of the now struggling men in the neck. Closing the tailgate, he put an arm around Martine as he handed her coat. Put it on. Ranch Meadows started the truck, pulled the shift to Drive – it rolled into the river through the brush. Come on. She was shaking visibly, mouth open.

CHAPTER 5

He half dragged her to the cycles. Can you do this? He held her by the shoulders, arms straight. MARTINE! She was coming out of it... They killed my Mom and Dad, burned them in our farmhouse. I came for their funeral today and... he cursed. Oh. God, Ranch!. Those two nerds in the cafe were all an act, Martine. They wanted to gauge you, who you were -what you might know, if you knew me and about the Vatican... The What?! Later. Can you cycle? Anything on two wheels. Let's go then. Where? Our farm after you get your bags at the hotel. Get some flats, we're traveling. On these? No choice, for a ways down the road.

They roared off, stopped in the hotel's alley. In less than five minutes Martine was back. Ranch lashed the suitcase handles onto the back racks of both cycles with the last of the Duct Tape. Let's go! He took a devious way out of town, unseen he hoped.

The Meadows Farm was expansive, Iron Gates ten feet tall, wide open now, unlocked, chains broken by the fire trucks heading in. The huge estate was burned to rubble. A dog sitting there by the back door area, dull, thin. Josh! The dog wobbled over to Ranch. He got out his phone, dialed. Come get my dog, Phil, I'm leaving and can't – his voice trembled...Come on, Martine, they rolled their bikes to the hen house. The chickens were gone, Stolen, skunks, something, he said. Inside the block building Jason Meadows had built for his wife Nan's languid hobby of selling eggs she didn't need to – Ranch tore furiously at the wall down near the rough concrete floor. A patch of block crumbled at his attack with the bar he had taken off the wall rack of tools. What is it, Ranch? The dust settling, he held a copper case in his hands. The eighteen inch square box lid groaned open. Her mouth dropped. DIAMONDS! Yes, and papers worth a fortune, Deeds, Titles, Martine - Dad was a millionaire and then some. Big Graphite deposits up at the north acreage. Five thousand acres of almost pure grade Graphite. Botticelli tried to buy and then...they beat him, threatened Mom - still Dad told them to go to Hell. Dad...Mom! That's why they murdered and burned my folks... His voice broke - OH GOD! He sank to his knees. Now she knew how he could have been so cold blooded. Why not, the Scum! She bent down and cradled his immense shoulders.

CHAPTER 6

It was dusk and the Dakota road Ranch knew so well from his youth was barren of traffic. Ten more miles and they were across the border into a large farm another oil shale town. The road here followed the large winding River. Ranch motioned. He headed there once more. A mile into the river's banks, he stopped. Cut the tape on the suitcases, shoved the cycles into the river's roar. They'll sink. Come on. He grabbed both bags. I can carry one...Shut up! Walking fast beside his long strides in the flats she had pulled out of her suitcase before coming down. She thought MARTINE!!! what have you gotten yourself into? Her eyes hoping for adventure and big money now wide open to the dangers ahead...

Back on the Highway it wasn't long into the cold night air that the Semi came on them. Rolling the window down the fat driver motioned, get in kids, too damned cold out there. Where ya headed? Next town a few miles, Car broke down ways back. Thanks for helping. The rest of the way into Southburg was quiet. This will do, Friend. Thanks from both of us. Good Man! Yeah, good luck. Go get warm. Martine smiled, Yeah...warm. Ranch lifted her down from the Big Mac cab. He smelled of adrenaline sweat. She sighed...God...What? Nothin, Ranch.

The large neon motel sat next to a new car lot, Ranch pointed, Wheels... Inside he spoke... Car broke down, got a lift here, how much for tonight, Two beds? A hundred and tax – TWO beds? The girl grinned - Yeah tired, had to hike. She nodded, Your choice, Handsome, she wiggled. Sign here, your license please. Martine was smiling shyly...

MONOLITH

The three small rooms were warm, clean, a cafe close. Get showered while I get us something. Any favorites? Anything that doesn't smile. He blinked...Vegetarian? Yep, You? Almost. He left his coat on the rack. Take your time, I have to make a few calls – alone. Safer for you.. She nodded, chin up wondering what that meant. How deep was she in this...

CHAPTER 7

An hour later, seven O'clock Clint came in the door loaded with sacks, the smell working the atmosphere. Wow, you are hungry. Aren't you? Guess we've earned this, Marty. Marty, huh? She wondered what that meant. She took some of the sacks to the round table, spread the items. Look at this!, Gee, Ranch., you did good! Her bags were open, items hung in the bathroom, steam coming from the tub. What are you going to do for clothes? Tomorrow a Four By and clothes after that. No big deal, I travel light from here on...Eating in silence for an hour they kept looking up at each other. Finished, she gathered the paper plates and plastics. You know, Ranch, I have some questions...You should. We'll talk in the car. I want to hire you to go to Rome with me- strictly business...no mood for sex or romance... after Mom and Dad, Relax.... No, I want to talk now, tonight -Remember, my life's just starting.

She went to her purse opened the wallet, pulled out a card, handed it to Ranch. Let's get acquainted. Ok, Martine Whatever you say. I need you, really do. We'll sit in bed. She smiled, touched his arm - Just sit. You talk, I'll listen and make notes on my I Pad. He turned the silver-card over.

Martine Salvatore
Global Private Detective
One thousand usd an hour plus expenses
Ms.goodenough@comcast.net

CHAPTER 8

Ranch sat down on the side of the bed...Looks like we have a bit of synchronicity here. You a P. I.? Yeah, OK, with that? He twirled the card in his fingers, scarred, calloused. She took his hand. Kenpo? Yes, how did you know. She showed him her knife sword, the edge of her hands. Leather, hard as rock...his eyes raised. You? She reached her purse, pulled out. The Certificate. Then rustled in her suitcase. Tossed him the gold inlaid belt. This is the Nationals! Yeah, Ranch I just won The Ed Parker Nationals in Milwaukee. That's an annual $100,000 dollar gig, MARTINE! – did you go co-ed? Yep. Beat both and Norton too. God, Martine– he beat me three years ago and he's better now by fifty pounds – a greased panther! Well, I guess synchronicity! Ranch rubbed his eyes as he looked at her. I GUESS I do need you! How much? For what? You and Rome. Is it about this Botticelli corporation? Yes, Vatican owned, hid under paper work, Huge megalith cartel. Well... how much, Martine, he smiled, Gonna make me beg?

He pulled off his suede boots and pullover shirt, laid back on the bed. She removed her robe - in pajamas. Ranch gulped visibly. She was a quivering mass of breast and muscle. No rayon pajamas could hide that. The neck open enough to tell things were Good Enough, her ankles and arms tanned to the extreme. He coughed nervous, How much -you didn't say.? She laid back on the pillow, arms behind her neck, couldn't believe her words: For your Mom and Dad, zero, Ranch! Partners this one – just my expenses and Romano – I need a break -so do you. He sat up, held out his hand. Deal, but I won't forget amenities when... When what?

When we destroy an empire, Marty - an empire...

ROY WOODWARD

After the bed sitting conversation she looked over at him as he got up. Shaking her head, she headed for the bathroom. I'll be quick, Ok? I'm going to have a hot shower -And a very long cold one - he looked her over from feet to crown. She winked back, Yeah, we did good didn't we? Ranch put his hands on his hips. You're safe from me, Martine, I had enough bruises last month. What happened, Ranch? Thugs, L.A. tried to get me, six of them. Are you hurting now? Yeah, but not from that...he grinned. She threw a pillow at him.

CHAPTER 9

Morning sun woke him up across from her in the other twin bed. He got up quietly. She had loosened her hair after she came out of the shower robed last night God, what a woman, he whispered. Minutes later he came back loaded with breakfast from the adjoining restaurant, placing the food, putting Honey on the steaming oatmeal, dividing the buckwheats, pouring the Grapefruit juice. She was up at his noise, sitting on the edge of the bed, arms overhead, stretching... Will you please do that in the other room, Martine? What? That...he put his arms over head. You men! I'm just a girl! Sure, just a girl - He shook his head again. Well...Yeah, well, just stop stretching in front of me, OK? Ok, Ranch, but...No butts either. He went over to the window, pulling the drapes aside, looking both ways, then closing the drapes carefully, switching the lights on. Let's eat. Give me a minute, Ranch. Well, hurry, we have to be out of this state. He frowned...

The car dealer shook hands, starred at Martine, she smiling, reached out for his handshake, gripped his hand. Wincing, blinked as his fingers emitted a slight crackling noise. He opened and closed his hand several times, looked over at Ranch. She used to milk our goats... But look, Fella, we need to get to L.A. right away. I have cash and my Visa - can you bundle a deal up super fast for that silver Suburban out there? How many miles? Ninety legit. Drive it. Good rig. Yeah, come on, Dear. Martine blinked and took his hand. I'll have to have your Drivers License and your Visa, Mr. Meadows. License is OK, no one touches my cards! Well... Ok, Mr. Meadows.

Putting Martine in, Ranch lifted the hood as the engine idled, Push the pedal, Martine. Easy! Just a tad...Ok, try all the lights for me. He went to the rear, motioned right, left, then moved his hands forward and back to his chest. The Dealer headed inside, wind was bristling and he hadn't grabbed his coat. We won't be long. Around the corner and off to a side road, Ranch maneuvered the 4X, trying brakes, steering, hands on and off the wheel. You know your wheels. Ranch. Dad's place, lots of years since a kid. He taught me things. I'll bet he did. He looked off in the distance. Five miles of road test and Martine was still gripping the seat. You OK? Think so - what a test drive!

CHAPTER 10

It is a good rig , Fella, we'll take it. Here's my Insurance card. You said it's a 2001? Yes. How much? $5,900. Wrap it up. Ranch tossed two banded bundles of $100s on the counter. I think there's five thousand there...Take the rest off my Visa now. On the Freeway, he unleashed the 400 plus horses and was pushing the 80 allowed. She moved over against him. Mind? Why, no, we're Buddies aren't we? She tried the radio with no luck. Here, I had one of these, it's tricky. He moved the dial to the concert station. Well, I'll be, he adjusted the volume down and started to say something. Hey, I know that - it's Wagner's Tristan und Isolda, Ranch. You like it? Just the intro, fantastically tender -He must have been in love with a real Isolda. Yeah, I always felt that, kinda tied to it lately. So different though than all of those repetitious up and down parts later, he frowned. Sounded like Lone Ranger music. She laughed and offered: It was like his life, Ranch, like his life. He never quite got over Love when he had it in the palms of his hands. Drank himself stupid...She remembered her Dad... The road melted away as she held his right hand and became strangely silent. He tilted his head, you OK? I hope so, Ranch...He thought better than inquire any further.

Three days later, bleary eyed and smelling of man sweat, he pulled into Pasadena. She had asked to tidy up several times as he gassed up. This isn't L.A.! An uncle, he'll let me leave the rig here in his barn. He raises horses. She smelled good - Rose Water and Lilacs. He leaned over to her shoulder. That Rose Water? Yep, and Lilacs. Not expensive. Kind of old fashioned. Do you..He interrupted., Mom vamped Dad with it for over sixty years. This synchronicity is getting to me. What's going on? She smiled, Gets me...Her tongue in her cheek.

CHAPTER 11

Uncles gone. Ranch slammed the double doors, hooked the loose padlock and opened his phone - leaving a message. Come on, Dearrrr.. He grinned. A block down the road they entered a Glass Shop -Meadows Auto Glass and Car Museum. Ranch grabbed his nephew, lifting him off the ground. Martine, Jon my best nephew. He looked Martine straight in the eyes. Ranch can I have her if you ever get tired of perfect? Sure, anything, Jon. She pushed Ranch backwards, he caught her arm, she chopped him gently alongside his head. Ok, see how you affect men, Marty? Sure...really tough on them. Jon, He pointed, I left my rig in your extra barn like before, locked it. Have a key? Jon pulled a key off his side clip bundle. Here, keep it. About you two....? Jon, eyebrows up started to ask. Business partners, Jon, buddies. We're headed for Italy on Dad's business that damned Graphite scam. He closed his hands. Bet you are. But stay cool, those prisons over there, you have no proof... I will... I hear they're rough. I know did my homework, but thanks. And hey, I'll call if I need you. Still willing? Eager, Ranch, anything, anytime! He blinked back a tear. His folks took care of me Marty, back then after Nam when Mom had Cancer– least I can do...They embraced. Martine, biting her lip went to him and gave him THE hug. He shook his head. Hang onto this one, Ranch. He nodded, absent mindedly -

Leaving Jon, Ranch scrubbed his foot, nervously phoning the Airport for the shuttle.

CHAPTER 12

The lurch of the wheels closing up, the familiar roar, the body rush of the big Trans Atlantic plane nosing skyward always thrilled and scared her. She squeezed his arm. Look at these, Martine. He handed her the tickets. Paris!? You told me… She turned facing him, Yeah, that's why I had you go get those newspapers while I got the tickets. But Ranch! Are you kidnapping me! He grinned - Kinda. What do you mean? Kinda? I thought we.. were going to Italy? Marty, I wanna show you something I once promised myself I'd see again - with a girl like you. It's quite a sight. You'll like it. Few days there to get that funeral out of my mind and for you to go nuts over French men and their pinches. Pinches? Yeah, they pinch good looking women on the butt in public. It's a compliment. Her mouth dropped, Really? Really. I couldn't do that. Even to you. Want to...? Probably.

Paris cabs were small to maneuver the old, narrow streets. The big bus, twin decked, moved around the Tower, then the Tunnel that got Princess Diana. As they passed through it Ranch noticed Martine's tears. He put an arm around her. Murder, Hon, pure money covered, aristocracy MURDER! He shook his head. Same thing with the Vatican. Plain as Hell with Mom and Dad! He stared out the window to the darting cabs below, racing each other After minutes in heavy traffic the immenseness of The Louvre loomed ahead, sparkling like a monolithic, faceted super diamond. The Louvre? Yep, I want to show you something. What, Ranch? Surprise. I still can't believe what I saw ten years ago with Mom and Dad. Just wait - you'll be shook up too...

CHAPTER 13

Below a black limo struggled among the rushing cabs. A swarthy man in a Burnoose, looked up at Ranch and smiled. Let's move, Martine... Why...The pistol handle Ranch saw easily in the loose coat, as he looked down at the smiling man, was enough. He had been wondering if they had tracked them. Money, power, technology. So different on the big farm when he was a kid. Ranch helped her into the seats across the isle. She felt nice to his hands. She looked up, direct eye contact and quivered. There it goes she thought...

Then a moment later, Come on! Lifting her out of the bus seat – Wha..? We're getting off next stop, Walking. It's not far. The bus rounded a corner near a group, visitors carrying souvenirs, models - the Basilica, paintings of the Apian Way, the many fountains, Peter's image crucified upside down. Ranch shook his head. The lying bastards...If people only knew – his words trailed off. Her arm went around his waist. I need to know those things, Ranch. Will you? It isn't popular T-V stuff...you'd vomit. I'm ready, try me. Ok, Marty, tonight in bed. Sex?.. No sex! Last thing either of us need- although you're pure Hell to look at... You think so, Ranch? Why? You have a lot of layers, Martine Salvatore! The outside ones are delicious. and they're coming off slowly. Don't hold back. I do like you and maybe I can help number 12 layer later, OK? How was he reading her? She stopped walking, spun him around. Lean down here, Fella....And Ranch Meadows suddenly knew why he was in Paris but sure as Hell he didn't know who Martine Salvatore' was except what that hall in the Louvre might tell them...Their lips engulfed their souls as the crowd watched and French men cheered Viva' la France and applauded. Ranch leaned, without losing a beat, picked her up and tried to give her what she had just given him. Martine Salvatore' fainted in his arms.

The Bus bench was wet from mid morning dew. He never noticed, rubbing that face to revive her. Marty! Marty? Hey, Girl! She blinked awake. Am I that good, Marty? Wha? What happened, Hon?... She stuttered, I, I, I'll tell you tonight. He rocked her in his arms for a good five. Can you walk? Sure, Ranch, but can I have a drink of something? At the small umbrella bistro Ranch held her close while the waiter brought the Lime Aid. Sure that's all you want? Yes, Thanks, I'm Ok now, just had a shock that's all. A shock? Tonight, Ranch, tonight.

CHAPTER 14

The Louvre startled both of them. The new remodel, the new packaging, the new 2012 footage enormous. You're not tired? I'm fine, enraptured, Ranch. Thank you, Thank you for Paris! She hugged him. He blushed as the crowd smiled at her excitement centering him.

Around the curve of the new additions Ranch guided her arm to a larger than life size painting. Over here a bit, Marty....He pulled her to the right a few feet. Now look there in the center, that family gathered around that tall old guy with the horse...and the sword. She drew in her breath...now look at the description at the side by the frame...She drew in another breath, squeezing his hand. My God, IT'S ME! That's me! Ranch, those people, that's my family, Dad, Mother, Gary, my brother! And that old man, tall, silver haired - IT'S YOU, Ranch! YOU! My GOD! She went up closer to examine the name on the painting. She ran back to Ranch. THE MEADOWS OF TYROLIA, Ranch, what's going on here? Martine I've lived with this for ten long years. That face, your face there - it never left my days or nights. Mom said it was an omen of my future. They sat down from the shocks rocking them.

Just then Ranch saw the gray burnoose and black longcoat far off in the surging crowd getting off the triple escalators., Hurry! Let's go! Wha...I want to... We'll come back. Trouble down there,Marty. The Burnoose hadn't seen them, he was sure of that. They must have plants on us... She asked, Plants? Devices. My watch, Something on the Suburban, in the motel, our suitcases...? They are capable. It's the Vatican Jesuit thugs. Walking faster they found the gold tinted elevators. The same guy you saw below the bus, Ranch? I'm sure of it. Get in! The doors slide shut, four floors down they opened to a promenade with fountains and gazebos – Tall fountains glistening in the warming October sun.

CHAPTER 15

On the bristling street Ranch waved a cabbie. Close hotel, he mumbled in near perfect French. A Motorcycle rental villa? One close to hotel. Martine recognized the words, barely - from her handbook of years back when she just 'knew' she was going to Italy and France as Martine Salvatore. In the cab, Ranch looked back fitfully, eyes red, chest rising. I shouldn't have brought you, MARTINE! I...Shut up with that! We're here. I love this. I love YOU! Her face glowed. The Cabbie turned back around to his chore.

The tall, ancient hotel dwarfed the crowds below its steps. Hurry! He handed the cab driver a hundred dollar bill, shoving his money clip back in his side pants pocket. We have to get back to the suitcases and check everything. They've obviously got us scanned... Look Marty, I'll go ge....Oh, no you won't! I'm your wall paper from now on. Besides I like foreign bikes in busy cities, it's like a .007 movie.

At the storage depot in the airport they got their two, re-packed suitcases and Ranch's military duffle bag. She had noticed the worn tag on the cords: IRAQ Special Forces, Green Belt, Sector 6.. This time the red and green Motorcycles had carriers with nylon straps. Outside at the lock bike racks they lashed the cases and the bag. Let's git! You remember the way back? No. Well keep close, it's getting late and traffics bad. Stay at my side much as possible. She looked a little worn at his words. OK, promise. Still, two different times Ranch had to double back and retrieve her. Traffic was worse than he'd figured. Making it to the hotel locking the bikes in racks, they got their rooms, Ranch taking out the card for the bike rentals, unlocked his phone. Ten minutes they'll be here to pick them up. Wow, two hundred eighty for two hours! He opened his hands. Rich city folks too besides the Cardinals. She smiled, Probably all lackeys with their licenses in hock to the Black Robes...He nodded.

Come here. She stood her ground. You.. I'm tired. He took the two steps up to the bed's dais. Picked her up and sat back on the bed. You do that well...just like Rhett Butler. Yeah, mind? Don't think so. What you thinkin? Here I am, Macho Man. She put her arms around his neck. You need a shave, Mac! Later. Just want you to know I'm proud of you, shocks and all...

CHAPTER 16

Hey, Ranch, Big P.I. Woman has to get her shocks and her joys. I got both today. You? Well, yes and no. I expected the worst, we're dealing with pros here. She smiled and cupped his chin, And who are we dealing with in that Louvre painting? You tell me, Martine...he paused, Marty... he touched her face, kissing her on the nose. She snuggled. Do you have....to go? Yeah, to give them the keys, inspect for any damages and pay. I'll shower, Ranch and order something, Ok? Anything, Partner, Save me some hot water, these older hotels are Hell on amenities. I Promise. She lifted her arms, pulling off her sweater. Hey, STOP that, will you! She slid her jeans down and off, her boots clattering. Beads of quick sweat showed on his face,\ Ok, I'll hurry. Sure? Yeah, we have lots to talk about don't we? She smiled...I'll say we do...she drawled. Now cut that out Martine! What... she grinned? Go shower you need a cold one, Girl, your motor's running. Turning her back to him she tossed her loosed bra at him. For God's sake! Marty! Running for the ornate door he tripped on the thick throw rug. Catching himself on the couch arm he reddened. See what I mean? She turned, hands over her breasts, You're just too clumsy, Ranchman. Ok, whatever you say. The door closed behind him. She locked the dead bolt. A SHOWER in Paris...Ahhh... She tossed her jeans on the couch, grabbed her suitcase. Paris! Yippee....Outside the door Ranch tripped again - on the rubber mat...fully flustered by mystery girl.

CHAPTER 17

Downstairs the inspection complete, keys returned, paid off with his Visa, Ranch didn't notice the blond girl in the black outfit snapping a picture of him. Upstairs Martine was dressed in a loose terry robe. She had ordered room service. Two Pineapple Smoothies, Blueberries, Yogurt and Bananas, Rye Toast with Almond Butter and Papaya wedges, placed the cart close beside the large poster bed -as she tilted her head, Nice choice?, she whispered. The room boy looked at the menu he'd rolled in, Vegetarian? Yes. Me also. He was lean, tanned, twentyish. Thank you, she handed him twenty as Ranch knocked.. Ranch looked him over, shut and locked the dead bolt – He ask anything suspicious? No, nice, mannered. Ranch looked at the tray near the bed, back at her.

Anything there that can't wait a few minutes? No, the smoothie is in a chiller, Why aren't you starved? He looked her up and down, a half smile, 'I have food to eat you not of,' if I can quote their Jesus. She went to him, raised on tiptoes. He removed her arms from his shoulders. Help me with these chairs. Wha...? Place that one here across from mine, yeah, closer - that's about right. Sit Marty. Are you going to interrogate me? Not quite. He sat opposite to her, pulled up closer. Give me your hands. She raised her eyebrows, puzzled, uuhh... I'll explain.. Marty. He turned her palms up, placing his to hers. Their knees touching, he asked, Comfortable?

Yes, you gonna hypnotize me? ? Nope, relax, trust me. Take a few deep breaths like this. He raised his chin, eyes closed, breathed deeply through his chiseled nostrils. Ok, we're going to just look into each others eyes. See each other in the quiet. I learned this in the Potala in the Himalayas ...on vacation with Dad. He winced and swallowed What happens, Ranch, Nirvana, she laughed? Better - Soul Amalgamation. Ohh.? Some Hindus do it before their marriage merge. We gonna get married, she giggled? I don't know, but we have to be a lot better acquainted for what we're involved in.. Our lives will depend on it. What do I do? Just breathe, look into my eyes. See yourself in my pupils. Can you? Yes, just tiny.... Sit straight! .Her tension finally vanished, worries about him trying to hypnotize her calmed...a little, what if... Ten minutes later a peace had entered her she hadn't felt, ever. Her breathing was deep, smooth, like stream water filling her body. Her eyes moist as if wanting to tear...She started out tense. A half hour later - That's enough for now, Hon. He took her arms, lifting her - Let's eat. Wobbling beside him from the experience, he seated her at the table. Ok? Yes, amazing, Ranch I liked that...I guess.... Me too. Good Trusting Girl, thanks. You were worried weren't you, Marty? A little, but....Eating her tray of good choices, he explained further Hindu secrets.

She didn't feel like talking, Ranch watched her flushed face. She had become nervous as her face flushed, deeper. She glanced at the bed. Finished, he took her hand. Get comfy, I'm going to get into my robe. After his shower - shave, he splashed on some Aqua Velva on his chest - he didn't like anything on his face but his Mom's Aloe plant gel. He shook his head remembering all she had taught him. He stared back at himself. I look too much like you, Dad. Mirror's can be too much... He let out a breath, flushed the toilet again, opened the door. SHE WAS GONE! MARTINE? Marty!, he rushed into the rest of the suite. MARTINE! Finally he found her on the balcony, face down on the chaise lounge, sobbing. He lifted her slowly, adjusting her loosened robe over her dark pubic hair.. Hey, Sweetheart, what's wrong? She began sobbing harder, clinging to his neck. Carrying her to the bed he propped her up on the silk pillows, sitting next to her, looking. She had calmed, but eyes closed, breath unstable. He'd leave her alone a while, bent, kissed her nose, placed a throw over her. Going to the kitchen he heated some water, tossed in a couple of Green Tea bags from the chrome container and tore open some Honey pouches. Frowning, puzzled he went to her. She was quite calm now, eyes open, tongue in her cheek. Sorry, Ranch, a lot of things caught up with me in that chair thing. I thought it might, me too. It's Soul Stuff, isn't it? I know. The old Lama said it was life in its finest and worst moments – depending.

CHAPTER 18

My God, I guess - it was like movies all crowded together, kaleidoscoped rushing in but now a peace...Ranch...She reached out to him. He took her hand, Slide over, Marty. Both on the outside of the covers, close, holding hands. She quivered. It didn't happen, It didn't happen! She whispered quietly. Then yelled out, It DIDN'T HAPPEN! Oh dear God, Thank you, Thank you! He pulled aside, What didn't happen. Marty. Wha...? She turned on her side, pulling her robe aside, hands behind his neck, ruffling his hair, kissing him, long, fiercely, digging her hands into his arm and neck. Finally, limp beside him, smiling she spoke, smiling He closed her loose robe. Ok - I have known many men, Ranch, a lot of boys – very few men that deserved the title. I love you, Ranch - like Heaven and Earth, Mountains and Oceans, War and Peace, Zhivago and Camelot - and I may lose you. - I know that, don't know how I could handle it. Still I know you love me - but few, real men could handle what I'm going to tell you...Ranch up now on an elbow, mouth parted...No, Ranch, let me talk while I can.. He laid back on his side facing her. Ok....he breathed. Before I tell you the Beginning I want to tell the End of my story - the worst: I've been a high class Manhattan prostitute, a thousand a whack for years. Though I'm clean hygienically - I'm filthy - in my head. He gasped… But... No, let me go on. Explaining won't be easy. When I was 13 puberty was showing up I had a habit- sleep walking, irregularly, walking around the house, usually outside on our large gated grounds. They had to put up wrought iron fencing because of it. One night I walked into my parents bedroom doorway, Stood there for minutes maybe hours before they noticed me... They were having naked, frantic, erotic sex. I didn't remember any of that...till later, around sixteen. Then they told me and more later when I was older, tested, hypnotized - being examined for my 'disorder'. She got up from the bed, placed the throw over Ranch. My disorder was still sleep walking, yes, with something else added: I was 'sleeping' with every boy in High School, had been for two years. But at eighteen it worsened. I began having almost uncontrolled orgasms whenever a boy just touched me! Sometimes when he just eyeballed me! I was a young beauty. I used that on them because orgasm had become my lifeblood! Ranch winched... Yeah, I warned you, Ranch... My parents finally found out what my life was, took me to counselors, medical specialists over half the country, once to Italy, twice to Mexico, New York four times. The best. It about broke Dad, heart and wallet. She bit her lip...Finally more Hypnotists, Psychics, Fortune Tellers, Kooks – all of what promised Mom and Dad hope for their 'Dear baby girl'. Catch was, by the time they were able to admit to themselves and the specialists agreeing to what might have been some sort of a reverse trigger, a kind of 'Freudian Female Oedipus complex' - Subconsciously I was hooked because of what I saw at puberty - in total innocence, loved what I was, what I felt, lived for sex, any sex, anywhere, anytime - never tired of my 'sin'.

She paused...The preachers had their turn trying to save me, cure me. One of them lost his family because he was caught with me naked, drugged, in his Cadillac, him drunk, by the local Sheriff. – She looked at Ranch, Yeah, he really got taken, T-V showed it all - you probably remember...big estate, rectory, jet, sport cars, cabin, boats. Prison. That's when I ran off... couldn't let my folks suffer any more of it...she started to cry, corrected, set her jaw. I refused to call them, take any more of Dad's money. Because of my habit I met a pimp. He laid me; easily of course. I told him, he placed me big time. A thousand a roll! - Drugs offered at 50% off. Thank God I refused another vice, seeing what my sister call girls had become - glassy eyed zombies part of their coked up lives. One died in my arms at a Christmas party, overdose of something in her drink. She shook to death in my arms! While her parents screamed. Ranch was breathing deeply, his finger tips gathered. Shall I go on, she shuddered? Ranch? He nodded. Well, I guess I wanted to suffer to hurt others because of my sexual happiness – guilt syndrome... a paradox, huh? So I began Martial Arts, everything I could afford and more at times because of the travel. Nick, my pimp, was fair with that, so I always came back. He kind of worshiped me. Only halfway love I ever experienced, he didn't know what to call it ...or me.

CHAPTER 19

She leaned back against the wall looking deep at him, hands behind her neck, pulling slowly on her hair -After I won that Nationals in Milwaukee and pocketed that hundred grand I KNEW I had my big chance. Didn't go back. Sent Nick five grand and a Valentine. No forwarding. His buddies weren't too gentle with drop outs...She stared into the distance. Well, you saw me there in Dakota changing my name with a very shocked Judge. Had to tell him all. He'd have found out anyway. Nice old guy...let slide a lot of things. Up to that time I had this problem. Men not only attracted me, I attracted them, they got interested easily. I still liked the sex habit - more so the attention, high end dates, clothes...Men, no matter what they were like - if even half way decent, touched me, danced with me, helped me into their limo. Yeah, orgasm - right out of the blue. No way could I control it – I'd get wet. You back there in that restaurant. You looked me over, Bang, I was drenched. No touch, just a look, all it took – but different...Then outside we shook hands... again it happened.. Yes, I WORE Pads... She paused, stretched, looked long at Ranch, immobile, hands still templed together, un-smiling, un-anything. She went on... When you did your thing with those murdering bastards, when you didn't make any passes at the motel after we dumped those rats, I began to feel something else. You. Yes, YOU and it felt good, better than any orgasm or anything I'd ever felt. I of course, didn't know love, didn't think I ever could because...well imagine...You look in the mirror every night at the nice gowns, every morning, see the big cash bills in your purse, toss it across the room - and you always go over and pick it up, count it again... She kicked the sofa, her long leg showing to the groin. She pulled the robe together....

MONOLITH

Ranch finally moved. Slowly went to her, put his hands on each side of her face, looked deep into her, I'm going outside for a while... You smoke? No, I need to...think. She watched in shock and wondered - as he closed the latch and door behind him. Suddenly wishing she smoked ..She went to the fridge.

CHAPTER 20

Forty-five minutes passed by, the latch moved from his key. He entered, red eyed, face wet. Walking over to her at the table where she was gobbling up leftovers. He knelt down, his head on her knees. Tomorrow, the Louvre again, Ok? We have to know, especially now. Let's go to bed, we can't take anymore of this - I'm shot. So are you. Morning came, under the sheets their bodies still in their robes, they were entwined, intact. Ranch, wake up! It's 10 O'clock. The Louvre. Yeah. Martine, He slowly got out of bed, smelled his armpit, looked at her soberly, Would you mind showering with me, I smell and I need my back scrubbed? She got up, rushed to him, leaped around his waist, robe dropping. In the shower soaping his back, she asked, Are you going to tell me? What? What you think of my damned confession! Oh, yeah... That... Her mouth dropped, OH YEAH??!

He took her face, Well look, Little Girl I guess if you can forgive me for unknowingly killing women and kids in Nam and Iraq, you'd be a 'good enough' woman to spend Infinity with....She screamed and did that indescribable kiss again. How...what happened out there when you went out? I asked Mom and Dad about this. And after we went to sleep, he paused, Just a minute... He began casually soaping her breasts - I dreamed we were tied together with huge ropes round a tree in a valley like that one at the Louvre – only I was young and your breasts were like those clusters of grapes Solomon wrote about...She punched him in the stomach playfully - And now? Tell you later, I'm busy here...Drying each other off, she asked. Don't you WANT me? Of course. But Ranch, we slept all night in each others arms, just showered, naked as soapy Jay Birds, kissed like newly weds and...and...she faltered, you didn't get an erect....! He laughed, I didn't want to - learned how not to - unless...She pursed her mouth, eyebrows up. You kidding me? Don't I please you, Ranch...? Look down here, at me, Hunk, all of me. She spun slowly. What do you see? He blinked, Everything that would drive men to drink if they couldn't have you. That's all. Ranch? No, lots more. That Potala and their long Hall of Records, the monks let me photograph reams of ancient scrolls. I know things... Well, aren't I attractive to you RIGHT now? You sure are, MARTINE, and that's why I'm in control. This is no small matter and you can't be hurt anymore. I know how to erase all you've been through, sure. But I don't dare mishandle this or you. She cocked her head, That's probably going to be the nicest single thing - anyone EVER says to me, Mr. Meadows. She took a long, hard look at each of their nakedness took the towel from his hands, wrapped herself. Let's go to the Louvre and find out about us...As she walked ahead of him, he pinched her bottom,...tried to, Platinum hard. She turned, grinning, Pervert! Viva la France Americonnn... he grinned.

CHAPTER 21

Their cab driver looked them over, Newly weds? He asked. He was obviously an Easterner, burnoose and all. Ranch said, Sorry, I forgot something, go on! Don't wait. Ok, I wait, no charge extra! He extended his right hand. Ranch reached out. No! I said, you go on! The man blanched as his hand was being crushed. He yelled, Yes, yes, I go! The next cab was Italian. The Louvre, please. The frowning blond girl nodded, silent...

Before the huge painting Martine – a Salvatore - stood in front of Ranch, his arms around her, looking down over her head as she read the yellow brochure the attendant had given them for a gratuity. She read quietly: "This life-sized relic painting has a decomposed date but it appears to be in the 1500s. Highly researched evidence tells us the silver haired, muscular, elderly man, the one with the sword, was some form of warrior- or mercenary seeking to purge their land of a tyrannical group of barons who had moved into the area from the west, probably Ireland's later Catholic power usurpers. The family hired him, the young woman was probably Martin Salvatore's daughter - part of the noble family that had for years resisted such intruders. It is surmised that the Salvatore clan thus hired the healed, unknown, deeply scarred, silver-haired man with the sword, as a sort of resident protector since the family patriarch was deceased from an altercation with local vandals. The other girl, a sister it is supposed. The young boy, a brother. The vandals and their origin are scant in our research but probably were hired by the intruders from the west. Little can be found except that previous to this, the man with the sword, perhaps one famed, Francisco of Sicily. It is said, unprovable, that he had been imprisoned for several years by the Roman pope for insurrection against the throne. Four years later he escaped, caught, tortured horribly, cast supposedly dead, in the Salvatore gates as a warning to all locals to desist from any aggression.. The girl washed and cared for him. They became lovers despite all the family could do to dissuade them. They knew if he was found alive. They both would be killed - for they were inseparable, traveling into many policed areas of the province, arming and training resisters to both throne and westerners. Being finally caught, they were emolliated, tied to a dead tree as seen in the massive painting. It was said their ashes caused a great vineyard on that spot to spread and flourish as if by magic for centuries. This all may be fable… but much is verified by our Louvre experts in Italian history. The almost faultless painting later appeared after the cruel pope died, reportedly by a family member, found rolled into a spliced leather tube, in a cave on the Salvatore' property. The cave is only a scant few kilometers from the Louvre's first structure." The Louvre thanks you for your patronage.

CHAPTER 22

Martine, shaking violently, dropped the brochure unconsciously, turned and embraced Ranch Meadows - remembering - the shower - the deep scars on his back and thigh - embarrassed to ask...He picked her up, went to the near bench, both crying like children at a Santa Clause story they wanted to believe in, but dared not hope for because they were told he was dead. Eyes red, somewhat settled they walked down.

Strangely, at the exit site, the blond cab driver was just collecting her last fare. They thought nothing of this, still reeling from their other-worldly trauma. Getting in Ranch felt a strange uneasiness come over him. The attractive girl turned and smiled. A whirring sound came from behind her, a thick glass slid up, the door locks clicked! Martine stunned grabbed his hand. Hurtling down the wide boulevard, the cab was in the Paris suburbs. A mist began to arise from the floor. A minute later, both of them were slumped over each other.

Good morning, Mr. Meadows! The large man, fifty pounds heavier and a foot taller than Ranch, blew smoke from his cigarette into Ranches retching face. Never mind the questions - let me anticipate: Who am I? Exactingly who you think I am – A Jesuit, protector of our Pontiff and acquirer of his rightful wealth. Ranch frowned....Ah, Yes you undoubtedly know of our history and tribute to our living Lord. I am Monsignor Durante. I need not hide my identity or role. After we are done interrogating you and your lovely friend to get what you know we are after - you will be in an outlying Paris trash bin - unfortunate lifeless victims of the poor lower class who often abduct travelers, raping them, relieving them of all valuables, stripping their clothing to sustain a living in poor, tattered France. Interesting that their lustful President has taken flight from them for a better tax haven, don't you think? Martine spit on him. Her bonds quieting her and Ranch otherwise. Marty, relax. She spit again. You bloated pig!

CHAPTER 23

Taking out his handkerchief, he backhanded her, blood trickled from her mouth. Not nice, Dear, not nice – He approached her, to wipe her lips. She pulled back...Brave aren't you, Lard Ass? He turned, Well, Dear, you will have time to see who is bravest of your duet. He left the room chuckling, tossing the bloody cloth behind his shoulder. Th heavy steel riveted door sounding like a bank vault. Ranch looked around their room. No windows, one door a steel door, concrete walls. Well, Ranch, maybe we should have gotten married before this, Huh? He smiled. I think we already are, Darlin'. He tested the plastic cords that held his wrists behind him. Leaning against the wall, sliding his jacket sleeve up. Don't you give up, Partner. She saw it – a Velcro sheath, small, only inches in length – a stainless blade, no handle, she recognized the Kung Fu trinket He moved to her, turned, back to her, Pull it out, cut fast!

Shortly muffled voices came through the steel door - both Ranch and Martine on each side. The heavy handle turned, the door creaked open. The four men looked around the room, their guns drawn and cocked. Before they had a chance to remark all four including the fat Jesuit were lying in a pile, unconscious. Come on, Hurry, Marty! Whe...? We'll figure that out later. Come on... The long corridor showed light – There, fast, maybe there's more of them in that side room. He tossed her a pistol, tucking one in the back of his belt. Outside the ajar door a Mercedes was parked, motor running – They must have been ready to take us somewhere. Yeah, how trusting they were, she grinned. Roaring down the gravel road, she pulled over to him... You cut that guys throat!

What did you expect, Kiss him? He didn't look at her – That Big guy? His throat? He was the lead man that kept after Dad to sell or lease our place, that's the best I could do in a hurry. I saw You in action, Marty, you broke one of those guys arms and you caved in another one's jaw with that kick. God! You are impressive! She snuggled up to him, you mean for a girl? For anyone! You are fast, Marty...God...what I saw out of the corner of my eyes would have made old Ed Parker blush...Ed, you knew him? Trained with him, set him up in Pasadena, got him an audition in Burt's Hollywood Gym after we did a few classes for LA. P.D. And the National Guard.. He damned near killed me a couple of times in expos. Yeah, I knew him! His temper and his ego got to him in his training bouts. Finally started doing cement blocks with his head – Damn FOOL, that's for juniors, not a pro like him! He didn't need to grandstand! She saw his jaw tighten...I loved the guy – too bad he left so soon. They said heart attack - It was those blocks.... He shook his head. Massive aneurism, I'd bet big money on it. She put her hand on his shoulder---I'm sorry, Ranch, I had no idea you... Yeah we were close, same birth dates, same age....

The dust behind them billowed in the Full Moonlight. It was late, she looked at her watch. Where are we? Don't know yet till we get to a crossroad sign but we're going back into the city. I got Fatso's wallet and his cards will tell us a lot. We are going in to the Vatican, one way or another, Darlin'.... I like that. What...? The Darlin thing - makes me feel feminine, Ranch. She wiggled. Well with those assets, he touched her breast cleavage you don't have to worry about feminine, Darlinnn...! She pressed her hand over his, moved it into her flimsy bra. More please. The Darlin thing? No, the hand thing. I love you Ranch Meadows, will you please marry me and make me a good girl again? He pulled over in a swirl of dust, turned to her, reached under her coat and blouse... If I can possibly, Yes. And you have to promise me...he was breathing hard, trying not to notice something stretching his pants... these lovely pieces of furniture will always be there by my pillow - No twin beds! Ok? She tore her bra into shreds, shoved her blouse and jacket aside...How about a preview for a quick five minutes? She opened his shirt slowly, his coat back, her nipples hot, pointed, throbbing into his very soul. Martine Salvatore, I do so love you, Where have you been all of our lives? That's all I can take, Darlin, I give...

CHAPTER 24

Breathing harder now, he pulled her onto his lap. RANCH! Do we have time for smooching, maybe there's more of them back there? Hush, Darlin, lay that lovely mouth right here on mine before I say Stop! Now my motors running! This is history...and I'm not going to miss it, Marty. You realize we ARE history - that painting it told ...She darted her tongue against his teeth as he realized just what he'd found – His wife from long ago and far away. Their lips opened and she moaned, fainting in his arms. again ....again...He grinned, knowing she was healed – Well not quite ...and she was his...to awaken to new things that just might astound her. She came back, reached up to his face, My man, at last you're here. Tears in her eyes, she smiled. He bent and kissed her hair.

Across the French and Italian border, back in Rome proper, he pulled into a service station. She was asleep, hair strewn across his lap...He pulled into the shadows at the side of the big Bed N' Breakfast sign and just sat there, looking down at her - hair a mess, eye liner smeared, her bra pieces on her lap, knees up against her chest, one shoe off - God, Ranch he muttered is all of this real? The painting, this girl - ten years of wondering? Shaking his head, she was awakening. She looked up -Are we there yet Daddy, laughing. How much farther, Daddy, I'm hungry, Daddy...? He ruffled her silky mass of hair - then smoothed it out with his intermeshed fingers. No, kids, he said, smiling down at her, We have a million miles to go yet. Anyone have to pee? Was your family like mine, Darlin? Same old, same old, I guess. Seriously, Marty - Do you have to pee,? No, I'm good to go for that million miles, Daddy. He helped her upright. You realize we're back in Rome now? Wow! I must have really slept...Marty, look, see that pickup over there in the shadows, and that alley entrance behind it? Yes, why? I'm gonna get rid of this car - you wait for me right over there by those tall landscape rocks. Got it. And DO NOT get excited about what you hear or see. Just wait there. Will do, Sir. - You sure you won't need any help? Not for what I'll be doin. He kissed her nose. She seemed to like that.

CHAPTER 25

Running fast despite the heavy coat, he felt his coat pocket for the half roll of toilet paper, He pulled it out as he got a look at the black pickup. Putting it back when he saw through the tinted windows. He approached the truck. Hi, Fellas, do you speak American? Rolling the window back up the passenger door opened, he got out slowly. The driver out, came around smiling falsely. We both can probably figure it out if you're patient, American....

Ranch noticed the bulge in the first man's dress blazer. The driver had the same bulge in his ski pullover- Ranch was ready when the first man pulled his gun out, a large .45 with a pearl handle. Just hold it right there, Glamour Boy.

Perfect English...Hmmm – are they Fatsos men or just locals grabbing touristas? He waited for them to tip their hand. You messed up, Stud back there, you know who you sliced? He was...With that Ranch was in action. Hands up he whirled, ducked, grabbed the gun breaking the fingers - his other arm catching the driver's throat. He sideswiped, pistol whipped his temple with a crushing blow from another whirl – The momentum sending both men down in a pool of blood. He took both of their guns and kicked what was left of life out of their heads with his stiletto boots. He collected their wallets and the glove box contents, registrations whatever...Stuffing it all in his large coat pockets, top and side, he grabbed both men by their collars and opened the camper shell, smiled as his small flashlight showed four five gallon canisters of gas tied to the sides of the shell. Quickly picking the two men up, he tossed them into the truck bed.

This is getting damned familiar he mumbled as the last leg was shoved in. Reaching in he cut the gas can cords and tipped the cans over toward the front angle the truck was sitting on – a slight hill. The toilet paper rolled out, he fed it onto the open tailgate and ran to get Martine. Come on! He gave her the .45. I'm going to move both cars to the alley. He looked at his bloody hand. Damn! He bent and rubbed dirt from the landscape rockwork as she watched. Too bloody much tonight, isn't it, Hunk. He looked up, said nothing. He looked drawn. Shut up, she said to herself, this isn't fun for him...Memories...

She watched him reach into his pants pocket. He handed her one of the two match books. Within five minutes he had both cars in the dark alley. Pulling one of the bodies out of the pickup shell he placed the paper in the man's inside jacket pocket, double checking with his mini light to make sure... Yeah, that's right...He switched the light off, ran to the pickup door, started the engine, slammed into the side of their car he had pulled over...Toilet paper still dangling down from the tank of their former getaway Mercedes, and paper streaming out of the tailgate of the pickup. MARTY! Come here – light the fuse on the Mercedes. I'll light this one. Run like Hell to the Bed and Breakfast. I'll follow right away. The soaring roar filled the dark night sky as Martine ran for the building, then a second flash and a third as all of the trucks gas cans exploded. Ranch was at her side knocking frantically on the door of the small motel. The door opened, the chain protecting the young girl staring at the alley flames. What happened? We were kidnapped by a man in that Mercedes. He said he was being chased by that pickup that ran into him. The cars exploded and the driver of the Mercedes hit the other men, took their guns and papers as another pickup came down the road and turned around - We ran into the trees - we are beat, sure you understand me?! Yes, I'm American too Mr.…. This is a baad… neighborhood for this sort of thing, she shuddered.

CHAPTER 26

She opened the chained door. Ohh - I thank you! Thank you Miss, please call the police and an ambulance. The man on the ground looked bad...Ranch was giving a good job of acting like a big wimp, shaking, holding on to Martine's hands, looking back and forth at the flames. She handed Ranch his change. We're the only place close that takes U.S. My Dad is a Marine stationed here, down the road. She pulled her bathrobe around her throat...Have a nice rest, folks. And you my, Dear, Marty whispered. Come Sweetheart, you need your nerve medicine. Ranch followed meekly.

In bed after their showers - naked now, she asked, Are your nerves settled down now, Sweetheart? He pulled her close. For a day or two, Partner. How did you register us to keep the police or Fatso's mob from finding us? Well, that pickup was from over the border in Rome. I kept their papers, put the pearl .45 in the guys hand on the ground after wiping my prints They might figure he was the bad guy in this. Wow, Ranch, this has been a night! Almost tortured and killed by Lard Ass and his monkeys and then this – They have us locked in everywhere we light. Wha... Not anymore, Darlin, look what was in their glove boxes. Her eyes popped - GPS? And then some, Darlin.

Ranch dangled two chains with flat electronic cases. This programs their GPS and any car they place a unit in – a monitor. And it can be worked over, ruined by these little buttons. Things are all screwed up at home base. It will take weeks for them to get back on line and maybe never. Oh, Rhett! You are so smart! My .007 she teased.. Kiss me! Did you take a cold shower, Scarlett? Never on Sunday, never at night...Never with you around, Rhett...dahlin. Pretty good! Ever been in the movies or TV. he asked? Sure with that Jesuit bunch following us even to the toilet – lots of footage. Well - not anymore... He pulled her closer, hands on the small of her back, her muscular lumbars like small ropes of steel aligning her spine. She stroked his face and pulled on his nose. Hey, what's that for...? Nothing, but just wait till you do something. They wrestled playfully. No one fainted. Marty, how you holding out, you know, the naked thing, the holding off of our sexual union, are you...she was up fast now, sitting over him, nothing hidden, no shame, memories gone that might have hurt. She cocked her head, Look, Ranch, far as I'm concerned I'm a virgin, your virgin, waiting on our wedding. What we do with each other's body till then is just lovely practice. No culmination till you say so. For that I can wait - but yes, I sure do want Ranch Meadows IN me just as far as he can get. Ok? He looked up, serious all over his face...I'll not disappoint you, Sweetheart. He pulled her down. They lay side by side, her thigh across his groin, his hand holding her breast. All seems well... he murmured sleepily. He looked at the coming sun through the blinds. He couldn't tell her how he was lying... He drifted off.

CHAPTER 27

A loud knock: Monsieur! Monsieur! Inspector Clousan... Please to open! Many questions. Ranch looked at the wall clock- Five.. He. grunted, looking over at sleepy Martine. Yes Sir. Coming, Sir. Stay here, Marty. The inspector was a thin, tiny mustached man, 130 pounds, wet, Ranch surmised. Yes?

Zee young lady manazere told us most of what vee need to knew. A few papers I weel leeve for you. She will return them to me. Passport please? Martine heard from the bedroom, Oh my God! Ranch went back to the bedroom where his coat and pants were. She questioned silently. He waved his hands with papers. Here. Sir. Oh, yes,! Monsignor's men, you must be zee new Americaan we heard was coming to his staff...Yes, Sir, they sent us these credentials last week, I hope they are in order. Ranch trembled in realty. He knew how rough French police could be on details. NO, No, Mistaire. Albert, no need to worry zee good Father works with us almost daily. The other papers?- No need I vill take care of everyzing.... Good Night, dear American friend. Oh, one more zing, zee young lady with you?? Ranch forced a blush. I am trying to become a little bit of a French lover, Sir and she just popped up in my hotel doorway yesterday – a sweet but very passionate little thing - but you know? "se la vi", Nothing serious, Sir. Good man you, are almost Frenched as we call it. Have you pinched yet? Ranch blushed, head down - and then some, Inspector, The small man almost tap danced in sensual delight. Go, go to zee sweet girl and help her happiness. Adieu, Friend Americaan. Adieu, Sir and Thank you so very much for understanding. Martin was standing behind the bedroom door hearing all of the charade. Well – you French – Americaaan lover that was quite a role you played there. He tossed her over his shoulder and sat down with her on the bed. She laughed, you've been doing that a lot lately, Macho! Yeah, I like the feel of you in my hands. Why? Just wondering ....He changed the subject:

These B and B's usually have food in the fridge, lets' eat, my nerves, you know... She chuckled and pinched his butt.. Not hard enough? Not bad, tell you later, Rhett... Now stop that!

CHAPTER 28

On the bus again headed across the border for the Vatican he looked long and hard at her....Listen Martine, about anything can happen now. So far they find us every time. When we were knocked out from that gas back there in France in that vault - they could have put anything in us or on us. She shuddered... You think?

At their hotel an hour later they checked and double checked their belongings for electronics. Well we went through all this suitcase stuff twice now, I had checked the car's underside but that's ephemeral, they could ...she interrupted, smiling, Do you want to check me out?...Quit that! He wrestled her to her back. When I do, I'll tell you. Surprise me, please, she jerked free, flipping all his 220 onto his back. YOU ARE GOOD! aren't you? $100,000 worth and a gold belt to prove it, Dude, she grinned. Give? Yeah, let me up. Let me see your watch. Ever had this back off? No, Why? Chips are small, Oh I see...He opened both of their watches. Nothing here. He put her watch on her wrist.

Funny thing, Marty, you're strong as blazes, fast as an oiled wildcat but so damned feminine and....And what? She lifted her head, What? Well, you do get to me is all I can say. Like last night and what you said about ...waiting till our wedding. Yeah, you agree? Sure. He kissed her nose, she wiggled up against him, turned slowly, grabbing his hands from behind her, placing them on her breasts pressing back against him. Yeah, that's what I mean. He picked her hair up in both hands and kissed the back of her neck. I didn't faint. Good, Darlin. Am I losing my touch? I don't think so, Rhett. She slipped one of his hands down to her stomach. What are we going to do, Ranch? If we try hard nothing till the clouds go away, Marty. She sighed, Then please kiss me for about ten minutes will you. I'm so hungry for you...for your hands on me, in me---for YOU, all of you. He held her face, And same to you, Darlin. I know what our love is, we'll make a great bride and groom. He lightened, Say, Girl - do you think you could find a wedding dress that would cater to that body of yours? Latts like a man, deltoids like Ulysses, breasts like no one I know, probably a 24 waist. That looks like a challenge for any shop or dress maker....She pouted, 25 waist, sorry. See my biceps? Yeah. I see. You are one real Humdinger, girl. Are you sure you want to marry this old guy? She teased, Well... probably if we get out of this alive. She pulled him close -Will you make love to me tonight, just in case.? Nope, but almost if that will help. She leaped around his waist, her long legs squeezing - OH, GOODIE! He shook his head...thinking, She's gonna run out of noses and then looking deep into her eyes kissed her nose one more time then that mouth,... so soft... longer than a kiss should last but just exactly what they both needed.

CHAPTER 29

Dizzy, they sat on the couch, side by side. She took his hand in hers. Tell me about Ranch Meadows, won't you? Isn't it about time? You know me better than I do, Ranch. Please....He laid back against the large couch pillows, hands clasped behind his neck. Well...once upon a time....She hit him on the shoulder. Get serious! Ok, what do you want to know? Everything. That can't be. Tough as I've become some of it is too deep or too pitifully hard, stupid, deep and impossible to describe, to even imagine it was me Look, let's keep it simple, to the point. Military of any kind doesn't make sense. Not just a no-brainer but it's not human! By that I mean you lose You. Best I can describe it. For you are truly brainwashed through your body – Drills, disciples, curses poured at you for weeks on weeks in boot. And then, if you are chosen for "better duty" as they call it - it gets even worse. Few handle it, some get sick, some commit suicide because of family pride being lost on them as failures. Things like Seals or Special Forces are common for that. Yet there are worst cases...He sighed.... Much worse. Tell me what you can...I'll try. It might be hard for a woman to understand that this macho thing men have adapted over centuries gets to be like a movie you have to live to...he paused...to really be what you think a man is. The "Don't cry" thing is but a silly piece of it. That other macho thing, "treat women like dirt and they'll eat you up," that's another falsity we coated ourselves with. And this next one will get to you as an example of how society tried to ruin men...

He shook his head. You're standing at a urinal, some guy next to you. You don't even dare cut a joke, mention the weather while you're pissing, no chitchat allowed - He might think you're queer. And maybe you missed a real friend like ships passing in the night and a listening rest room of guys voids it as you void your bladder. Just a piece of what has happened to men so real men hide behind sports, big arms, 400 pound bench presses and fancy Armani suits and shirts – and why they, quite simply... screw like it's a Saturday afternoon game 'must do', sex everything they can attract and win for a week or two. Or a lifetime of fooling themselves and draining their Temple...She winced, did you? No, glad to say the other things got to me, not the sex. I had Eddie Owada, my special friend and true guru, his invisible Professor Thind, a Sikh, Swami Thant Thakar Sing and Dr. Bernard Jensen. Men, real men that 300 hundred pound line backers couldn't budge in a tussle. Her eyebrows raised. He explained: Discipline, wisdom, control, respect for everything - especially Woman...even in her least stature. And when I learned that - after first laughing at these guys diet and austerities I began to see what Mom and Dad had inadvertently taught me – kind of unconsciously. I call it a reverence Dad had for her and more than that - a duty wrapped in gentility. A 'paying attention' which till you, MARTINE, I never even entertained, but I did stand in awe of what might be waiting for me – and her, one day. Then the trip to Paris, the Louvre the painting, you there with the old worn out silver-haired guy. The look on your face as you seemed part of him and yet impossible for one so young and lovely...She interrupted...But Ranch he had been in prison for years, tortured, he...Yeah I know that now but then when I first saw that painting it didn't make any sense. I knew you, yet I didn't know him even though Mom said he had my face, jaw, eyes and body... made no sense. Fairy tale stuff and yet....Impossible? I still wonder about our ages, you, your life ahead – the What Ifs...he winced.

CHAPTER 30

What about your love life? My love life? My God, that!. I hurt women. Lots of them trying to be to them what one girl-woman-goddess made me want after I lost 'her'. My stupid fault, my youth, my anger, my inability to forgive her for loving me,' beyond the call of duty'. And over the long years following -losing her, I bit into women, 'affairs', marriages... like they were knives, unrelenting knives that could cut out the pain of years of being sorry, of guilt.. Knives I used like they could cut out *her* memory. Sounds almost impossible I know, but she wasn't just any girl. I had to stick those knives into any form of love that threatened me forgetting 'her'. You, Marty are the only woman that has made sense since then. I almost had your problem in a way.... but you opened something Eddie, my Japanese Buddhist friend taught me, rather 'prepped' me for when I became really ready. What was it, Ranch? The reason I couldn't take your new virginity, Martine -

He took her chin in his hand and pulled her close, looking into her tear filled eyes - Any more than you could *now* go back to *then*....She held his face, sobbed I LOVE you, so very, very much, Ranch Man. I love you...I know you do and that's why we have to win this crazy game of life, death and love we're playing. That's enough for now. The rest is Eddie's story. And you know, Marty, Ed is Japanese royalty, related to the reigning Princess if that makes him any more noble than he is. He's over 88 now and still doing it all; traveling everywhere, giving, helping - tough as shoe leather, holds World Records in Judo and has held years of first place in world class weight-lifting contests! Teaches and mentors unsuspecting Seniors in Colorado, two adapted sons, a Buddhist-American wife...Martine blinked at Ranches background tale...That's one whale of a life, Ranch...look what I'm getting. Wow! And you ask if ?I want you? The afternoon talk had turned past their meal and the sun had long gone. Bedtime.

CHAPTER 31

She came out of the shower, robed, smelling like soap and roses...About tonight, Ranch. She hesitated - tried to laugh...After all those years... years....I just STARTED MY PERIOD!... You're safe and I WILL wait till we're married if you still want me. He chuckled and then thought better of it. A grand and noble decision, Martine Salvatore. She pulled the covers down, You stay on your side, Ok? Don't think of testing me... please. I'll do better than that... Marty - he walked to the double bed... you're safe, Wonder Woman.

Morning light saw two different people who had budded like bashful flowers to each other's hopes and dreams. He stood over her, ruffled her hair as she looked up at him, solemn, smiling deeper than faces can smile. There's a lot more than just the Eddie parts isn't there? Why do you ask? I had a dream, Ranch, and you were on top of a mountain sitting on a rock like the statue of The Thinker - but looking far out into the vastness, your brow furrowed. You felt your arm, your chest your legs and you stood up and said, Yes, I have to tell her...What is it you have to tell me Ranch? Is there still someone else? He bit his lip, holding her by the shoulders - I'm eighty-six years young, Lovely teenager. 86 long years of becoming what you see and think you want. WHAT??!! My GOD! Ranch you look 30! Even THAT is a mute point. I see people, women looking at you – you looking at them with a shake of your head. How did you stay so....? Well... Darlin before that you'll have to beat a few bushes in your upbringing about age differentials and what you presently want out of life and marriage. Her mouth was still open in shock. Marty, Dear, all I have going for me is you and that Louvre mural – without it and your uncanny self, I'd be giving up. He put his arms overhead, But let's eat out for Breakfast while you decide if you can digest 85 - I'll tell you about that and how we'll get into the Vatican. I have a friend who has a friend. He watched her closely. Went to her and kissed her nose. Her mouth still open. You asked for it, Lovely One, You asked for it, Marty, girl - I tried to stay aloof, stay deaf to your words, your wiles, the pro in you - but you have ways that are hard acts to follow.

CHAPTER 32

At the wending creek a mile from the hotel they placed a blanket on the river bank away from the crowds of people on the boulevard . How did you know about this place? I read folders, he laughed. Like it? Oh, what a setting, Ranch! It's us, Isn't it? He noticed she looked at him differently now – a look of love, coupled with awe and wonderment. And he wondered. Silently he murmured to himself, Can paintings lie? Will my age blow this? He had told her everything. How much could she hold after all her life had done to her. But she did. All she had to say to convince him was: Mr. Meadows, from now on I work for you for free and I will sign anything, go anywhere, do anything. I AM YOUR WIFE – I NEED NO MORE CONVINCING. FROM NOW ON IT'S ALWAYS AND FOREVER. I GIVE! How could those words and that kiss have been his whole life he thought, as real life hit him headlong - on a blanket on a river bank in Rome, Italy

Minutes later – after his calm came - Do you get it? The plan was outlined with Vatican inception, sketches Ranch made as she watched, curled on his lap, head alongside his shoulder as he leaned against the broad weeping willow – the rustle faint in the breeze. We get in here at point A. My friend is waiting for our call. This is the formal Visitors Center, Here is the Popes residence-apartment. The Pope, she gasped, we are going to kidnap the Pope? No, his aide Luis. How will we ever get out with him?1 He'll go gladly because of what we tell him. Watch.. Well why him, Ranch, what is he to your Mom and Dad and the land grab they want from you now? Do they really need you alive? Probably, but they don't want me to believe that - they think I believe they can manipulate the land titles and land patent Dad set up. I know different. It's a real process that could take them years, maybe never unless they forced me to sign with true witnesses and notary and some kind of Blackmail Threat –maybe you, Marty. Or how much I could take of torture no man knows when it's done by former Inquisitors – He laughed, half- heartedly. And then, yes, maybe they plan on using you to get my signature. Maybe why they just threatened us, held us when they could have just put a shell in our heads? I think so, Darlin.

Wow, this is complex Ranch. It sure is and that's why I wondered if you should go on with me… Tomorrows the day the Pope is going to announce his choice for his Step Down. You heard didn't you? Yes, but I had no idea I'd be here – involved in it like this! Ranch, you think this aide, Luis can tell you what you want to know about the insiders, even the Pope having anything to do with your Mom and Dad? Well at least, Marty, he has the Popes files on his computer and on paper as well -They take no chances, my friend says – lots of duplicates of every transaction or plan – or secret...She blinked, And they must have plenty of them, right? True, Marty, true - centuries of them and we may get to grab a few if my friend can work it through Luis...he rubbed his palms. There's one Sant Thakar Sing my Sikh teacher urged me to find - never knowing this would maybe be the way it turned out. Those basement tunnel archives are twenty miles long and three stories high and deep underground - three layers of wealth beside gold, jewels, artifacts, records. Things that would blow society apart if...he hesitated, if....

Hand me a bottle of that Red Grape Juice, will you? Ranch I notice you use a lot of that – she paused...is that how you...It sure is, A real cheap Fountain of Youth once you get your Pancreas and blood sugar levels in order. Some wait too long for that and it does more harm than good. A long battle. Well then help me, Ranch, I want what you are...Deal, MARTINE, deal, but only if you're sure. Completely sure…

CHAPTER 33

She reached out and shook his hand, hers lost in the expanse of it's size and the mystery of this man that was her Grandfather...My God, she breathed... and I thought my life was weird...What Marty? Nothing - just talking to the new Marty I'm getting acquainted with....

He smiled, I'll bet...You know anything about Quantum Physics? Heard a little when I rubbed shoulders with a few deep Martial Arts guys – not much though. It was like they kept looking over their shoulders for the guys with the Butterfly Nets, she laughed... . Is it that unprecedented? Not really, but religion in general hasn't much patience with even the mention of it. Mostly, "of the Devil" type reaction. I have done it a lot along with Remote Viewing. I was chosen in our Special Forces squad due to my Zen and Hindu experiences and training. Profound things happen...he raised his eyebrows, Tell me. She sat up straighter, Well quickly, - all you do is get quieter than you ever thought possible, hearing only your breath and then, not even that. At first it drives you nuts, so many thoughts try to crowd in and ruin that quiet – finally one day it rolls in like a silent surf and you see where you want to see, go spiritually where you command your Self to go.,. Your Higher Self? Of course, although people and nations use it adversely – 'Low Self Idiocy', I call it for it *ALWAYS* backfires when you...I get it, her eyes were aglow, her face radiant. It answers questions then - ? she got up closer... If, he put a hand on her cheek, you know how to ask them, if you're as clean as a Lesbian Nun, like we used to joke. But that's cruel, for they are so used and betrayed. Pregnancies never known by outsiders...Oh well, that's a part of what we saw going on there and in palaces worldwide - especially London, Tel Aviv. Gee, Ranch.... Yeah, Gee indeed, Marty – a whole nearly unknown, unseen, unbelieved world of duplications and deceptions that could drive men mad if they hadn't been weaned off the false breasts they kept trying to get milk from. Ranch, you are one deep, Dude, aren't you? If I am, it's because I stay open and dedicated to our Father-Mother Source, Marty - that's how I am. Her turn to kiss him on the nose. And she did, curling up in his arms, the Willow Tree, sighing, matching her contentment – and apprehension about the morrow and an eighty-five year old Mr. Universe type bridegroom.

CHAPTER 34

Noon on the morrow, their rented mini-car turning them back across town to Rome and the parking attendant at the Vatican. He looked at Ranch and Martine, smiling broadly, his accent not quite clouding his fervor: Americans in much love, Yes? Ranch put his hand on the boy. Try it when you're about forty, Son - it doesn't come through till about then...The youth cocked his head, quizzical. Walking up the range of steps Ranch grinned at Martine - I think he wanted to pinch your butt, Marty... Really...she laughed, maybe I'd get used to that if you did it more often. You are a flirt, aren't you, Girl? For your pinch only, Man.

The uniforms were everywhere, guards, robes, foreign dress – a hodgepodge of color and smells, noise and dialects. The hucksters at the side of the great Reception Hall selling or giving Vatican particulars, directions, warnings, glamorizing of the power evident, Over there, Marty, see him? The tall guy in the green Tyrolean' hat? Yeah, that's him, Come on.... He took her arm, pulled her close...Play dumb, Ok? I get you, I'm shut. The man walked slowly toward them, turned toward the opposite wall, motioned. They followed his nod. He pulled a newspaper out of his coat, opened it, leaning against the wall. Ranch moved near him, bending over with his handkerchief polishing his shoes. Speaking through the paper Green Hat spoke fluent English: Here is the Cardinal's apartment number and his aides secret phone number. They are expecting you. This wasn't easy, Mr. Meadows but it was worth it...Call Luis, then wait here till 1 PM. Luis will come for you. They are scanning you now. A slip of paper fell from his newspaper at Ranches feet. His handkerchief covering it immediately. The man folded his paper, coughed, turned and walked away. Well – that was a real cloak and dagger meeting, she breathed.

There's a phone booth, I have to call...She waited outside, wanted to be inside. This was fun...she lifted her eyebrows. Yes, Luis? RM here, One P.M.? Yes, I know... we will be here. She is my secretary. Yes, very.. She heard, giggled. He hung the phone, opened the door. Half hour, we wait outside by the step railing by the tall flower pot. Let's go.

CHAPTER 35

Up on the block above the steps Ranch saw him, lighting a cigarette, then heeling it. He was not what they expected but a large athletic man, tall, broad like Ranch, swarthy of complexion, dark shoulder length hair, immaculately attired in a white suit and Italian boots, a red scarf over his neck. Coming down the steps toward them he took each step as if he was a ballet dancer. Sir!, Yes, Luis? Yes. Come. Past the Vatican guards at the end of the hall, cleared by Luis and a handful of papers, they entered the ornate elevator. He put his fingers to his lips...please.... Ranch nodded. Seven flights up they exited, moving behind Luis to a far Guard Post. Again the papers...A few feet more and he took a chain of keys from his neck and a card from his pocket. Standing before the oak doors he placed his key, entered a card when the key caused a unit to come from the thick door. Then placing his face close to a metal disc on the door a whir sounded. The doors moved sideways into the wall. Sir...he motioned ahead of him. My Holiness the Cardinal.

CHAPTER 36

The man before them was in bathrobe, but such a bathrobe. Forgive, Children, I am at ease today and holy robes have deference only to commands, Please, he motioned, Sit?.

Couches facing, they sat, Ranch waiting for a queue. Mr. Meadows I understand your visit to Rome, to me. Please define even more now that we can communicate more safely. Cardinal, my friend and your associate from Bulgaria told you of my visit to the Himalayan Potala and what I saw and copied.... Yes, in somewhat detail but safely so... Well Sir, I as you - which I know, have entered into a life of meditation and much discipline – austerities… he paused watching the Cardinals eyes as he also looked him over musing to himself. No pushover, mentally or physically...And Sir, call it what you will, I was ...uhh, accepted... and got invited for a tour not given to usual visitors. He waited, watching looks between Luis and the heavy man in the bathrobe. Yes, Mr. Meadows, go on.... Sir, I sincerely believe you or someone in this organization needs to see what I photographed there....If I understand, Mr. Meadows, it is... he hesitated, beyond the third vision of Fatima – shall we say, Earth Shaking? At the very least interpretation, Cardinal He turned to Luis, back to Ranch, and what do you two suggest?

Martine swallowed hard, trying not to act surprised. That you, Sir and Luis meet me and my secretary at our hotel incognito, if I may, for all of our safeties and I allow you to photograph my records. And the price, Mr. Meadows...? Three million dollars usd if you are convinced it is that valuable. And only then after we send the last section of the photos to you will I expect payment to my account in America. He waited, The Cardinal placing his fingertips together before his full chest of air....Are you not taking quite a chance of me being, shall we say, Dishonest? Not at all. Our mutual friend from Bulgaria assured me that even though there is a lot of intrigue in this so-called Holy Place – I understand that you are free of guile and pretense. Martine gulped. Well, assuredly, I try to stay aloof from venal and political sins. I accept the trust of our friend, more so of you. Mr. Meadows; Three Million dollars on a handshake is no small matter, he smiled. Even amidst all of the wealth I see pass daily in my office proceedings. Cardinal, a lot of people, millions - will die if I don't trust you. More than deaths will occur – perhaps Rome itself will not be able to escape what is written in my possession. Know this: I understand from the Potala Lamas that they have since - buried the originals so no one knowing about our meetings will seek them by violence to their Potala or nation. Do you see the enormity if I am right about what I alone have? He un-clasped his fingertips, stood with athletic ease for as large as he was. My dear Mr. Meadows, the pittance of your amount required is of no matter – I will take it from my personal account. May I further say this: The much ballyhooed tales of Fatima are to me non-discreet. My dreams have said much comparatively. We, you and I, the Holy See, the planet are at a Crossroads. That I know and I see in your eyes all that I need to see, as I pray you also see in mine, that we are both trustworthy Brothers who care about life as we know it. That crucible called Love that can bring it All Together Now despite all of the defeats in the past. He bowed, as did Ranch.

Those three striking words: 'All Together Now' the Cardinal had used brought a start to Ranch – A memory reborn, or a time blasting into his future. What was this feeling? He looked for awareness at Martine. She smiled and winked. What's going on Ranch thought…

CHAPTER 37

Seeing Ranch disheveled at those words he smiled and winked also. Ranch was shaking slightly…Peace, my Friend…he smiled again… Luis will arrange the 'incognito' date and meeting time after we go into the Basement Archives within the hour. First lunch, then my robes…he smiled. An aside, Mr. Meadows, I know of your 'dismissal' of Monsignor Durante and of those rascals who play act as our protectors. Well done! Were I younger I would have played .007 against them - incognito of course. This may be fun, he chuckled, smiled broadly, then frowned at his levity. They shook hands, Luis embracing both Ranch and Martine. Luis, the lunch cart, please? The silent lunch as was his fashion, then his departure for his attire and they were ready for the shock. I believe what your Sikh friend wants is easy to find. I read it often under guards.

Later in the grottos the vast Archive was indeed an adventure of unimagined wealth and mystery. The Cardinal photographed the needed item with Luis standing close hiding it from the Guards.

CHAPTER 38

Moving to their waiting car she asked, Did that surprise you about ... Yes it did, but they have quite an intelligence grapevine, can't forget that – good and bad...It only proved to me the Cardinal was playing square with us. If he wasn't we wouldn't have left that room. We'd be in some torture chamber or Sodium Pentothal delirium spilling our guts. No, I trust him. This unit proves it. He swung the chained container. There has to be some real Wheat among those Tares in that pile of gold and marble. As he shifted gears, she moved to his shoulder. I sure do love you. He ruffled her hair. I kind of like you too – You can stay if you want, kinda used to you, Marty.

In the earned quiet of their suite three hours later they sat across from each other at the dining table, a fat vase of fresh cut flowers Ranch had ordered cheering the room, and Martine. The evening meal done, she stood up and washing the dishes explained, I want to get in the habit for you...He laughed, If we get Dad's contract closed with some honest company and that three million, you can have a housekeeper or two, Marty. Promise? Well, give me a little time...He opened his suitcase and then his duffle bag, pulling the cord out of the bag slowly. The razor knife from his arm sheath sliced open the housing where the cord had been. A plastic tube revealed in the loose recess. He had a pair of large tweezers in hand, pulling a brown leather-like parchment from the tube. RANCH! That's IT?! Yep, this is it, probably The Downfall of the fiercest farce ever done in the name of religion or God. Reaching into his suitcase he laid a large book on the table – Blackstone's Book Of Law. Opening it she saw that it was hollow, something wrapped in thick foil, filling the square recess of the book. Wha...? Got it from FedEx when we first got to the airport....a special unit they gave me at the Potala.

127

He unwrapped it gently. A shower of bright violet light almost blinded her - Ranches head turned away. Several flatly encased crystals in gold were holding some sort of electronic device. The other side had a silver backing. Watch, Marty – He unrolled the scroll, placed two glasses on each side to hold it down, took the crystal device in his hands after a silent prayer, repeated again...Watch....

She was still rubbing her eyes. This is....No wait, Marty.. Slowly the scroll began changing in texture and coloring – it seemed to relax, stretching out flat as if liquid. Where hieroglyphic type figures were, slowly changing into....English! Ranch, MY GOD, it's doing ENGLISH! I can read it. They both stood, Martine now alongside Ranch, holding his hand. His arm around her waist. They read slowly in cadence out loud....

CHAPTER 39

"Children of Earth, My blessings on you who view,
What you will find is deeply true,
Held in store for ages as if a child in womb.
It's former pages gone but some here for all to plumb,
Kept by men hardy, noble, true - at home in eternal snow,
This prize though grim opens men's lives anew
If held as this unclouded one who shows its view.
Read now My work, long withheld, centuries blocked,
With bloodstained sins by men, mere beasts. Soon shock,
Shall now be poured upon their plans,
To more enslave and decimate Man."

Suddenly the scroll turned into a scene like a video but in many dimensions. They watched as a large man with a Sun Crest on his robe, crowned and around him a populace of robed, pious appearing men, while behind their tall chairs stood garlanded women of many nations, shapely, smiling. Wine goblets lavish upon the tables before their male companions. A similar cross stood garlanded with flowers and cloth behind the man. The scene, royalty personified changed to revelry when a few men left among the rioting party of worshippers. Outside in the garden's dark they were cut down by heavy swords and thrown into waiting carts...A new scene came and went, ages flew by fast forward, Ranch and Marty in silent awe. No, I hadn't seen this much, just a preview there in the Potala. Look, now...there...It's Rome being built, the Vatican rising up – see...God, the details, look! It changed to the Inquisition tortures. Marty had to hide her eyes from the dismemberments....Then to the present age. Popes, expansive grandeur, wealth in the halls, on beds of silk, jewels flashing, harlots in Nuns clothing, and other gentle Nuns resisting assault, babies torn from fat wombs, buried in slim graves across the world. Assassinations of noble, honest men. Fear placed in others to still their knowings. Young boys, promised positions and then forced to position themselves... in first and often agonies, kneeling before grinning pontiffs and lesser prelates, faces smeared with liquid lust from men who knew no holiness while only the hole in their minds held sway – It was all there and then it exploded.

The sordid scenes, the grandeur of Rome aflame, rockets falling - while away in a distant city with a slender triangular tower - the city around it flaming, people running, autos, piling the roadways, the sky darkened, the bright Sun hidden. The unit gave a final sound and was still, the scroll once more taut, wrinkled pulling up into its former condition. Ranch spoke slowly, The Lamas promised an additional message would come after I had made my proposal...to the Cardinal - I have no idea what it might be...I asked about the payment. They said, "Use it for the weak and honest"....

CHAPTER 40

The hours went by, they talked longer hours then the doorbell announced the Cardinal and Luis. Greetings Martine and Ranch! May the God of ALL bless this meeting. The Cardinal was dressed in a Nun's habit and cloak, Luis, face blackened in a servants garb. They seated across from Ranch and Martine. Quite good disguises, Sir. We hope so. Things seem to be stirring in the papacy. His retirement and the coming election of a new Pope has rattled more than Vatican dishes from last weeks Earthquake This is a large quake for us. But I fear there will not be a lengthy stay for the next officiator. I agree, Sir. Nostradamus, remember? Yes, indeed, he did see this end of Pope rule, didn't he? Ranch arose, Come men, to the table...In a few minutes the Cardinal and Luis stood stunned, shaking at what rolled on before their eyes. UNCANNY, Dear, Ranch, uncanny! Such glorious technology from the past! And it has assured me of your legitimacy. Your money will be transmitted to your account immediately. But, hear me, Luis and I have a fortune together as men, not homosexuals.

We have been convinced as nothing else could - Your requested Three Million dollars? I will make allowance for what you will need to also convince nations and men in power. Your account will find Ten million instead of Three...He embraced Ranch, tears flowing heavily, his voice shaking. We will be making harsh decisions in our quarters, be assured. Please, your bank information... Ranch handed him a card from his shirt pocket. The Cardinal smiled. Ah Yes, North Dakota, the land of great stones and you, my son, Ranch appear to be one of them.. They embraced a second time. Luis grim, looking down at his clasped hands. Sir, I will send you the copy I promised - of all this as well as a small copy of our painting. The Lamas told me how to facilitate it. The

'Nun' and his black companion left, quietly strolling to the elevator. RANCH! TEN MILLION DOLLARS! What a gesture, huh, Marty? They embraced for long moments. Get your coat, it's snowing in sunny Italy. Where ...? To the Airport Industrial complex.

CHAPTER 41

They stood with the agent looking at the Lear Jet. Can you place two more fuel tanks on those slender wings? They're designed for three more. Two on each side will do. About the payment? Here, my parents account in the states. How much? You have come at an auspicious time, Mr. Meadows – This craft is here on consignment by one of our board members who is in financial straits...and yes - it is an earlier model but in extemporary condition, just checked out...

Well then? Ranch anticipated...Nine million, would he take nine million, Cash? Let me call him....He opened his phone case, punched numbers -Deloy? I have a buyer tentative to your approval. I believe it is appropriate. An American, yes. Nine million. Sir, would that would be a cash transaction! Of course, by FedEx Yes, Deloy, FedEx He closed his phone, Done. You just bought your Flying Carpet to new vistas! Ranch looked at Martine, Thank you, I'm sure you have minimized the role this bird will be in our futures. The agent cocked his head...'our' futures, Mr. Meadows? Yes. You included...

CHAPTER 42

You're a pilot, Ranch? she breathed as she hurried along beside his strides? Yes, flew these when they first came out - for Lockheed. Part time test pilot after Nam. Easy ship to learn. Lear did a marvelous job of simplicity. He called it' The little guys plane', simple everything. Wow, Ranch, Wow, our very own Jet! She tap danced and gave a leap in the air. Wow! Ranch smiled at the little girl in the woman's body with the manlike power. Yep, our very own...

Being advised it would take three days for the tank installation. They moved to a different suite – in case. Ok, Boss teach me -we have plenty of time. Like what? Everything you think I need to know - especially about you. She layed on his lap on the large couch, a pillow under her knees, one on her stomach. I was married, told you that. Her name was Carole. We had seven sons, two daughters total from former marriages. Yeah, you guessed it, my past before Carole had another marriage. A naïve one of no sense whatsoever. Lust. But not that with Carole, sweet, lovely, talented. Vulnerable to worldly types she met in her modeling and decorating world. Had to lose two husbands to booze and drugs, went through Hell with them, abuse both mental and sexual. Two of those men's boys went to prison. I came along and rescued her from all that Hell. We worked hard at that marriage to know adventures and love, everything different -yet both still kids in reality. Carole taught me love. She WAS love but I learned too slowly- her last years came crowding out our immense love as we worked to whip her Tumors How long? He watched her face change....Forty-five years, Marty... That's enough of that scene. It still hurts to watch her in my arms at the end...I understand, she placed fingers on his chin. Go on..

MONOLITH

I was an enigma to myself, my longevity learned, formed by my Dad – the Lama's diet, his studies covered up his youth. He was eighty when I was born, had inherited the homestead, wealthy from cattle and investments. Very wealthy. Millions. I had it all, trips to everywhere with them, with my relatives. Mom didn't like to travel – worried about her Chickens. Mom, Dear old Mom - he sighed. You would have loved her. Well, all of our kids, mine, Carole's finally went their ways, some wise, some talented, some spiritual, most world loving novices at life - thought Dad and I were freaks, never really knew us or all we had learned. Wanted other things mostly, but at times---we talked and they took it as fun fantasy. Good boys, though, precious, men finally, as the years and tears taught them what me and Dad tried to. He stopped for long moments, took Martine's face between his hands. Can I tell you something pretty deep, Darlin? She looked at his seriousness, mouth slightly open at his gaze...Marty, I have a lot of reasons to believe you ARE CAROLE...returned.

She blinked, gulped, sat up straighter, leaned forward to him – How? She breathed in wonder at his words… A Walk-In… It happens infrequently among mortals when love finally gets known for what it was intended and death suddenly knocks it out of the equation. As if the Gods won't let it go to waste. She was fully alert now, erect in awe at what she was hearing. I nev…I know, Darlin, it's big stuff to lay on you but you can't kill love. Get that, You CAN'T kill love. And Oh - how I loved that Girl! How does it work… I know about Reincarnations, Reimbodying, but Walk-Ins?

Ok, then hang on: Sometimes on the Otherside pacts are made between people who know some of what will happen when they come to Earth as Mortals. If a life is meant or needed to be cut short by whatever and something didn't or couldn't get completed one party stepped in as the other stepped out – Walk-In – Get it? Well, yes it might make sense if… He went on, History has cases where it becomes concrete, where love was so grand and vibrant that it was as if the Universe was aflame with wanting it full and pure, unending – even no more death as we know it…He looked to see how she was reacting. Very unusual people were always involved. Like us…Marty.

Since I first lost Carole, when I first saw the painting at the Louvre of us - I saw things in and about you, Marty that was a near duplicate, yet more perfect… of Carole. Tell you something also so strange, Over in Tibet when they lose a Dalai Lama they start searching fast for his Reimbodiment. And they turn over every stone, look for every hint, Birth Marks, Locations, Similarities, Familiarities of the expected child, reported by omens - that new baby. As he gets older, responsive - they interrogate him, pin him down about past lives, abodes, friends, favorite things, pets, appetite. How would we, I… know? We won't unless it's TRUE! Then if it is - it will engulf us in its beauty and fulfillment. I'm open for anything Ranch. It is true - this love I have for you has had its signs and wonders for sure… I'VE CHANGED SO with your patience and concern –your compassion wipes me out, Ranch! Don't forget that when we stood there at the Louvre and you didn't want to face you as that old scarred up warrior, it was ME that stood up for our love. I saw it, felt it, knew it! She yelled it out. And I'm feeling what you're saying right now just like then at the Louvre. How will we know though? It won't miss, never does, we're talking Om-niversal stuff here, Martine Salvatore.

She hugged her pillow. I love this, Ranch, go on…Everything…go on. More important Martine is you now. I, all this bewilderment could be a very hard act to follow IF you do want to follow me. Oh Yes, Ranch. Ok, I'll list some fast things in your mind then…Hang on. And for three glorious days and three equally strenuous days Ranch taught Girl-Woman Marty. The list was long, exotic, all new mostly to her ears except what Ed Parker and his entourage had dropped to their students and they, suspicious of a woman around them, let drop at times in part, till she had gone back to her kicks and jabs – her envied speed and power, Ed shaking his head at the small dojo in Hawaii - at a near equal in speed and dexterity, 'and a Woman!' Those leaps, he once said... Fantastic, Girl...who is she? Ranch, quipped, I never knew that was you that I once saw at a meet in London...Marty.

CHAPTER 43

Hours later, into the night he instructed: 'The Clapping', wringing hands motion for centering positive and negative palm polarities, The index fingers in the ear tunnels blocking temporarily the blood and nerve flow to the Pineal, Pituitary and the Hypothalmus glands, the Telemeres for renewal length and far more. The value of the sea foods, kelp, dulse, chlorella and others for the Thyroid's perfect control over all body organs and hormones. Acupuncture meridians, hidden things known only to Tibetan - Buddhist priests, learned with silence when in captivity of long years in Burma/ Sri Lanka. Control over body temperatures in fearful climates, the Breath, (his prized love and youthifier) - Breath held for minutes without tension or injury. The various postures, inverted, seated, Yoga and Americanized new findings by open minded Masters of many arts. The Dry Brush Bath, Hippocrates many cures with a single liquid, the nutrition of Pythagoras, the Rishis and their secret longevity and curing power - learned also by the high mountain Hunza of Pakistan.

The Sanskrit sounds, Egyptian mantras used to ward off attackers, to lift and fit huge stones - So effective a small Master could not be lifted by ten students...All this and two days and a half night Martine drank of Ranches eighty-five years, until she, exhausted, slept in his arms on the couch, Ranch picking her up undressing her and placing her in bed beside him till the moonlight and soon sun caressed them into smiling wakefulness. Ranch awakened seeing Martine on the floor by the foot of the bed, doing perfect Namaskar Dands, stretching her silky tan, nude body up into the air. He arose, moving to her with her robe. Put this on, you'll get chilled, he grinned. For God' sake, Marty, have mercy!

MONOLITH

She leaped into the air, five feet above the carpet floor, high kicking the tip of the chandelier. Anything, Boss, anything.

Ranch grinned, as he recalled – And Carole hated Yoga, thought it was "heathenish". Good luck Carole he breathed. Wish you were here. Are you…

CHAPTER 44

At the Air Terminal, having made all transactions, examining the new tanks, the new tires he had requested, Ranch was maneuvering the small Jet onto the nearby Tarmac, heading for the man with the set of flags. The wide concrete strip adjoining the Tarmac at Roma Atlantica had another plane, a large super liner, passenger jet pulling over toward the Lear Jet. When nearly wingtip to wingtip the flag man dropped his arms, nodding his head. Both planes idling. MARTY! Look! He pointed at the big plane....See? Those two faces in the front window? Oh, its the Cardinal and Luis, Ranch!... It sure is. Looks like they had to make a fast decision before the vote Or maybe...what they showed the other Cardinals...Martine said slowly. Yeah, maybe things got rather sweaty? I'll bet, look at those smiles. Suddenly the flagger gave Ranch the go ahead. Ranch punched the throttle, pulled the flaps to level and they were roaring down the slab. Marty, pull the gear up on three! He counted - There, he motioned. Now when I say, pull the flaps up to lift position-full. That's it above the Down Flap glass. There's a good co-pilot. She wiggled excitedly, Wow, our very own flying carpet, Huh, Ranch? He smiled as he began the steep climb at four hundred, then a half bank to the right and they were headed south over Sicily, the blue Mediterranean gleaming rich gold in the Sun. How about that sight, Marty? She stared ahead and down as the ship burst into its maximum power, the Atlantic now only a few hundred delightful miles ahead.

The excitement had drained her, she slept against the right bulkhead, pillowed by her thick coat, Ranches over her legs. He looked at the screen, LaGuardia! Come on, pull up! The screen changed color and a relief outline traced blue lines to a section marked LaGuardia. Good Boy! He curved the plane to the right twenty degrees, cut speed to 200.

Wake up, Marty, ready to land. She was up and running in excited joy. Her, Oh, GOODIE! made Ranch smile as he reached over and squeezed her shoulder. Ok, Copilot get ready, flaps down one quarter, SLOW now, slower -There,. Now gear down full power, hit landing lights. That's it there ....she was holding her breath. Hey, relax, Sweetheart, you're doing great, Ok? I guess...Gee, this plane is so easy....It just loves your touch, Darlin. Ok, Sit back it's my show on in. He wavered the ship back and forth testing the flaps and the rudder, decreased the jet fuel monitor. The air control tower screeched on.... THREE MILES AND COUNTING, LEAR JET. RM ITALIA - ON COURSE, PATH CLEAR - RESUME LANDING OPERATION – Move left to strip Orange 4. Roger? And out, Tower, coming in....the landing gear quivered, the plane jerked slightly, tail downward and they were rolling slowly toward Orange 4. He cut power a minute later and pulled the brakes. Put your coat on Co-pilot, don't want these guys eyeballing my woman. They laughed exiting the door. Leaping down with their luggage tossed before them. A white Jeep pulling up with a trailer behind. Mr. Meadows, expecting you! Good drop, any problems over that Atlantic storm? Martine blinked... What storm? You slept above it, Darlin, no storm for you. I saw it on the Tele-Screen and climbed way above it, didn't want you seeing me playing through those clouds. If I had been alone I'd had a ball with this dream of a ship. They hugged, the Jeep driver cheered a whistle.

CHAPTER 45

Where to, Sir? Rent a Car office. Right over there, Sir, close. Ok, Store our plane overnight, here's the Registration. We'll be back at 10 a.m. Sharp! Fuel it, check those new tanks for any drips, check lube and oil everything Ok? Ranch handed him a hundred -You bet, Sir, will do. 10 p.m. sharp and go. They got out of the Jeep, retrieved their luggage, walking into the Rent A Car office. The rental Buick was a new experience for Ranch compared to the old 1940s Buick Roadmaster of his Dads, colors the same blue as Dads he murmured. Hmmn? Nothin, Marty - just remembering back a ways...Ohhh, she saw the mist in his eyes. Sorry...

Driving along the East River a light stopped traffic at the Intersection. A Mexican boy holding newspapers ran to Ranches open window. Big news, Senor'. One buck? Ranch dug into his coat. Go buy yourself some more papers, Son. The hundred shocked the boy, his mouth open as they sped ahead of the traffic toward the U.N. Building in the distance. Really? Yep, they need a chance to change too, like the Vatican. She unrolled the paper and gasped. Ranch look! The kid said Big News! Look at the size of this headline!!

Ranch pulled the new Buick over to the meridian emergency lane. Let me see that! She handed it to him. He read out loud in shock: "Moslems riot worldwide - outgoing Pope orders all Moslems out of France and Italy. Martial law begins in both nations, streets aflame with rolled over autos and police units. Smoke fills skies, airports jammed."!! The Cardinal – he must have gotten wind ahead of time! I wonder how they reacted to the scroll showing, Ranch? Doesn't matter, looks like they've kicked over a hornet's nest with some very untimely poor judgment.

His eyes scanned the sidebars on the right of U.S News and World Report. Listen to this, Marty... He blinked as he read, slowly, "The France based Louvre closing doors to public for gigantic remodel." Yeah, remodel, we know what that means. Sure do, Ranch – Relocation. Wonder to where? Good question. And here, Marty, "Russian volcanoes erupting in major multiple alert. Asteroid hits city of one million, on Kamchatka peninsula, California, Cuba, Europe report many meteor strikes. Yellowstone evacuating due to numerous eruptions and three quakes"!! God, Ranch, all Hells breakin loose! Remember what Sid Roth said two days ago on that T-V show with that Rabbi Jonathan Cahn? - You mean about Harbingers? Yep, Our planet's warnings the world is screwing up? Sure do. Been waiting for this to blow worldwide. Cahn and Roth are God's men of the day for the Sincere Christians and true Jews You think? I sure do Marty, right on and getting the attention all this deserves. He tossed the paper to her lap and punched the gas, screeching down the wide boulevard

CHAPTER 46

Hello, Mr. Secretary, he was speaking over the U.N. Lobby Phone. Ranch Meadows, Cardinal X notified I'd be contacting you...Right? Yes, Meadows, Ranch Meadows. Yes. He wants you to see what we brought from the Potala. That's right. We have it here right now. Yes or no, Sir?... Good, we'll wait. Minutes later in the large planning room on the second floor the show was played and over and over. The six men, the Secretary General, three aids, a secretary and the Uzi carrying guard - stood perplexed, shaking. The Cardinal wants you to call his cell number right away. Yes, we will parley immediately. Thank you, Mr. Meadows. Shouldering the bag Ranch shook hands. Be wise Mr. Secretary – be wise....Rushing down the great steps, they looked back over their heads, remembering the Hopi prophecies and their last repulsed visit to speak with this office they had just informed. 'House of Mica', wasn't it called, Ranch? Ranch! He was in deep thought. How did they spell it in the prophecy? Don't remember but it means glass. Look at all that glass!

Next stop, the White House, Marty, the Cardinal gave an itinerary he thought best to contact first - then South Africa Sunday. Wow, Ranch what a route!

CHAPTER 47

The Oval Office, seated, waiting. In he came with the press secretary, Wolf Blitzer and Henry Kissinger. Both of them shocked at Kissinger's appearance, one foot dragging, a cane in hand.. Mr. Meadows, he growled, the good Cardinal told me a little – Vat is dis scroll and the accompanying device? Ranch stepped in front of the men, moved to the mahogany table, unwrapped the scroll and crystal unit. An hour later, Obama insisting to view it twice.... Ranch went to the president, whispering into his ear: Watch your ass, Mr. Obama - it's chicken roosting time... America needs you to change horses and get rid of your handlers, those skunks in the hen house! He smiled at the cane holding Kissinger up, gathered up the bag, took Martine's hand, walked casually out of the office, led by a pair of Ak-7 totting guards.

South Africa was a no-brainer wasn't it, Ranch Man, Yep, they got right on it! I was really surprised what they said, what they did. You? Intervening their congress, showing the film of the scroll to the whole nation - WHAT a fast decision that was. And the others cheering for us as we were escorted to the airport! He waited till her enthusiasm died down...Marty, South Africa has some real sharp ex-pats from everywhere. It's also supposed to be safe cataclysm-wise. No earth faults, the Cape tides leading out 24 hours a day from both east and west sides - no tsunamis - even if they do have a fault they don't suspect.. The blacks respect the white element of expats that are sincere with them. The lower area tribes and Zulus are settled in – Watusi's civil - all respecting each other somewhat. No more warfare. Labor is not just cheap, it's willing to go the second mile and then some..

The Lear pulsed like a silver cat going through purple clouds of breathless size and shape. You don't mind? What? Going into these clouds? Oh. NO, it's sooo immense and wild, I'm getting goose bumps! Before the next thunderhead, he rolled the Jet over on it's back, rolled twice fast, leveled and hit the cloud at 600 hundred miles an hour. She tried hard not to pee her pants. It's been a long time now she gulped as her hair roped down over her head in the rolls. I love it!

CHAPTER 48

Four hours of fueling, checking, eating in Kansas City, off again in clear skies -North Dakota came into view on the screen in the short hour that followed. Soon the plane was circling the Meadows homestead, Martine looking down at the thousands of acres expanse. A long north-south ribbon of cleared land stretched out from the burned out estate building. Heading north with a sharp turn, Ranch came back at passive speed, I'll do it Marty, you look for anything unusual. She nodded, nose to the Plexiglas. Down easy. Headed toward the chicken coop, the plane locked and chocked, the two motorcycles were still there, dusty, intact, waiting as if lonely for fast riders. Ranch dusted them off with his handkerchief. Leave your bag here, I'll tie the scroll onto the rack, my suitcase under it. We can buy what you'll need, What...she looked shocked, puzzled at his words. Do you remember, before Marty - seeing a big silver spire over the trees east of the park entrance? I do, wondered what it was...thought it was a Mormon temple...nope. What then? She was even more puzzled when he kicked the start and whizzed off. An acre down he waved her to come ahead as he closed his cell phone. The town was quiet, disturbed by the two bikes momentarily. Come on.... They walked past the tree growth into a large blacktop clearing. She looked up at the spire two hundred feet in the crisp air and back down at the man standing in the doorway.

CHAPTER 49

He spoke as they got closer, Maja said you had just called from the farm...Yeah- Roger, - Martine here. We're getting married and you're it. Got anything to eat so we can make it till then? She will need a seamstress for her gown - Gripping Ranches hand, she shuddered and fell, fainting in his arms. Do you have this effect on others, Ranch? I really doubt it, Rog. That's another story. But she does seem to really like me. They went inside, laying Martine Salvatore' on the large padded pew before the altar. Roger gazed down at the disheveled woman as Ranch straightened her long legs. Where did you find her!!! Well, Rog it's not so much where but when, -probably a few centuries ago in sunny Italy – Could you handle that?. Just then a sunbeam came through the colored glass window above the altar, striking her opening eyes, turning them to violet gold. I think I can believe anything now...Ranch. That's the first time that big colored window has let a sunlight beam through since the time when Maja walked into this chapel and I fell in love...

AFTERWORD

(Roy's predictions as Mankind is creating)

The farm returned fast, money does that, but their love pushed it even faster. The north property was leased to a German mining firm. A wall went up twenty feet tall to hide the noise and equipment. A small lake became the perfect setting for their new Italian villa. The huge Louvre painting arrived in a month by special van finding its way into a separate structure adjoined to the house, now preserved in plastic laminate for perhaps another few hundred years. Headlines became more volatile. Rome was totally destroyed by fire ...again. Paris was down to ashes, only the Arc de Triumph and the bent Tower remaining – Nuke! The Seine still running joyfully leaping in bubbling spurts as if knowing her children and the birds would return. Obama, Rahm, Kissinger. Rove and Bernanke fled to the quieted Solomon Islands – the quake rebuilding needing laborers and they hoped – politicians. Russia was tapped hard by heavenly forces or...man....never knowing what the myriad coincidences were from or from 'whom'. The 20 volcanoes on and under the Kamchatka Peninsula and many others far out under the waters, breathed their last bursts as the Urals and all of the Nuclear bases hidden there in underground facilities were covered, sealed – in cooled, hard lava and everlasting dust. Too dense to blow away, flowing down the streams and rivers to nourish dead soil for future children.

Vladimir Putin, once Europe's bad boy KGB buff - held his bluff and won. The Crimea thing and the rest of Mother Russia was his again, rather 'his kids' as he referred to his salvaged, wiser Russian family and military youth. Beijing's riots ruined the old regime', the students taking over by pure population force against all China had to repulse them within rural and city alike. Slaughter to be long remembered by all who believed the sword is mightier than love among worn out neighbors with needs and a dream. North Korea finally got its invasion after two small clean Nukes were dropped – The U.S. tired of wondering if an EMP in the high altitude would ruin America's electronic empire –and a war win. The Chinese and Japan shook hands over the disputed islands, The U.N. building and Rockefeller Center, many other large complexes turned tail and became social centers, centers for feeding, clothing, jobs –opportunities. Huge land west was opened to a Land Rush like old Oklahoma had long ago. Millions participated. Free grants put down wells, planted crops, trees, orchards - neighbor Americans of every color co-oped helping homes and barns go up overnight. Above all that delighted Ranch and Martine, government validated, staffed Orchards began replacing the former cattle businesses. Slaughterhouses went dry from new public sentiment as that "other Scroll" was released publicly. It slammed into humanity and rejoiced the 'NO Animals For Food' cause by shaming everyone that ever ate without thinking or feeling for our harmless friends. Summed up it simply said:

"For thousands of years, tears, agonies, blood and greed My animal creation has groaned. And you my human children, killing them, eating them have killed one another because you learned and practiced death upon innocent, defenseless beasts without concern except for your belly, your taste and the enterprisers that sold you once loving, gentle, living creatures. You murdered, you became the murdered ones in endless wars. Karma, children, karma unleashed, simply earned, justly allowed as you chose it in sorrowful future after future."

"Indeed you finally found by this decree and utter simple Deduction - that all Effects have their Causes – As you planted in bloody deeds and appetites – just so you earned an indelible bloody crop. That blood washed away slowly as it blinded you. Let the bloodless day unfold, its rays of Light stun you all with your new Earth. What in Plenty, Love and Unity I designed. You nearly lost. War was not your enemy.

MONOLITH

You were your enemy. You shall not longer kill in war or dietary. Your Earthly Mother will cast you off equal to your deeds."

Yes, that overdue bloody crop had to be harvested first. All Hell hit - as if to get things moving positively again. A mighty Exclamation Point on that letter to Earth or anywhere. So it all merged in chaos or unity -:

Taiwan and the like nations: Japan, Hong Kong with it's stable/early success at independence, China, Shanghai the new, true neutral nations and capitals ...Japan's Fuji finally blew - parted from Tokyo - a million dead, an approximate ten million more homeless, wounded, irradiated – The new Tsunami a mile tall covering technology and hopes for centuries to come. Mud , skeletons, wasteland. Remaining people moving as things settled from the belching nuclear plants, believed, by the world ...to have been closed down before Fuji shuddered ever harder and caved in with roars and ash heard and layered worldwide.

Then as things had quieted, life returning, that illusive, denied, ridiculed Planet X came by- an enormous 'grin' coming, some thought, from its head of flames and black debris. Hurtling past our Moon inside our path it closed closer each of the seven days of its hidden journey as Nostradamus warned about. ("The King of Terror") But believed by few, lay or astronomer. NASA, placing its hopes in the lies and years of facades and air brushing out of any believed photo evidence... gathered its forces, the few who they chose at gunpoint and repaired to their ready missile buses for the Moon and the new Sky Labs --- But this is the other record below for your eyes to read or your heart to doubt.

What happened when X plowed through our atmosphere causing the Moon to stagger and ring like the bell many had said it was – manmade, an alien space base brought in after the hollow 'God' created Moon had moved away from Earth during an earlier bypass of Planet X wiping

Mars and lessoning Venus' dome residents? The legends are told in the Kolbrin bible – Earth, the blue planet with the two Moons, peopled by the wise Martians who were warned by what was in their path unseen, till a month before it struck. The scant few making it to what became Atlantis, then Egypt, then turmoil amidst its pyramids and peoples.

In North Dakota Ranch Meadows, Vice- President, of The New American Pioneers Party typed that story as he read it nightly to his forever bride in her healthful pregnancy.

They titled it becomingly:

"ALL TOGETHER NOW" Thanks to the Cardinal who worded it so carefully, slowly in his Nuns disguise. Remember? And their child when it came – young 'Card' Meadows.

G'night Mate...

A PRELUDE TO ALL TOGETHER NOW COMING UP...

"THERE ARE TRUTHS THAT MUST NOT BE TOLD – AND LIES THAT MUST BE REVEALED"

Oh, Really, Citizen? Shall we look at a few things you might want kept from you?

- You don't want to know your wife is sleeping with her boss?
- Your daughter is on Cocaine and Meth?
- Your 16 year old son is going to prostitutes?
- Your brother is cheating on his wife?
- Your baby's milk is full of pesticides?
- The IRS is an illegal function robbing you blind?
- The Cathlics burned 1,000s of books God intended you to read?
- The car you just bought has a poorly re-built trans and engine?
- Your congressman is a secret card carrying communist?
- Your preacher is in it for the free ride and the nice rectory
- Earthquakes can be predicted to the very hour?
- Roosevelt could have warned Pearl Harbor?
- Your new Orthopedic mattress has bed bugs?
- Christianity was composed by demonic, mercenary men in black?

Let's stop right here for that should be shock enough – For you may say such a fact "Should NEVER be exposed because people, good Christians by the millions, would throw up their hands, give up being spiritually concerned, would become immoral, suicidal - God should have revealed this before it led so many astray into insanity and divorce! "Really?

How far do you go if you are reputable and an authority on deciding such things - Lies, half truths like Christmas, Easter, Halloween, Molestation in prominent or religiously famous families. Shop lifting by celebrities, masturbation, rape, illicit fantasies with chains and flagellations, defending teenage sex in your family, a child window peeking, cheating on tests?

To many in our present society the above list is inconsequential, just a part of facing and dealing with life ... Ho Hum Is it important to expose lies and tell hidden and covered up truths and scandals? Describe what YOU want kept from you on the basis of the few shockers listed above – Items that are to some just rudimentary happenings in a struggling, developing culture... How far do you go – What do you hide from yourself or others - allow or condone?

What if an enemy invasion, a hurricane, tsunami, earthquake was imminent – Should you be warned? A dam ready to burst above your city? Ho Hum?

IS IGNORANCE REALLY BLISS?

A few years ago famous research group, The Brookings Institute, did a project to evaluate how much the public should be told about secret or difficult information, 'Difficult' namely, due to potential disruptions of mind sets, religious beliefs, and historical-religio understandings from basic– high school and college promptings, placed on non-evaluative average citizens. About UFOS – Good or Bad? What would be the effect on people in general... if they knew....

Their analysis was amazing, actually scary, for it decided 'we' weren't ready for the Truth. To the writer, me, that is like the ancient Catholic

Inquisition and the book burnings by them and later by Hitler. WHO decides for me? I do! And for you?

That is the point of this article: Are you responsible for yourself and how you might REACT to difficult news, new revealings, shocking factualities withheld for years or centuries – Who decides what you know. What you believe, what and who you worship? Is it anyone's business?

I believe you have OPTIONS, CHOICES in this thing called life experience and no one should keep anything from you because you might be 'fragile'. If adult, a parent, an official you have an office of authority over yourself, your family, your wards. Each must be resposible to their office, to themselves. Teach, promote the Truth no matter how difficult – Any person, nation or religion based on a FALSE premise has gone down! Check it...lies destroy themselves but in doing so they take many people into Hell or extreme anguish. Especially in religions. More Wars over religion than any other factor, more millions of lives lost over 'isms' – Prepare your self, your loved ones with coats of steel for what will come as THE SHOCKER soon – Not just beginning things on December 21, 2012 - but far more involved for each of you – Not just a financial crash worldwide, not just huge physical earthquakes but physical and spiritual shocks we all NEED to be fully awake to our individual responsibility and soul survival.

STAY TUNED

DUE TO THOSE WHO WERE OPEN TO TRUTH - INSTEAD OF THE LIES - AMERICA HAS ENDURED.

Most of us tried hard to believe in words - those printed, those spoken, those promising better lives, better health. But the dollar won against us.: Big business, big Pharma, Fat Politicians with slim waistlines and big Egos. Who do we believe? No one unless we are wise enough to fast and pray, meditate believing our Infinite Source does care and will answer. This has become my Ultimate Truth to believe and to give out. People, (and you know who I mean) - have done their positive-negative jobs on us. The hurts have made us all smarter even as the wounds smarted, Right?

So try to listen up, Fellow Learner, at an amazing story, prove it out as above described and get the benefits: Learning that Service To Others is an ultimate blessing on both sides, I finally got around to changing my life. As I did I got hooked in to 'Upstairs' my Source, the Infinite - not some blood and guts warring super alien god who had me and you (?)... transfixed from our Sunday School teachers and later our Televangelists who used the super weapon, fear of God and Hell Fire and never ending punishments. As a Dad later on with nine kids, it wasn't hard to stop that kind of thinking/memorizing for I wouldn't do it, you wouldn't either - and we aren't even Infinite yet.

Some don't get it yet though. Maybe they like guilt trips, blaming others, needing some Animal to be sacrificed for them or some nice Guy who learned about overcoming a sideways society. And BTW, such a Guy just happened to be one of sixteen others down through time who really tried to be our example - not our Scape Goat. I'm talking Responsibility for our self - not cop outs — not atheist, not doing any old thing that feels good. Responsibility, excellence in living and doing those "Good works" that seem to scare Hell out of lots of Christians and others.... "Only God and Jesus can do good works!" Phooey on such misleading doctrines and obvious Brainwashing by the money nut pundits. Love figures out what to do, how to live, when and who to give to. That Love is yours from Infinite Father-Mother if you seek it wholeheartedly. Call it religion if you need a word...Pardon, but my fasting, praying, meditating freed me from churches, meeting hopping and workshops and all of T-V's desperate preachers who come up with a new tape or book every five minutes to occupy your mind and ears so you DON'T THINK. Don't miss this point – you ARE fished for by men that know the Truth but just don't give a damn if you do!

Example? A close friend, a well meaning non-denominational minister, went to Rome, hoping to get a glimpse of some of the ancient Catholic archives in their twenty mile long basement (20 that is!) . He got acquainted with a Cardinal, had some talks and in one of them the Cardinal had a heart attack! He weakly asked my friend to help him to his Vatican apartment.

He did, the Cardinal got well and talks continued. Finally he told my friend he would take him into that basement that contained copies and originals of what the 'dear brethern' had burned or stolen from the Alexandrian and Memphis libraries in old Egypt. J........... was flabbergasted at what he saw and moreover what he learned. That was passed on to me, as was another friends experience in Roman deceit. A deceit that earlier composed what became molded Christianity from pagan Catholicism. Things you and I have believed, taught our kids, were baptized into, memorized and held tight to without dare questioning. You know WHAT I mean about questions...

Should mention this one you still hang onto and some of you would kill over it... The Sabbath Day.... Sunday is not it. Catholics placed that in your Bible because their hero Constantine was a Sun worshiper back in the 300s B.C. And Saturday isn't either like the Jews have been brainwashed with from their false Genesis records. What IS? The same world hopping friend that got into that basement met with Mohandes K. Gandhi of India - that great little liberator from the

Brits rule over their opium fields. Mr. Gandhi made my friend J....wait a whole day before the interview. Why? It was his Sabbath. Oh? But next day he took him into his back yard. He showed him a huge rock with inscriptions on it. One line for every authentic Sabbath Day from Abraham's (ABRAHM) time. He was a Brahman by faith and practice! Thus his name. Dates and testaments now kept secret by guess who worldwide? Yes, Friday, same as brother Moslems revere - because they recognize Abram of Chaldia as most religions do, as a true holy man and inceptor of true beginnings. And poor believing Abe, didn't get his guidance always from the Infinite. That phoney god told him to sacrifice his beloved son Issac. That 'almost act' made Abraham quite a hero to lots of us down through time. NOT.

You might begin to dig through the fog about now; at what I am getting at. Downright LIES have ruined lots of lives, made Hells out of a possible Heaven on Earth, ruined marriages, created suicides, started wars, turned people insane when they began to get a whiff of the real Truth. Are you that fragile? I don't - I can't - believe you want to live a lie. Or do you? If you do stop here - To go on gets dangerous for wimps...

Notice you and I usually hung to things that felt good, tasted good, made us gushy and warm all over at Holidays? Ever thought about that, where did it start? Babies from Virgins, Easter eggs, Halloween, Devils waiting to devour your Soul? Sound a little like someone wants you living in Fear, Guilt, Shame? Right on, Friend, Pilgrim. And it sure has worked for centuries, hasn't it and few have spoken up --- till now.

That isn't easy to do. Imagine.... You can attract Bullets, IRS, Swat Teams, Excommunication, loss of your loved ones, credit ruined - Gee, really? It happens, 'Been there; had that. Call it 'No Wimps Land'

MONOLITH

The point of all this for you is this: You live a hard life of endless laws, restrictions, false beliefs, robbery of your hard earned bucks and now, here we are, Americans with 17 Trillion saddled around our necks, politicians admitting a near disaster of untold size worldwide and these guys scurrying around like Ants in a Honey Jar hoping to keep getting rich over your Ignorance. Did my fasting, prayers, meditational seeking bring me and you any answers, solutions? It did . IF you can handle it.

Money, gold, wealth, daily bread, bank interest, gas prices eating you alive like Piranhas while you are tied in their pond of lies and greed and your lack of knowing what in Hell is happening...?

National debt? Answer: Simple... Kill the Federal Reserve, jail it's traitors. No more interest rates,

Everyone rich or poor, pays 10% total taxes which includes all taxes. No more sales tax or property taxes or drivers license taxes – all an illegal Gestapo force. But that's minimal as a solution for 17 Trillion in robbery by the Fed. Here's the cork on the bottle: HANG ON -

Everything I am now going to list you will rear back at or call insane, impossible, too drastic....But, Friend American, What's more insane or drastic than us going down the drain? So think deeply now and Remember Rome and Greece and today in Europe. Same scene, different players. Do you like the movie?

Every piece of our blessings of Mineral Wealth, from water, gravel, coal, gas, oil, gold, platinum, wind, diamonds, precious gems etc. was placed here by whom? Our Creator-the Infinite - not men, not Rockefeller or the men you give credit for our beginning wealthy nation. Right?

We're talking something here you forgot about: MONOPOLIES. By a few who had know how, guts, start up capital and public trust. Where did it end up? A Monopoly in all of the above listed Mineral Wealth.

Without thought you and I gave up our God Given Gifts to those men we respected and trusted. What happened? They got super rich. We, the owners, collectively - got screwed and paid through the nose and through laws passed for those Monopolists to keep their strangle hold on the "ignorant masses, the useless eaters", that those so-called "forged" Protocols describe.

Action, Solution? Since we are at a point of no return, bridge out situation and since we are the actual owners of this vast Mineral Wealth by common law precedent – Pass this Law: Each Company, Family, Corp. that has control of the above listing of Natural Resources is divested of all further ownership EXCEPTING that given by a new law which states: Those former owners, families and corp. heads place 90% of their stock in a public trust while their management receives a salary allocated on production capability and simplicity. PROFIT INCENTIVE has proven to always work.

Some of you will shout: "That's sharing the wealth!" Nope, it's putting the natural wealth of a Nation back where it belongs. Equal to all its citizens. Is it communism, socialism? Of course not, Shallow Thinkers, sharpen up your pencils and your insights -Again you have had Newspeak and Politically Correct jargon placed on your mind to make sure YOU do not rock the boats of the elite skunks that wrote those Protocols making it appear as if the Jews wrote them, planned it all – NOT SO, but they plastered that lie on the backs of the Jewish population instead of the Rothschild etc. dynasty called today ZIONISM out of Telaviv that does have typical and orthodox Jews very carefully fooled as we Americans drench them with our money and weaponry!!!

Wake up Jews and Blacks – you are being used, pitted against us and each other and you who are Mexican nobles - you are swallowing the same bait by causing your flock to become antagonistic to commonsense border laws and to rebel at Gringo's easy life. Arrogance is easy to spot in many Mexicans who really do want a very wrong share the wealth program.

Now what happens when the Mineral Wealth is put back in the citizens hands and semi-management? Fifty percent of the trust money goes to infrastructure needs, military's sensible requirements and development of land, wells and allocation of small farm plots for families that want them – or training programs for occupations they can perform. NO FREE HANDOUTS. WORK for what you get will be the hard rule. Talents rewarded by community awareness, more land if you are proficient- productive. Stops if you wallow in laziness and poor production. Fair? No free rides, Pancho Via, or whatever color you are. Be an American 100% resposible.

Did you miss where the other 50% goes? A Public Fund allocated, given to each individual whether rich or poor – It belongs to all. But 10% of each persons amount goes into an interest drawing pot – A better, safer form of Social Security which is managed by their local community, chosen officers who job out that 10% by investing in overseas products or companies. As a Nation we will no longer bill our people for interest – others may until they see our progress and better way of life – No more stress, mortgages, fines...We help each other pioneer style – We each build, farm and plan for a sound future. Sure, there's a lot more to what I got from 'Upstairs' as sound advice for a crippled nation and our wondering families. If you've handled this much you're ready for some more, all of the delightful details that really, only Heaven could have sent to a common man who cares for something besides money, acceptance and praise. Thanks to all of you who have already contacted me. Spread the word, Share what has to happen if we are to make it. Copy this Newsletter, Watch DAVID'S SLING '2013 and you' on MANTA.com (Email for more:) ROY Rwoodward28@gmail.com

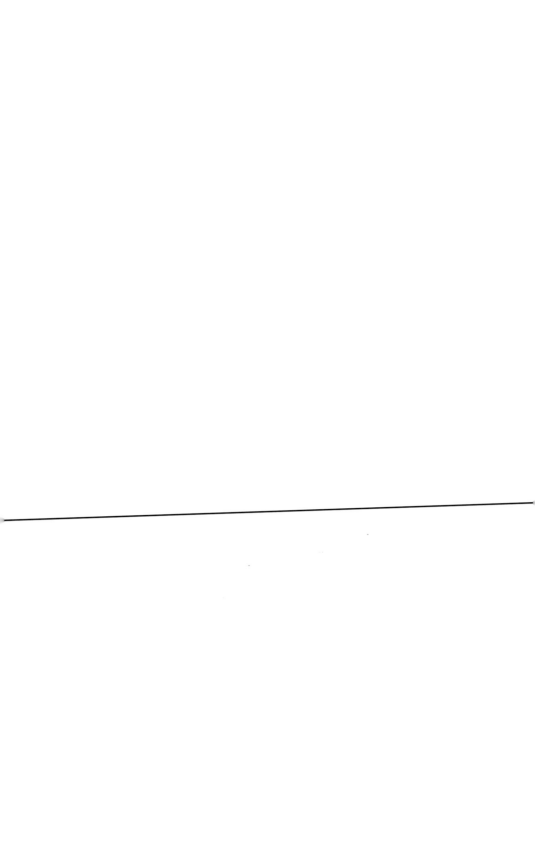

BOOK 3

ALL TOGETHER NOW

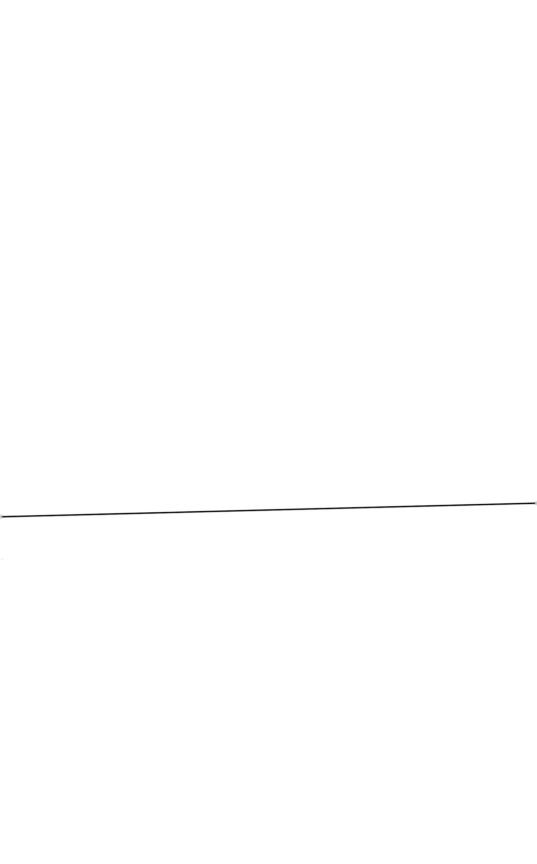

- ALL TOGETHER NOW -

THE LEMURIAN - ATLANTEAN CONNECTION

"Factual fiction of 2010, 2011, 2012 – and millions of years before - what has happened, what is forthcoming and how it will affect you and your loved ones."

Necessary as a fictionalized account expressing some of what Professor Churchyard saw in Tibetan archives about far ancient Lemurias demise, what he and others hoped would warn us and cause our investiture into a frequency adaptation without pain or loss.

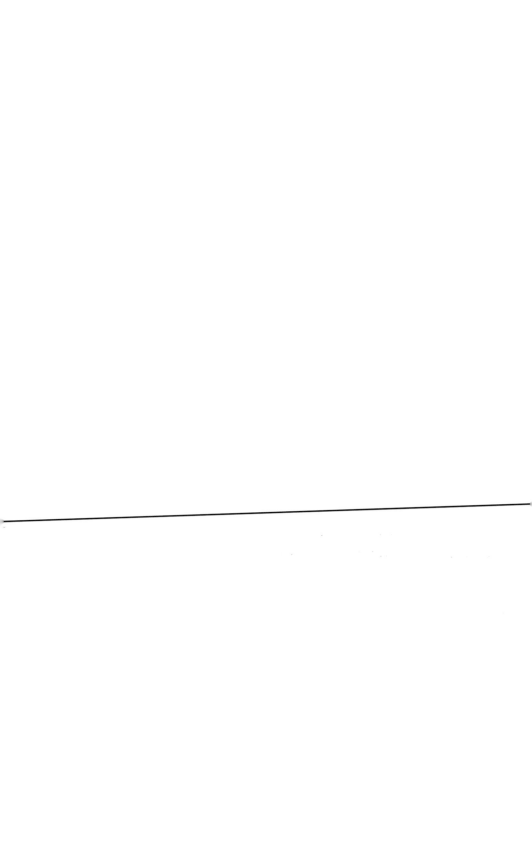

FOREWORD

It has been with some reservation that the author presents this book. If I had told it like it happened over many years in my spiritual growth and various unusual experiences – few would have believed it and probably done little to change their lives in this present age of extreme controversy. Telling it like I have here; may leave a bit of mental strangeness in the reader but that may further your interest in checking carefully what is told and found in some of the end pages Bibliography. Whether you decide if this has been my past lifetime experience and a Romeo and Juliet love - can be your adventure. I assure you it was mine and continues past death - and loss beyond telling. But, as in Romeo and Juliet's case, nothing worth living comes easy. Joyfully the author found there is no death where love dwells. And more poignant and mysterious: There is no boundry line between Heaven and Earth. But we were not taught that were we?

As I watched and thrilled to the Metropolitan Opera, Romeo uttered words that struck cords of sweet music as well as bitter-sweet happenings:

"I see you - and my heart rejoices!"

Flesh, Spirit? Both? Which? Wait till you find out. Can anything separate Love that originated before the Mists of Time?

This book, an epilogue of horrible drama, death, destruction, adventure and the love that endured through all of it – millions of years in fact, Reader, has a warning and a hope for you and billions of population. Read well, ponder more so.

- June 27, 2010 Carole Mae's birthday -

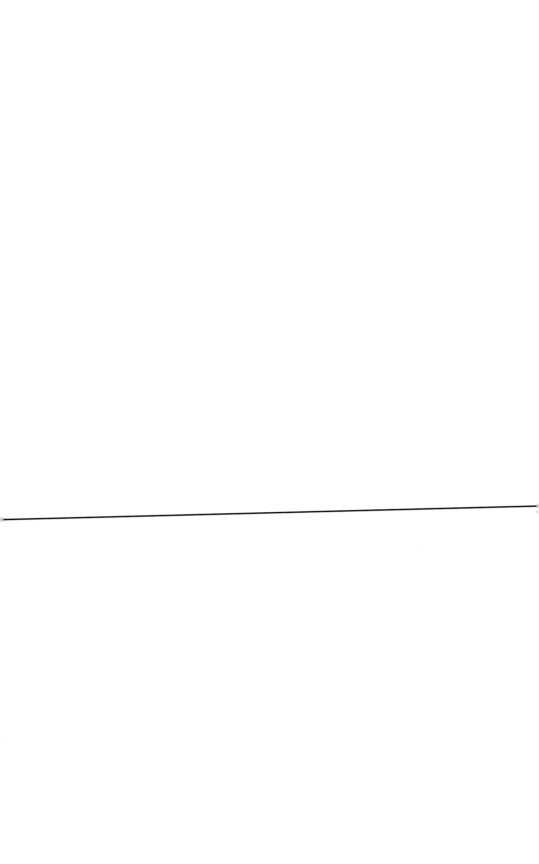

CHAPTER 1

The Lemurian capital's seismic dept.:

Tan, the needles at it again —just squiggles but hundreds of them! Well, don't alert any more than we have: This is definitely Cosmic in effect —all of it agrees with those 'perturbations' happening months ago to Neptune, Mars, Venus and others out there. Not Sun spot activity or renewed Earth Wobble excuses as NACA tries to convince the confused public! I know Jag, they worry so about public reaction, stock market collapses, land depreciation, dollar values. Crazy logic!

Yeah, call me if it gets bigger. Maybe we'll hear from Mars if they see it closing in. The Blindside, Sun glare down here has us pretty well stymied for photos or telescope details. OK?

The two men placed their four palms together, their eyes meeting, tears forming at the unknown enormity of what they thought they knew was happening. Six months of painstaking watching, re-checking worldwide and with outer world neighbors, rare scrolls from the mountain peoples across the Earth.

The Red Giant wasn't changing it's course.

CHAPTER 2

He lay back in bed looking at her sleeping face – What a masterpiece of delicate Humaness! Morgha rolled over and kissed her hair. How long had it been –How, when and how they met? Laying back across from Franaa, Morgha decided on a few more hours of sleep, his muscles still aching from timber cuttings stacked in their back yard.

Already the two glistening moons had their night sky alive with shadows and silky light. The double moons reflecting their dual suns rays in multiples. He slept, the circular bedroom windows, oval longitude; as she had wanted them - letting in the mid night breezes from the ocean and it's edged palm trees.

And he dreamed of 'Long ago and far away', the words of their love song – one of many – and his eyelids fluttered as the reality of love invaded his sleep: "Long ago and far away, I dreamed a dream one day – and now that dream is here beside me. Long the sky was overcast but now the clouds are past – you're here at last... Chills run up and down my spine, Alladin's Lamp is mine –The dream I dreamed was not denied me - Just one look... and then I knew... that all I'd longed for Long Ago was you..."

His hand subconsciously reached to hers... The Mists of Time melted and it was future 1965. Lemuria and then Atlantis and the Egyptian plateau were washed away now and archeologists were still arguing the cause of the 'flood' – Sunspots, Undersea Volcanoes. El Nino?

Morgha was now Roy, Franaa had become Carole Mae – Time to meet again in the Grand Drama of Reimbodiment that had the worlds spiritual competitors as mixed up as the past archeology of ancient civilizations and their demise. Each body woke up that day to a strange lurch in their Solar Plexis and a tingle in their hand.

Tan, The Atlantean seismologist, had decided to return to track down the next pass by of that infamous Red Dwarf, Brown Dwarf planet, whichever had been decided by renewed Telescopes and worn out Astronomers. Now decided to be 14 times bigger than Earth. Planet X's mass unbelievable, magnetic pull outdoing itself among the planets as it passed by them creating quakes, slides, storms, havoc. The often scribed Elliptical Orbit laid down by ancients as well as the Mayans telling all to look ahead to it's regularity it's destructiveness as it barely missed hitting Earth each clocked time.

Maybe he and Jag, his former Polo Player in Lemuria's state parks, could figure out – at least alert this generation, maybe technology could 'nudge' it aside, further out in it's ellipse of fury. Hadn't it wiped out their neighbor Mars, pulled in Venus from stars away?

CHAPTER 3

The 'High Strangeness' of this word Reimbodiment may be a diverse way of skirting around the controversial subject/belief of Reincarnation. The author makes no pretense here –but only gives you a chance to see how much you can believe other than what past teachers, books and tapes have mis-taught you. Both words: Reimbodiment – Reincarnation may well mean the same thing to some and have a totally different appeal to others. Reincarnation, though does prevail in the belief or fact, that all things created from stone to Man came up the hard way –sometime, somewhere. Here or out in the vast Cosmos. Progression from minor beginnings – Yes, maybe even apes?, you ask. "With God all things are possible?" Yes or no?

When faced with this last scripture from your unchallenged Bibles, Talmuds or Korans, you flinch as to evolving entities; don't you? Otherwise HE can do everything but that, Right? He's then limited according to your ability to understand Him and His ways? Hmmnn...

But nevertheless here we have two men and a woman said by the Writer to have been re-born in a new era, new location to warn, maybe even help avert a cyclic disaster akin to none known previous. And a woman tied closely with those two men – and YOU. How so? Maybe your life and future fulfillment rests in their story as you decide to judge it Truth or Fiction...

Yes, it's different than you and I were taught. Each time some of us have tougher shells and need a bigger hammer. If you weren't a carbon based human, you followed conventionality –customs, beliefs that someone else thought out for you. You like to think little and trust big, remember? Life by your design has to run smoothly, too much thinking and trouble comes. But, recall history which never fails to give hard evidence – Thinkers always had trouble –or were killed. At least ridiculed. You ever ridiculed a person, concept or belief not common to your teachers or books?

This being a Love Story, most un-common - should hold your interest. It shouldn't be too hard to step outside your beautiful, plush-lined, perfumed, stainless steel box and read something that will stir some remembrances in your clouded past before this life...

Add all this up to the most marvelous of all Human Gifts: Love coupled with Understanding. This is what I do now. Not much time left before you may have to return here or some other Planet – (or stay for a long term orientation session in a level of 'Heaven' you thought you deserved better?) Yes, usually true after the Death Experience. Warnings either bore you, frighten you or discourage you from trying to survive all this Earth's problems and frustrations. But know that you will be very disappointed when the 'change' takes place if you didn't try an awfully lot harder for yourself and loved ones. YOU OWE THEM!

CHAPTER 4

Better than Heaven, better than surviving for Eternity or Infinity is... What? Finally knowing and having Love –your own love. Doubt it? Don't - for love is the sum of all creation – What Father Himself learned so as to make us a pre-determined Pair –Mates – Twins. Out of the flame of His personal Being which had once been alone except for His Consort. Wife? Yes. Children come from, came from love uniting with it's own. Divorce, Murders, Suicides come from missing the mark. Wrong choice or Choices. You got ahead of yourself and God to make it plain... You chose the wrong one. Hell then became your invention, instead of the Hollywood Heaven you had expected. A statistic instead of an ecstatically happy bride or groom – miserable, maybe still hoping, dreaming – fantasies? Or ready to do something about your life?

Better enjoy this story. You may decide it's true and can give you tools to help your Dream. If Heaven, super scenery, vistas of majesty, even golden crowns, streets of gold, harps and the Bible lot - as you learned it in Sunday School – If all that, (and it adds up to stuff and ego satisfaction - rewards) doesn't get you nearly as excited and hopeful about your Afterlife, well maybe you really are looking for ultimate Love –and not stuff and sensations? I mean him or her – small h's. The Guy, the Gal – The One.

CHAPTER 5

So stuff without Love is madness, at least boredom, Heaven without your Twin Flame –true mate is, just recess till you come back down and try again to understand one simple thing: Reimbodiment is meant to be THE Law for your happiness and fulfillment. You don't get this Law in your Heart until you live FOR LOVE – him, her, everyone. You don't learn that one till you try it over and over again. Look how petty you have been in so many ways in this lifetime! Try harder and the gold ring is yours. (See Meryl Streep in Defending Your Life – A video you need yesterday!!!) Maybe too the video Heaven Can Wait)

Ok, back to the plot? You ask... One moment first:

When things don't work you have to ask Why, if you're normal in gray matter or spirit. And you'd think this would have sunk in after a number of lifetimes and false starts. Slow to happen, that's why HE made Reimbodiment or Reincarnation at the beginning of Time. Slow learners take longer classes. I hope you read your story here, there's lots of 'boxes' being pummeled from the inside by some super serious people today. Not much Time left to get outside. How big is your hammer?

Every so many millions and billions of years, our Earth is reformed and repopulated from deceased Souls who had recess from their last event or location in the Cosmos. Hold that thought because Science, Archeology and some Religions have proven it:

CHAPTER 6

UPSTATE NEW YORK

General Morrison, this just came in on the Ham Radio! The slim Corporal handed the paper to the worn looking soldier: Thanks, Son, you, better get a few winks –almost morning. But you, General, there's... The General pushed the boy out of the tent, Go to sleep, that's an order! But, Sir!...

The first faint tips of sunrise light were striking the tall pines of the immense clearing. Jeeps, Half Tracks, unusual Boom Trucks with aluminum dishes hanging from their ninety foot lofts, stood even with the blue green pines. Above all of this in the clearing, stretching windwise hundreds of feet from the clearing's perimeter was the camo balloon, it's gray-green surface dying in from above with the New York State forests where dozens of other such clearings and balloons were in action. Action? No, rather, Waiting.

The General picked up the field Phone, punched it and only static. Damn! He flung it down and reached for the Ham Radio cord, plugged it in to the generator...Morrison, here, Come in all fields in Relay 123. Got it? Soon amid crackles, of yet unrefined Ham, voices; began to emerge. The General wrote quickly on his writing pad, then punched in 123 on his special hand computer: Got it. Thanks, Men. He settled back on the canvass lounge chair the Corporal had brought him from town with the coffee. He grunted, closed his eyes and slept, his wrist jerking fitfully from the Afghan shrapnel scars and then even that old wound settled down...

MONOLITH

His eyes moving back and forth under their lids he was back there right when the news hit from NASA and Palomar, as well as the European Space Command Network that had been strung all over Europe and part of Eurasia. It was entering premature, traveling far faster than they had expected the Earth's gravitational pull to trigger such speed. Twice the size of Jupiter? God sure did it super size, they had remarked at Palomar when they saw it first coming around the extreme lower edge of the Sun's glare. That had made it hard to photograph, let alone visual. It wasn't pitted, it shone like metal...

CHAPTER 7

Well, we know we've been lied to before, What do you think? The NASA super, looked down at the floor steadily. When his head lifted there were tears in his eyes, his chin tightened as he stared hard through his slowing tears...They screwed us, Zach, screwed us as if we were snott-nosed kids! DAMN!! The desk shuddered under his fist. Zach, you knew their promises, saw the batch of high tech in our Dulce bunkers down there –What'd you believe? The tall Gyro Technician scrubbed with his feet – looked out the large shoot proof window, I believed them. What I saw them do, I believed and I believed you – who wouldn't have believed all our team saw there – ancient history, nations falling, Rome, Pompeii all down the tube while we saw their ships hovering over it all... Yeah, Terrill, I believed, who wouldn't?

OK, that's past, now the fun begins, Zach. He wiped his eyes. All the Military has finally admitted their blindness for a Tech trade-off for the Alien Bases. Eisenhower, way back then, fell for it with a few reservations but at Edwards, his reluctance mushed. When those ships landed and then after the occupants got out and the talks were over – and they just evaporated in front of two thousand Militia and twelve Tanks – well...Yeah.

Don't forget that over ten companies of our boys were melted down there in those lower archives at Dulce and Trolley Square under Salt Lake City. Even the Pres tried to explain that to the parents, but...Yep, bad times, bad stuff. Bottom line, we were so hyped on technology like their civilization was, that we bit hard.

MONOLITH

What's the plan then, Terrill? Pentagon and all foreign based troops, home fast, Zach. All those Micro - Fused mirrors on those balloons are faced inward partially; so that when the noon Sun hits they ignite more gas pockets inside the balloons and they almost shoot straight up into the Ionosphere. Then at the peak altitude of one hundred thousand feet the War Heads start moving out – How many Terrill? Don't know Pentagon wouldn't tell us but they are strung all over our deep forest lands here, Black forest in Germany, in the mountains behind that Yalu River Dam in China, and –he paused, looking worried...In the bare Sonora Desert in Mexico...

God sakes Terrill, they can be seen, up close and personal! Sure can and all of us except the Pres has screamed. No use, he says he has sealed orders from higher ups and they figure we need all the ground we can cover – tree cover or not! The two men walked over to the 8 X 8 wall screen bleeping and squaking now. What's this mean? Hang on! Zach hit some buttons on another smaller screen. It lit up. It was Sonora. What's this Zach? Don't know yet! Suddenly 400 hundred miles of desert sand and hundreds of camo balloons flashed and were gone –no explosion– just a flash. MYYY GODD!

CHAPTER 8

General Tank Morrison nearly fell off his cot when the Ham started calling in. Grabbing it shakily, he rubbed his eyes –Yes, Morrison here, What's up? Keno 4? Go ahead, Keno! General, Sonora's gone; vanished! Whhaatt? Yeah, lasered, something... we don't know, Sir. My God, Keno, the others know about... Yeah, Sir, all of them worldwide. Any others bothered? So far, no Sir. What's the move now then? We're waiting for European Space Command to reply, we just don't trust NASA anymore. You know they said for years X wasn't real - if it was no threat, It would pass by far enough – Yeah I know, Lying bastards, Keno; they've hid it for years, now it's here and...Sir, Keno 4 here, got to go fast, will re-contact, something is... KENO! KENO! Come in, come in...!!

Far off in the early morning mists, General Tank Morrison rubbed his eyes in disbelief. Maybe a hundred miles away from the shallow edge of the pine clearing, there they were, hundreds of them. The Ships.

South of Morrison, yes, about a hundred miles, silver blue elipse shaped ships were darting, almost playfully among the balloons tethered thousands of feet down to Earth. Like kids popping penny balloons soon all of the hundreds were dropping on their cables, deflated, smoking while a blue colored ray followed each one to the ground – where something white and red just popped and melted. Then the fumes and all ... just gone! Nothing. The ships darting back into a large white cloud with the Sun shining prettily on it's underside where they disappeared.

The Ham came back on, startling the General. Sir, Keno 4 back! Yes, Go! Did you see off in the distance there to your south? Yes, Keno, Yes!

MONOLITH

Well that's why I conked out, Sir – those ships just dropped out of that big cloud and all hell started! Are you OK, Keno? Yes Sir, shakin like hell, Sir but WE'RE ALL OK! – Not a soul even singed and all the trucks Ok too, WHAT's going on, Sir?!! Keno, hang on, I've got calls coming in on my Multiple Pak, can you wait? I guess, Sir, but for God's sake the men are goin nuts here, hurry! Roger, Keno – out.

CHAPTER 9

Grand Canyon Dam Core Complex Naval Intelligence Headquarters:

Have you got it, Stevens? Just through from all zones. Yep, all destroyed, no one hurt, ordinance sound. All communications Zorro! We're back on Com. The staff of hundreds cheered after the deadly silence of the last hours. Je sus Kee Rist what a morning!! Stevens slumped in his chair and pulled a rag out of his jeans, wiping his neck and forehead.

Iron Mountain Bunker: Retrieved complex for government officials and the President. One of three readied years past –

In a far corner of the plush shelter Henry Kissenger, Barack Obama and George Soros along with underlings like Rahm Emanuel and the puppet from the Federal Reserve tunnel were dabbing at their microwave breakfasts, hardly looking up at the Military Police hunks standing over them. A speaker announced loudly, Rothschild and Blair and the 300 will be here by Chopper in 30 minutes. "All hands stand down! Till the Elevator clears, then on your toes, Men. Big time stuff coming on! The Bunker's cheers rang out as the men with the dark countenances at the table; all dropped their forks.

The shootproof glass wall between the traitors and the staff clouded over so the staff were now unseen: Canders, those ships we used to see on Sub duty in the Northwest Pacific – tell me, did they really have bases underwater there? Like the Sigorney Weaver movie? Sure did, Tom, lots of em – over 200 we counted but couldn't get down to em. Some kind of block or ray or curtain – nothing penetrated it. Lost 2 Subs, 110 Divers who volunteered. Never found a trace... Well, what's the program here with these ships blasting our ballons out of the sky, no personnel hurt, even scratched, all the ordinance intact - I just don't get it!

OK, here it is but 'for your eyes only stuff'! See? Or else! Yeah, Top, huh? For now anyway...Their eyes met as friends for over 20 years but they knew the rules and –

He began, These Monkeys over there, He pointed through the misted glass wall, They suddenly got fooled too, like we did. What'ya mean? Radio dispatches started getting captured because we had, shall we say, 'tips', about their loyalty. These intercepted messages said those ships were going to take 'them' out of all the destruction to our cities and to be ready on the White House Steps for a 'Beam me up, Scotty' date two nights ago. We knew then we had something fishy, for this meant they and the ships were one. Well, yeah I figured that but... Wait! When we went to pick them up with the Military Boys, strange thing happened: Right above us a small ship drifted in with a Speaker going. WHAT'D It Say? Hold on now, you're getting too excited. The speaker was in ALL languages at ONE TIME but we heard English! What? Yeah. Said some of the bad guys, those Whitney Streiber Greys had got together with the Bilderbergers and the Club AND the British BP Oil Blair boys. And, Yes, The Bushes - and made a compact making Operation Blue Book a reality. You mean that was a real plan like Bill Cooper exposed? A phoney Saucer invasion? Sure, he was the original good guy till someone in the CIA or the F words shot him down in his doorway after they wrecked him a few years back and took his leg! WHY? They thought he was nuts, exposing too many people in gov, making it hard to move in all our other problems. Then? That ship overhead spilled all the beans right there while we all were waiting to see What's next... they even dropped rolls of metal tapes down with all the secret dialogues between these fish market crap heads! By the way, Tom that so called Star Gate Portal Yeah? A planted rumor to get military out of Baghdad while troops were deployed to Afghanistan – No portal. Just OIL with a capital O – and the Gulf of Mex leak? Planned too - to rob us of our oil here so we would have to pay huge prices from overseas, gulfs there, mountain vastnesses, plus plunge our military bucks into a knot hole. Sad, Tom – Conspiracy? God Yes, you'd have had to be blind not to see how it was all orchestrated outside the White house, outside of No. 1 Downing Street. Puppets, Masters, Strings, Threats, Murders, All sides selling both sides weapons, CIA starting this and that and we get in to finish it – and make a fortune out of it. Cooper and I were buddies from Nam, Tom. He taught me the following and I always looked for it in every headline and every order we got: PROBLEM, REACTION, SOLUTION and gave his life for it all. What'd he mean? If you want government or military power just create a big public problem – The people will react in fear or anger or want. They'll DEMAND a solution. Give it to them, telling them they must give up something for it to be done for them – you mean? Yeah, Iraq. Freedom? Try The Patriot Act and Blackhawk and FEMA – CIA's old fashioned comparing them to Mossad and Scotland Yard and British Intell ...sleep nice, Tom. The two men retired for a two hour rest from sleepless nights of wondering.

CHAPTER 10

Showering, the two officer friends sat down at scrambled eggs and oatmeal... Details are this Tom: Greys are phony, some were Area 51 produced - by other aliens and Jack Parson's labs there and elsewhere. The Nordic type aliens too, but the Etherean Hosts...The WHAT? Ethereans, you heard me – Way out past our Atmosphere on other dimensions, Octaves they call it. Able to go anywhere, any speed beyond light through the Zero Point Field. That? Yeah, it's true, real, no limitations in the Field. Einstein knew it but few listened. Parsons knew it used it at White Sands and Sandia at Albuquerque was working on it overtime. Plan was, by the bad guys to make a stab at a hologram fake invasion by Aliens like Reagan hinted at in a speech he made for his Star Wars Shoot down program. "Kill em all, ask questions afterwards!", same old military myopia! I never wanted to believe all this Operation Blue Beam stuff, Can! Well you'd better; because it has happened but in reverse, Tom! How? They, the contracted Aliens turned on their benefactors, saw them conniving to kidnap some of their robots and reboot them their ways. But, by the way, they had it all planned out, told us, "How long do you think the One will let this go on?" The WHAT? The ONE! – God, the Source, Him/Her their version of the Pos and Neg, Yin/Yang, our Big Dad, fool! Mr. Cosmos machine/person/power – you tell me! Uhhh, you're telling me we have friends instead of Sumerian gods called Annanaki on our side? Well, Tom, get this and I'm glad I wasn't shy about asking their C Chief as they called him...What? I asked him, 'If since they had actually cloned and populated Earth back then with thousands of years of profound High Tech lab tools and really made themselves a slave race out of cave men types called Drudgas and Ihins - if they were still of that 'bent' wanting to do the same to us?' Answer he gave, "No, that was thousands of years in our bully, pride, power trip when we actually usurped our Father Anu - who did come down with us to review things with our earlier Creations – at least an experimental being we might further develop. That good effect would have happened except that two royal Brothers started fighting over it all and your population leveling flood happened over there. One brother, whom you Earthlings called Noah fought to save the then half developed Earth Man and Woman. You won't be finding any Noah's Ark right soon – it was one of our Mother Ships, room for everything and then some, Brother Cander. We must leave now for your Back Countries where the populaces have been waiting for the Rogue Planet you mistakenly call Red Dwarf, Planet X and your NASA's long list of peppered titles – all pseudonyms for their lies and fears of being in league with the wrong Brothers. You do see, Mr. Cander, that we all belong, many alien races here, some well meaning, some just curious about your Best Bombs - quite an admxture, hard for you to have decided correctly (high tech connivers some of us, but we learned.) We all eventually learn or die trying. We all change eventually if we can get honest and quiet with ourselves and environment...don't you agree, My Brother?"

Well, Tom it was like talking or being taught by God Himself, streetwise. I crumbled to my knees, not in reverence or anything like that – just totally whipped into absolute childlike awe. He topped it all off this way: Said, "Once they were exploratory, DNA researchers, experimenting with mutant life forms cosmically - for many had weathered or been genocided by races far more aggrandizing than we biblical, so miscalled, "Sons of god Yahweh." Nor were we that - but stragglers with a Father almost at one time as greedy for power as we became. He convulsed at our lusts and waywardness – left us, went back to his galaxy by way of your Black Hole, we use them to short cut through Universes, Can. He told us to learn Mercy and Justice – to learn what that meant and then to check back in. Brother Candor, WE HAVE LEARNED! We mean nothing but good, Love you call it. Simple Brotherhood – helping others help themselves, Huh? We watched a few people like you and your team, not churches and seminaries – just mindal and spiritual people who - like us; finally found out, had a portion of the Source's Son stationed behind the Fifth Ventricle in their hearts – That un- researched mystery figure standing gloriously upright inside that small Pyramid Chamber – you would call it –'The God within..." Suddenly the hatch started to close, the violet light intensified. He flowed back up the ramp, WAIT, I yelled! "Yes?" What's with Planet X now, is that your planetary vehicle, an Orbiter? Will it mess up Earth, Moon and Mars and scatter Venus? "Yes, X is our home away from home – we still work for Father Anu with a bit more delicacy. Your planned balloons to shoot it aside would have sent severe radiation down and ruined your planet. Silly idea, Son; but you were frightened. Desperate men do desperate things." He turned facing the hatch, his powerful, broad back to Cander and said slowly, very slowly...

"Son, try hard at remembering what you are here FOR – Each Other." He waved his powerful arms out and over the landscape. "Just keep it clean, we will do the rest, Can; Adeiu!" And they were gone, Tom. And I cried like a baby dripping snot, not even giving a big Damn!

CHAPTER 11

Worldwide Six Billion humans clung to each other, looking up to the Northwest sky, the stars now gone, the Sun hot, glaring, eyes tearing at both the glare and the drama – Planet X was coming into our orbit between us and the Moon. The first vestiges of it's shape now showing through the Sunrays. Crowds were singing 'How Great Thou Art, Rock Of Ages', Zipiddy Doo Daa by the Hippies, anything else they thought was appropriate or that would ease their fears of almost sure evaporation or being mashed or drowned. It was all here now, the Books, the Tabloids, the Mayan Prophecies, Taggert's powerful book, The Field, The Marches, the Fasts, The Fists up at God – Sadly too, the Suicides, kids with them, even pet dogs. Fear...

Morrison now back at the New York Urban Center Military Compound watched in disbelief in how far people can go with fear or religion when the chips are down – He shook his head and looked up again. Something was rearranging the cloud formations. Deep into the clouds, the moon seemed to be trembling. Clouds mottled like buttermilk curds at first, now furtive, roiling, like they were anxious for something – And it happened. Zooming in between Earth and the trembling Moon, now being pulled into the mass of X, it quite simply shattered into pieces of silvery, red substance, piece after piece zooming up and toward Planet X. Doing so, it came into X's path and crashed into bits by magnetization as a mass of water, Yes, WATER, splashed out of where the Moon had been, it flowed up and out into Planet X's path – headed at Earth.

It has been told since that scientists experimenting, researching on The Field had found that water has Memory. Primeval memory. That heavenly mass of Moon water, old H2O; hit into X broadside - the entire surface glowing white hot, steaming and as the steam cloud swirled away into the distance that Planet, four times the size of Earth just glided up and out from Earth as – and some said this was fantasy – colored PENNANTS were seen streaming out from portholes in the underside and sides. Flapping grandly, disintegrating swiftly, trailing down to Earth. Me and Tom have parts of one of them, Bright blue with strange markings. They say it's Sumerian...

Our people Earth wide seem to be different now - something good seems to have happened inside our heads and hearts. Crime is down amazingly. The prisons emptied themselves in mass, maddening riots as they stood in the fields watching, some on their knees, others shaking their fists at suspected death. Our Water Tables are up. Where the oceans slopped over and up landwise we have huge areas of new agriculture – some places, whole ocean beds bare now, being farmed and orcharded. Animals, and that's the best of all we are seeing, come up to you, no matter the species, even snakes and alligators. Yeah, we pet em, believe me! Husbands and Wives either hung it all up or stayed together. Ones who did are like school kids in love –The others being taught by such – Crazy stuff happening everywhere. Some say we have migrated into another frequency because of Planet X, others, say God has just 'raptured' all His kids because it was almost ruined here and something drastic had to be done. I don't know - but I have ideas I ask Him about...

I went walking among what looks like a new Earth and smells like a new Atmosphere the other day and I found a piece of torn paper in an abandoned house, drifting around in the wind. Had a few words on it in magic marker: Know what it said?

"I SEE YOU – AND MY HEART REJOICES." Know what? That's from the Metropolitan Opera I once saw with my then, Invisable Angel, Carole on one of our fantasy 'dates'. When we left, me driving home, her there, invisible at my side; me bawling, tears wetting my shirt – she yelled out loud. Yes, at times I did hear physical words from her dear lips: "Stop the car! Pull over, I've got to talk to you!!" And she did, Oh, how she did - and I became convinced, far beyond fantasy and hopes. She told me what it was like THERE, what choices meant there, what she had decided about us, how at the funeral, she in that damned Casket, me blubbering over east of it on the bench – she 'put on' Frank Sinatra's STRANGERS IN THE NIGHT – our song - for me. Old Frank singing his lungs out, the brass playing, that shrill fabulous Trumpet blaring me unmercifully – and I knew, just knew it was her way of saying – I'm not dead, I'm not dead – like my Dad had come to me and said long years ago – Tell your Mother, I'm not Dead, Son, I'm not dead!!

So you can take this or leave it all in a pile you WILL one day sort out. What you're reading here now isn't fiction – it's real, just believe it if you can. I don't care anymore about convincements. You get it or you don't.

I really believe if Carole hadn't been able to yell at me to stop that Subaru, that I wouldn't have made it another day. It was just too bloody much! Too bloody much…She saved my life, put breath in me…God that moment will never leave my memory!

Right now, I'm in our big, new bed. Those strange, regular love songs that I told you kids about, always cropping up - out of the Nowhere – almost every early morning from her… She's there, Magic Girl, my Carole Mae back here on her blue silk pillow. She sleeps very sound now, no groans, no whimpers.. I'm propped up on my elbow, just shaking my head..soo beautiful, so very, very impossible. Look at you, Darlin, just look at you! I'm looking at her; this new/old song playing in my head and heart – wonder if she's hearing it too? It's a real old one from the 40s: Listen to those words: "Innn… the weee small hours offf the morning, when all is covered with the dew, In the weee small hours of the morning, I'll be lying there again with youuu…" All seems so familiar.

The New Start

PROLOGUE

This didn't get written till just lately. Four long years after Carole left Earth… I figured you might have figured out what happened about me and Carole Mae. Sometimes readers like to imagine – but I got a lot of complaints because people said they had – if you can believe this – "Fallen in Love with us"

Well, Carole, Yes, but me, I have to think about that... What did happen is that Carole Mae, my little Darlin died in my arms about when Planet X was coming into life in our orbit. Astronomers agreeing NASA was hiding it from the public- even trying to convince or scare amateurs that they were having hallucinations based on mass hysteria or 'telescope viruses'. Carole Mae had told some friends, sadly, not me – that she just wanted to go if such things were coming – she was half afraid for her kids, herself and half convinced that she or God could do anything to keep a rebel population from their folly. Colon Cancer, 10 Tumors. She wanted to whip it with Alternative Treatments, knowing the so low cure rate (10%) with rad and chemo – and the horrible pain and nausea. She fought and got discouraged, fought again and prayed with me, tried everything but that strong will to overcome a crazy population hurrying to their personal Hells.

All this time of the 6 months they gave her, we found a love we had kept covered, like a flame under a basket –barely flickering due to many obstacles, money, mixed kids from her two deceased husbands and particular hazards you can see spelled out in my next book: I KNOW A SEX SECRET.

Fact is, had we both have known this secret, Carole would have had the way and the will to win her halfhearted battle. But life gets funnier as you cry more – The ironies capture you and throw you to the ground.

So how did IT happen – that most remarkable episode in several lives we have known since she 'came back'? Came back? Yeah, Came back, flesh body, eyes, ears nose, all packaged in just a slightly different but same body – corporeally reimbodied.

How? I don't know –it would sell a million or so books overnight probably and help a lot of people who were really, really IN Love, not just money, T-V and sexing each other.

Well, during my care for Carole Mae that last year one the farm, Mike gave us - we found out what love really was and we dove in head first into the grandeur of it, it's wonder, sweetness –the 'paying attention kind' I call it – more even than that. Unexplainable. Gentle, quiet times, caresses, whispers in the night of our darkness that was trying to dirty up our future as we kept putting more wood on the fire of love like we never had slightly imagined could be possible on Earth – even Heaven.

Of course I expected shock if she couldn't whip it, thought I was prepared – we wouldn't talk about, made her mad because I started crying like, well – Then it happened that long night of her groaning pains and that short, short morning of her just suddenly being gone. The flowers I placed in her hair and in her hand, her coldness instead of – Oh God!

Somehow I got through funerals, sympathies, cards sent in appreciation – wet pillows night after night. Then she came to me inwardly as my very counterpart Soul – my true mate and flame bred by Father-Mother the Infinite. She said, "I'm not going to leave you here alone, your knee paining you, the operation coming up – No, Roy, I've been THERE and I've decided my Heaven is with you! I told them that if Heaven is eventually coming down to Earth and I have choices – then I choose you, Dear, always and forever. Your invisible Wife. And I won't give in to any other plan – it's my choice!" Not only did she mean it, she demanded it! And she has stayed, day after day, nights besides me talking sweetly while others who I mistakenly told thought I had lost it, was fantasy bound - or that Carole had attracted low deceiving spirits counterfeiting her voice to me. Chief argument was, "The Bible doesn't allow the Dead to come back. Hey! Lazurus did, Jesus did, a little girl did, a little boy healed back in Mom's arms. Don't Bible me, Friend, I know it's pages almost backwards and side ways. Tell you something, 'God' didn't originate Death, He doesn't want you or me or Carole Mae to die! We do it to ourselves – then we blame God because we feel guilty or mad at him – knowing so little of "As you sow, just so you reap!" Jesus said that, remember? Don't forget it ever again. It can ruin Death and bring people BACK! I promise.

All those long months I prayed, called out to everything good and holy I could think of and she would always be there instead of God, with God, just talking to me in my Soul – that chamber in the heart. Then Father God, our Infinite started coming and filling me up with hope that I needn't die and go to Carole – "Heaven, Son? Thy kingdom come, thy will be done on Earth as it IS in Heaven –"Remember your scriptures?" Right Father, eventually you and it will be down here if we ever get it straight and learned to love one another instead of in the back seats of mortgaged cars! I talk to Him like that, He replies same way – very street wise personality.

You may not buy that though, can't blame you after all the Seminary and Bible wielding Televangelists have had a field day on your memorization mode!

Yes, it had to happen, we promised each other and Him and He promised us – That if we offered to be available to Him anywhere to be example, to teach or do His work of showing what real Love, His love is and can do to re-make lives - no matter how far distorted even if others really weren't twin mates, flames from before Time and Earth Creation - even that could be phenomenal.

But your 'view' isn't that important if you can just visualize such a thing – Even that HE, through Carole; has shown me that there is a far more sophisticated, tender and un-animal like sexual experience awaiting those of us who can simply accept it through trial practice... and reverence too for her body instead of 'me firstism'!

One day she was on my mind and heart. I WAS lonesome first class. And there was this girl – so very lovely, Carole Mae's eyes and sly smile, the hair, the slender and new curves that took my breath. She just stood there. I couldn't move. She had on that horizontal wide stripped orange and yellow sleeveless sweater – I have her picture in the car in it from back 'then'. My mouth hung open, my eyes bulged as I focused and re-focused. Her and in a slightly different all renewed form, a new package, same fabulous person.

Her lips formed some words, I unfroze: "Hi, Roy" My knees went limp, I sagged to the floor, tears erupting. Carole, little Darlin, it's you isn't it!? "Of course, Silly, who'd you expect Meryl Streep? Would you like to see if we could make a go of it?" I grinned, ran to her, she leaped up shamelessly astraddle of my waist, her white toga rolling in the wind. That kiss was eternity wrapped up in everything that's Truth, Beauty and Goodness.

We're here now – it's 2016, things get better every day. Neighbors from the Heavenly places – The aliens; they call them, 'The Starry Places' – We have battery paks that run a whole farm for 10 years at no cost, just 24 hours in the afternoon Sun. Water out of places that X caused to cough up from it's magnetizing pull, our animals talk to us telepathically; we don't kill anything anymore – just raise our orchards and gardens with love to feed us in the old/new Sea Beds and soil, flowers grow magically, enormously everywhere. Children run computers that are wired to sea water and crystals heal anything – wrap one on and...amazing –everything is amazing now.

Especially Carole Mae, she's been there, done that, given it all up for me and our love. Well, not quite because it's all down here now – as promised. Remember?

P.S.

We still tell folks about that Meryl Streep video, it's one people like: 'Defending Your Life', tells so much about Reimbodiment – so simple, and that moving narrative Rip Torn gives at the peak of his performance and then in real life he dies a broken derelict. Yeah, a picture's worth a thousand words...and living has it's varied moments out of The Mists Of Time – Look harder, it's out there...

SOME MISC. HELPS FOLLW:

EVERYTHING YOU NEED TO KNOW ON PLANET EARTH 'CHUCKLE'

COMING SOON:

MY BOOK CALLED SELF: IT SETS YOU FREE. SURPASSES BOOKS FOR DUMMIES... A NEW BIBLE, KORAN AND TALMUD. COMPACT STUFF THAT GETS THINGS DONE IN A HURRY...

- 1.The impossible made easier and faster.
- 2.How to overcome almost everything that troubles you.
- 3.Your religion - what it's doing to you or for you.
- 4.Great wealth or peace of mind – Both?
- 5.Get to the mountains –and hurry up about it!
- 6.What your thoughts and words are doing to you –and others
- 7.My God! That attitude!
- 8.Paying attention –Who does it?
- 9.The Eve syndrome – He, She, They made me do it!
- 10. Helps for anyone that's serious –or ready.
- 11. Beyond religion, preachers, popes and priests.
- 12. One, two three, let's all go to the Hospital!
- 13. Four, Five, Six, let's go natural everything!
- 14. How'd you get those wrinkles? Could it be attitude?
- 15. I rub the best things into my skin but it gets worse and...
- 16. Paranoia, Discouragement and Resentment –A closer look.
- 17. The many Genocides you don't recognize, Fella!

- 18. Fresh, Clean Air, Sun and Quiet - But WHAT kind of Water?
- 19. Wine, Beer or Grape Juice? You poor trusting Humanity! Alcohol the accepted Social Killer
- 20. The best Plastic Surgery isn't! Try this for free.
- 21. Rapeseed, cattle feed and profit. Canola Oil. Does it make cattle and people go blind?
- 22. About "ROY" – Who is he? Why he can't be 'elected' President. The ancient prophecies about him. Things coming before and after Planet X passes near Earth. Election farces, lies and machines.
- 23. Monopolies are killing you, stifling the REAL Americans.
- 24. That "S" word, Socialism, could it be remodeled into something better – like Cooperation? That Hugo Chavez, goodness....sakes!!!
- 25. When enough is enough and people are ready for a new type of fraternity.
- 26. When you need a Pet – Man, Woman or Animal. Marriage, Live Ins' or Sleeping Around? The real skinny. Homo – Les.
- 27. The ridiculous Orgasm-Masturbation LIE and the truth: Yale-Harvard report.
- 28. Bartering is naughty? Try Poverty, IRS will feed you.
- 29. The REAL Signs of the Times are invisible. How people like YOU fool themselves with Denial! Why denial is never seen by the Denier.
- 30. My Doctor said Mylanta! Those drug commercials. E Gads!!!
- 31. The real Cancer is...Dr. Lorraine Day MD, Surgeon, her book, her cure! How she survived by forsaking conventional treatment. Her Book: CANCER DOESN'T SCARE ME ANYMORE!
- 32. "I can stop smoking or drinking when it's my time." The joke of all jokes. Do it now!
- 33. Yes, of course, ask your Doctor. Excuse me... doesn't God answer His Kids anymore?

- 34. Every 3,600 years we have a Visitor that passes by Earth. Have you been lied to about Planet X? – By geniuses? Stop being so damned trusting and get prepared! If you don't believe me, watch the Skies and the Earth Wobble and Quakes that's showing the signs of its entry into our orbit!
- 35. That new Atmosphere and Soil called "a new Heaven and Earth." In the Bible. The other Bibles: The Kolbrin, Ohaspe, Koran - Contradictions? Proving it…
- 36. Will YOU make it through what's coming? Safety? Where? Will you be satisfied with what you get when 2016, does it's thing? Rapture, 'Beam me up, Scotty' and things like that...
- 37. That "R" word: Reincarnation people fight against. Facts some religionists won't dare discuss without anger –usually... The ZOHAR paragraph…
- 38. The best way to sleep, think, speak, eat and live –and where.
- 39. The New Small Villages – Shangri-La 'The Big Experiment' and hope from here on - Contact Roy.
- 40. BE everything good and up-building! The Answer. Stop putting names on everything. and everyone. Gossip, ESP, The threads of Aku. TRUTH BEAUTY AND GOODNESS
- 41. A time to live, not die – Why Immortality is scoffed at by sick, sick people – Beyond cloning and transplants.
- 42. "You're a very Bad Girl, go to my room." Rome and Hollywood, New York and Every town.
- 43. The only way out of all Forecasts... and Prophecies. Does it work?
- 44. Mother Shipton's Prophecies. Check them out NOW on the Net. Compare with General Washington's Vision at Valley Forge...

* Above subjects are available by regular postal mail. Inquire…

IN THE MEANTIME -GET TO THE MOUNTAINS – AND HURRY UP ABOUT IT!

Why? Well, Friend, if you don't see the fast disintegration of present civilization, economics, government and religious farces, then you had better get a 'Seeing Eye Dog'. The cities are, as have been said, "Death Traps", as blacks discontents riot, food shortages, radiation, dead foods and unrest occur worldwide. Can I make it more plain without frightening you? Maybe I should frighten you: "FEAR IS THE BEGINNING OF WISDOM." Get what I am saying – People don't like changes, notice how they procrastinate even *good* changes? And you need to be as open as possible in these trying times for half way decent survival – and comfort? Yeah, you get that, don't you?

If city life is changing and will get unbearably dangerous, think about an alternative wilderness place in the mountains – Think about ocean changes due to ice caps melting, tsunamis, quakes, hurricanes, volcanic eruptions – (Notice, have you, that Mt. St. Helens is again erupting, a new dome rising up, lava flowing, ash floating into your fresh air? Yellowstone threatning world covering ash and jarring? And what do mountain climes offer you? Well, little crime, fresh, pure air, pine tree scents that are antiseptic to your lungs and bloodstream. Wildflowers everywhere that you don't have to plant or water like your city gardens. Skies so blue, mountains so impressive that you find you are a different creature. Is that enough, or shall I mention the lack of Bad Spirits roaming the cities, trying to hold Angels at bay. Bad spirits? Yeah. Bad spirits, Earth bound spirits that get their kicks from sex perverts. druggies and drunks, acting out their former degenerated lives through you unsuspecting people who sing "Eat Drink and Be Merry, for tomorrow we die!"!" All true, but Yes, exotic information, strange words you're hearing here. And diametrically opposite from what media, religions and the society establishment want you to know about your *environment,* right? Yep.

When Discovery Channel and Public T-V tell you what I am typing to get across to save your physical Butt and when I have been shouting all this 50 years ago before such media was even thought of – Well; that

SHOULD get your awareness that Father-Source is working for you through people like you and me. Ok?

Angels, Good E.T.s, are His Helpers, Messengers. The controversial, ridiculed Zeta Talk Web page by Nancy Leider gave good stuff from Aliens that are Service to Others that are at least a thousand years in advance of Earth technology. Can you handle anything that DOESN'T appear on Star Wars screens? Does truth have to be as YOU see it in fictionalized entertainment? How many Suns are out there, Pilgrim? Suns like ours with planets like ours orbiting in Father's quaint way of keeping them spinning, developing in their various civilizations! That Zeta page contact is: Zeta Talk GLP. Type it into your Computer and beware of the cynics and disinformation that are blasting it. It's true stuff and certain factions don't want you to know what it tells about your future. There's a lot of geniuses, ridiculers; that are trying to make it look like lies and sci-fi hype, lots of other counterfeit web pages copying it to confuse your judgment. E.T.'s ARE contacting us –Angels if you prefer - messengers, aliens from our Source. Feathery wings? Nope –Silver ships, elliptical shaped, like those elliptical clouds you wonder about up there that hide from rocket toting jets in every country. Note their 'rims' sticking through every once in a while. How they can dissolve…high tech for sure. HIS.

When you relocate to the mountain wilderness places don't settle under lakes, reservoirs or DAMS –they will go in what's coming – nor close to rivers. Mom Earth is out of orbit, wobbling, quakes are being caused by this wobble! Use your head, don't go broke building a fortress, get your foodstuffs in freeze dried and vacuum packed cans. Lots of canned seed stock for gardens, sprouting later. Wet canned goods isn't too safe due to the can's linings of tin and lacquers. If they are vacuum packed, freeze dried better. Important you build with big Quakes, high Winds –Volcanic ash –Flash floods in mind, no heavy roofing or rafters to fall on you, no bricks or block walls. Poured Concrete is safe if you reinforce with plenty of heavy Rebar. Think it through and you will be guided - or contact me for some ideas that make sense and save bucks.

Land in Wyoming, Nevada out west is still practical, fairly inexpensive. But get busy, do what you can anything is better than moaning. This warning is legit from 'upstairs' – do some praying or asking about your next move. Ask before sleep and your Sub-Conscious will give you His answer in the early morning. That part of your mind is HIS tool (your Source, the Infinite) for keeping you on the ball. Use it!

Reading these words of a closely predicted future and – Surviving it is not easy to take. I know and feel for you as a Dad and Husband – not easy to think about loved ones suffering. Plan ahead so they won't! That love you say you have for them is THE priority. Remember - those crises you already see happening all over the planet, horrible disasters and cataclysms became real overnight for millions of dependents. Now your family is in the picture - DON'T LET THEM DOWN…Be strong. Be confident. In America we have been given a rare warning and blessing as we watched Japan and the West Indies tsunamis take out partial civilizations in minutes.

Plain talk now – If you call this Calamity Crying, Dooms Daying you're a goddamned fool that deserves to get whatever comes. Buck up…

WHAT YOUR THOUGHTS AND WORDS ARE DOING TO YOU - AND OTHERS

Here's an 'Open Sesame' for everything you want or need, so pay especial attention. It challenges most people - for they are doing, thinking, speaking just about the opposite of what they should every day and wondering why things goof up or why prayers don't get answered. You want action and help? Here it comes, Big Time:

Everything we are, have or see - started out with a THOUGHT, then magnified, multiplied with lots of thoughts. Creation, you, your present life, body, health, your job, talents, income – your future is nothing more than what you THINK. THOUGHTS! And what you SPEAK THEM TO BE. Your love life, mate, squabbles, divorces, debts – everything hinges and is made of YOUR thoughts. Don't blame 'God.' Or bad luck! He (Source), watches you make those thought decisions and action choices...especially the words you speak so casually at times.

For a very convincing experiment try this: Get quiet, centered, alone in your nice chair, comfortable, feet on the floor, do some deep, slow breathing through your nostrils, out fully with your mouth – blow it out, all of it! before the next breath. Then with your eyes closed, hands in your lap, no tight clothing etc, Say aloud, I AM WHOLE AND PERFECT IN EVERY WAY, PHYSICALLY, MENTALLY, SPIRITUALLY, NUTRITIONALLY, FINANCIALLY, THOUGHTS, WORDS AND DEEDS AND I WILL IT INTO CONSTANT REALITY FOR ME AND ALL MY LOVED ONES! Keep saying it over and over for a few minutes, Then say, I'm in, PERFECT HEALTH; a few times and feel these words sinking into every cell of your body. Smile inside of your Soul as you love those words. That's it. It works wonders.

During the next few days you will experience some good surprises. Work on being QUIET in public, at work, at home. Stop rattling. Feel the Peace working in you and others. When you talk be positive in words and references to others. Build them, don't tear them down. Like you, they need help.

This next paragraph has to be shocking to get your attention and you will know who it's for. If it isn't you, you can smile good naturedly and hand this to someone who needs their chain jerked hard. Ok?:

WHO THE BILLY HELL do you think you are??!! You bluster, you play the hurt little thing, the silent one, "Oh, nothings wrong", you say, when you are one sulking mess inside, You get mad over anything that doesn't suit you, You stomp out of the room when you should be solving the conversational impasse, You jump in the car and roar away from the house, skidding around the corner, You call up an old Girlfriend and have 'get even sex', or you play up to that Hunk at work the next day...etc., etc.!

I repeat: WHO THE HELL DO YOU THINK YOU ARE? I'll tell you – One spoiled BRAT!! A brat that hasn't even begun to know your self – That low, sulking, sniveling, hot - headed self that brings you down into purely carnivore animal REACTIONS. And those reactions are twofold: One is chemistry imbalances, nutrition lacks or excesses. You just haven't grown up emotionally and intellectually enough to see what a mess you are and why! Two is **REACTING** instead of getting calm and thinking of what the next WORDS will be that come out of that brats mouth. NEVER JUMP TO CONCLUSIONS ABOUT ANYTHING. Ask, "Am I understanding what you are saying?" or, Hey, that's interesting but seems like you had said something way different before..." or "Let's talk about this. I could be wrong..." Get the idea?

So get smart on your Blood Sugar situation or your Thyroid Balance. Do you use enough Kelp and Dulse to feed your starved Thyroid Gland? Be sure you are Ok there, not a basket case of imbalances, ruining your Thyroid, Pancreas and your associates... A sincere wellness pro can help a lot – See them.

Understand also, that if you don't exercise *progressively* you will always be out of whack and a sack of embarrassing flab. Stress happens, stress can go IF you exercise with lots of Deep Breathing for the Oxygen and Prana but ENJOY your workouts, keep consistent twice a week sessions or a bit each of 5 days. IMPORTANT: Short fast bursts of 5 reps and 5 sets (after getting warmed up) gets you BREATHLESS like those 100 yard dash boys –notice their bodies are VERY polished, muscled everywhere, not just legs and they have lean muscles, fully developed symmetry - not just bulk and NO FAT anywhere! Maybe you should be thinking 50 yard dashes and then walk 50 etc. for getting rid of belly fat –if gut exercises don't do it?

Do you know what SELF is! Your self, not every other persons self? Your basic self, (undeveloped Low self, uncontrolled self) is animal like, selfish, survivalist, "Service to Self", it's being called, instead of Service to Others. Is it corny to think of others in your dealings and conversations? Do you really want to be upset half of your life, killing off millions of otherwise healthy cells? Answer me, Dammit! Come on! Solution: At night before sleep say, "Hey there, Subconscious, I understand my role and your role. I need your help keeping calm, poised and wise in all of my dealings with people – especially with myself. Thanks for helping me know how to be calm and poised in all situations."

Keep at this for a few weeks and Watch!

Get the little book published back in 1882 by Levi Dowling: The Aquarian Gospel of Jesus Christ. Never mind what your take is on Jesus, whether you are an atheist, agnostic, serial killer, or a New Ager – This book will startle you with understanding and tools to change the Brat. Be advised – Read carefully, slowly, there's things there you could miss that could leave holes in your life...especially those first few intro pages! DON'T PREJUDGE ANYTHING. That's stupid...and you should know that.

The other Guy or Gal is important. His words, his needs, his problems. You, nor him are islands! You NEED each other. Hear him, hear her know their experiences. Shut the blazes up, and pay attention, Blabbermouth. "Open mouth cannot hear.", says a Chinese proverb. So true. Will you remember it? People are so wrapped up in their thing, their ego gluts, their "I wants" that they don't think of how they might help the other person by paying attention. "How can I help?" This should be your first concern in conversation. BUT don't offer unless the person is a Basket Case of befuddlement, sick, near death – or ARROGANT, full of Low self and needs a few shocks to come awake to who he is. Shocks can come from 'God' or from people

Ever think about what you might be missing or did miss when rattling on and on about YOU? That person over there has something to say you might need? Enough? Burn this in – it's your life and you usually screw it up. Don't!

MONOLITH

In that Bible story of the Garden of Eden, you and me are nailed with this one: – Because Adam and his Clone ate some 'fruit' (or did something they weren't supposed to. he he!) they and you were banished from a Paradise and now you are suffering for their rebellion! It's called Original Sin, it's very original all right; and will keep you feeling guilty even if you didn't have any say in the eating or 'doing'. Wow, huh? But that's how twisted some things got when scribes, quasi-prophets, prophetesses, translators and Constantine's scroll gatherers gather up OR EXPLAIN varied nation's religious precepts, records and MYTHS. Personal favorite things –not always 'Father's Truths' but put in ink to fool you or capture your Soul or Wallet. Sometimes they didn't realize their sin, mistake or foolishness...

Well, back then Adam put the blame on Eve, remember? And it didn't help one danged bit – both got kicked out of the Garden and had to start farming and working at WalMart –two jobs at least nowadays... Point is that you can't get away with BLAMING anyone or anything for what you are, how you react, or what happens to you! BLAME you! You have to answer for YOU! Yep, it's so simple for me to research this, to Fast and Pray for 50 years to be sitting here typing this - but DO YOU GET IT? When you know that Reincarnation figures in everything you did, or earned, the good or the bad or the *unknown* - then you can get the picture easily. It's called JUSTICE. JUSTICE! Notice that word the 'UNKNOWN'? Meaning no matter the lack of knowing of something – it can still hurt you. You walk out of the shower and step on a needle...didn't mean to, didn't put the needle there...see? Did you once place some pins in your brother's bed (in another life), just to get even for him eating all the Brownies? The Vatican and easily led Catholics and Christians hate the word Reincarnation and such dainty comparisons - because it places total 'Responsibility' on you to become LIKE their Jesus (Yahoshua). Ridicule against that word hasn't stopped its spread to 3 ½ Billion far eastern people you might call heathen... They checked it out and saw the Commonsense and Infinite Law of Justice in it.

And it is inescapable in analysis that it is FAIR from every angle. God - Source designed it fair so you couldn't complain. But you do, don't you? You covet the other guys good fortune, his wife that doesn't nag and you call God a monster for letting all those Afghans and Iraqi civilians get machine gunned and those babies whirled up in that tornado and for taking your Husband in that hellish accident... Yes, you blame God, no matter what you name Him or what religion you cater to. Listen...You're a baby that just hasn't dared grow up to certain infinite, primary things because you were scared away from "those awful heathen doctrines" that just happened to be DELETED from your Bibles, Talmuds or Korans so you wouldn't have to take any blame or responsibility. UGH!

Blame your KARMA, blame his Karma. It all has to happen due to fairness and what you Thought, Said, or Did (or didn't do that you should have done). You never can see what happens to another person that doesn't have to be what he or she deserves!!! Karma! Now think before reacting to what I just said: A guy thinks he can beat a train at the crossing. He doesn't. Who should you be blaming because he doesn't come home by five? Yourself because you and he had been fighting before he left the house? Naw!!! Blame him only, not the Train driver, not the old Railway Sign that wasn't readable or working – Him. And him doesn't mean God, Allah, Jesus, Yahweh or Lucifer! BUT GET THIS: God-Source did SET UP AND DESIGN the Law of Reincarnation, of Karma so no one could ever blame Him. He loves you, loves that guy that raced the Train, loved those exploded Babies, loved those bloodied Afghan civilians. He IS Love or you wouldn't have been created and have the opportunity of Life and Choice – YOUR CHANCE TO OVERCOME WHAT YOU MUST EVENTUALLY OVERCOME from a low, primitive, self way back when LIFETIMES ago! Yet strangely you are somewhat designed NOT to remember until YOU ARE READY TO… Surrendered... You have to change, repent, develop, grow up – Graduate, accept His ways, not yours alone…

* So please do your doubting, mixed up, used up, lied to, angry, whining little Self a huge favor – Get the book – REINCARNATION - THE PHOENIX FIRE MYSTERY. It will make you feel like an idiot for not recognizing the number played on you by the religionists that wanted to turn your guilt trips into sin forgiving money, tithing money for their mercenary pockets as they brainwashed you with: "Jesus, Yahweh, Mohammed, Adonai will take your sins and make you free. No problem..." Oh, it sounded so good, so easy, so simple. But so lazy and irresponsible. First you get mad and then you get smart...at these words then you finally hear the Truth. You were fooled! Deceived by scalawags "in sheep's clothing". Wolves fleecing you. So ask this Question: Who had YOU fooled sometime, somewhere, somehow? KARMA is an Infinite fact of every life and was removed from the Bible, scoffed at hated by Catholicism because it stops off their income. They get PAID for forgiving Sins! It's called Confessionals and Indulgences See... Sure, parts of the Bibles are pure Truth, parts also men removed, added to or played games with to gather power. Who? Jews during their captivity in Babylon, they wrote it in as if God told them that, "We Jews, are the Chosen People." Oh? Like Hitler's chosen Nazi Master Race of Aryans? Close and so...similar. Don't buy that one, folks! And, Hey! If you never knew what The Vatican's Jesuits did to history and still do to American and World governments you better find out fast who the real terrorists are! Read: THE SECRET TERRORISTS By Bill Hughes. Honestly I couldn't stop reading it for two days!! It's a Bombshell that has to go off in your life so you can SAVE IT! And HEY! Jews and Christians: Check out the ZOHAR section on Reincarnation. Be surprised.

Get the Books! I don't sell them. My fingers are getting tired typing. Educate yourself. Bless your hungering heart. You are about to be free. "You SHALL know the Truth and the Truth shall MAKE you free indeed!" That's one Truth they failed to keep out of your hands.

- NEWSLETTER AVAILABLE -

IF YOU HATE WHAT I HAVE TOLD YOU BUT END UP LOVING WHAT IT DOES FOR YOU - MAKE CONTACT - THERE'S LOTS MORE... Rwoodward28@gmail.com or: Roy, Box 36, Baker, NV 89311

P.S. I'd be doing you a big injustice if I didn't most heartedly recommend some other books you need to open your life to full happiness and capacity. There's some hard stuff you haven't learned in them, probably; but what a blessing they are: The Biggest Secret, Children Of The Matrix, 9/11 Alice In Wonderland, by one of the worlds best researchers and lecturers – David Icke. LIFE CHANGERS at least !!!

THIS SAMPLE NEWSLETTER IS FOR COMPANIES AND FAMILIES THAT ARE IN TROUBLE!

It has urgent information that has been withheld from you!

HAVE YOU BEEN THINKING AND SPEAKING WRONGLY? DEFEATING YOUR HOPES FOR A BETTER LIFE, A MORE PRODUCTIVE COMPANY AND HEALTHY, ATTRACTIVE BODY?

MY NEWSLETTER IS A MUST! LIFE CHANGING SCOOPS. PLEASE DO NOT UNDERESTIMATE ITS IMPORTANCE.

For long years positive thinking books and lectures have been around. You probably have read the many books, tried the contents for a few weeks, failed to see immediate results in more money in your wallet or any cure for your pains. Was something missing in what you read or heard at expensive Workshops? Most certainly you only got the tip of the Iceberg. Knowing the rest of the story can mean very unusual changes in your life. Your income or your health are at stake in these troubled times and this Newsletter is designed to help you help yourselves.

Yes, you read the books, tried to remember and practice what they directed in changing your life – and you, as most other people, failed and stayed in your 'average' bracket of income and health –maybe even lost fortunes or became dependent on others to care for you. Have you given up? Some few of you have not and are sure there is a key factor that you have missed in this Positive Thinking and Speaking science. Now THE ANSWER can be yours. HERE NOW FOR PEANUTS!

The Writer knows your plight:

- Sky high costs of living, taxes, food, child care and driving your car or truck,
- Jobs lost due to overseas bidding and fiascos,
- Mortgages unpaid and homelessness looming like a fearsome giant,
- Stocks and pensions lost due to government and industry crime.

And you ask, "What can one man or woman do in such enormous crises?" You wait for government to do something, a miracle of legislation –a pitifully small handout is given and still you live from paycheck to paycheck – miserably lacking your needs or your peace of mind. Yes, I know –I've been there and then I found the KEY. Does this key cost an arm and a leg? $5.00! Is that more than you can afford?

Then just send me an 8 ½" X 11" SASE and a Dollar Bill, I'll trust your honesty. After your first experience with real facts in this first issue, you will be able to afford the $5.00 monthly cost. I guarantee that! Other issues will startle you with facts kept from you that endanger your life and make you feel helpless as world events encircle you. Do something! So why spend more hundreds on advertising or on T-V hype that wants big money you don't have? They get richer off of your gullibility and desperation. Stop that! A five dollar bill can change your life and that of your loved ones or employees!!!

MONOLITH

HINT: I have two U.S. Patents and 30 other Inventions we can all be sharing in development or jobs. I'm not greedy. Let me help...

SEND YOUR NEEDS and M.O. TO:

Roy-David Woodward,

Box 36, Baker, Nevada 89311

*SHARE WHAT YOU HAVE WITH OTHERS IN NEED. COOPERATION WORKS WHEN MONEY DOESN'T... SEND A LARGE SASE FOR SHARP BARTERING DETAILS.

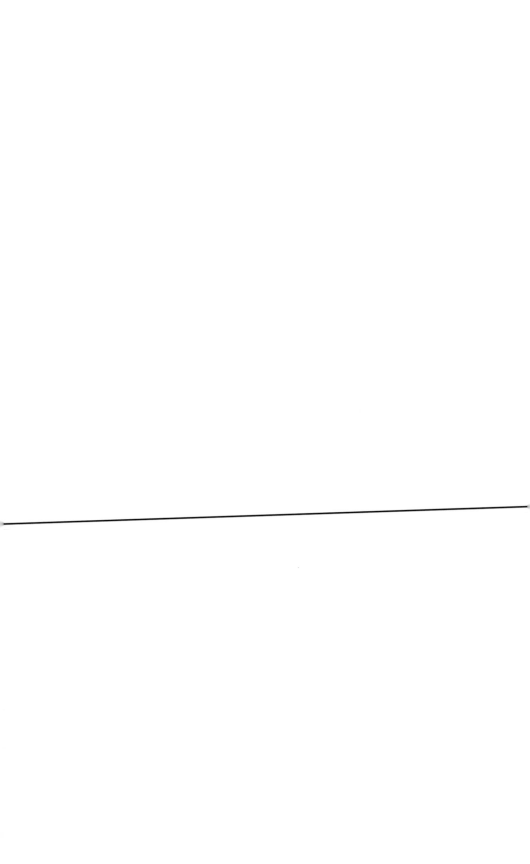

FITNESS, WEIGHTS, NUTRITION IN A NUTSHELL 'THE REAL SKINNY'

No matter how many notes or courses, programs or tapes a person has - it is not conducive to good discipline and method unless it is simple in explanation - short in telling. You, as an individual Soul, Brain and Body are more adaptive at Doing instead of Following others. You are always alert to new things - but it seems you usually have to find them yourself to appreciate or use them? That is due to your creative nature. You must Create what is best 'for you.'

Seeing this, as you do, there is a way that super simplifies everything for you:

Here it is:

1. No matter what it might be that you need to know in Life: Fitness, Workouts, how to do it, how many times to do it, when to do it, Whatever – this will work by depending on The Holy Spirit, your Source, that just loves to help people get disciplined and healthy. No matter how ELDERLY, WEAK, FAT or SLOTHFUL you are (or have been). There is ABSOLUTELY no excuse for not moving some part of your body each second, at least each hour! Some part, a toe, a foot, an arm while watching TV or on the toilet, before sleep, in the car – KEEP MOVING and fat and weakness goes fast. FACT! Move, rotate, lift, even a few inches, Fatty! Your ankles, wrists, neck – something at all times and WATCH the results! Movement DOES reduce!

Keep bothering a nest of Mice and they move out –Same thing with FAT! Take water out of a bucket, a Thimbleful a day and it shrinks. Take exercise calories out of your body and it shrinks. (But also tones up beautifully. Patience does it, Be Slim! Be Muscular!

2. Just STOP, get still and go within, then ASK for that particular 'need to know'. You are a Child of 'God', get connected, ask and receive!

3. Accept the first thing that comes into your Mind. That will usually be the correct one IF you dedicate this process to your Father in Heaven (Source) No notes needed – Spirit, Sub Conscious will inspire you, and at the right time.

4. For long term needs NOTES ARE GOOD, but for now - do the above.

5. As for reps, sets, exercises –that's easy: 5 of 5 with Barbells, never more than 50 to 75 pounds - or 5 to 20 pounds on Dumbbells. FAR LESS IS BEST WHEN BEGINNING. PLEASE! For women less accordingly –Enjoy, don't strain –TRAIN! Takes longer, but no injuries.

6. Two exercises (Bent legged Dead Lift and Barbell Bench Press) are the only ones you will progress to VERY HEAVY Weight. Reason for that? STRENGTH! You must have strength for life in everything! All other Exercises are to be super easy, fluid, rhythmic and fully ENJOYABLE –working off all STRESS of the day. Save your shoulder Rotor Cuffs. DO NOT TOUCH CHEST TILL WARMED UP WELL.

7. Twice a week do a full easy Workout for no more than 45 minutes changing to different exercises each workout, similar ones; but varied in style. And always do the 1 and 2 DB Swings for coordination, balance, shape and WIND - use them as warm-ups and get breathless with reps or a moderate weight. But do get a little out of breath for heart strength!!!

8. Every OTHER WEEK do those 2 heavy exercises (Dead Lift and Bench Press with the HEAD END of bench raised 4 inches.

Then pour it on after SLOW PARTIAL warm up movements! A MUST DO! Push for more and more STRENGTH. On those days also do your many exercises BEFORE the 2 Heavies! When you do Bench Presses come down VERY slowly and up faster. Gives better definition! After your heavy presses do one set of 30 reps with light weight. Enjoy this commonsense way of gaining huge strength.

9. First thing Mornings: Sitting on the Toilet (after you drink 2 large glasses of Lemon and pure filtered Water), resist your THIGH strength with hands on outside and then hands on inside of Knees. Smoothly, fairly fast (This is for Prostate and Bladder.) For women for Uterus and Ovaries tone and health. No Sex Organ herbs necessary for these organs if you keep the circulation up.

10. After your Bowel movement, stand and do the Abdominal Vacuum, in and out at least 20 deep pull in reps and then try pushing on one knee at a time, sucking in the side muscles in a rhythmic movement to tone organs and pull up hernia potentials! This Vacuum can only be done by letting all of the breath out 'before' you pull in stomach muscles. To do this Abdominal Vacuum keep your Hands on knees. You are bent over with knees bent slightly.

11. Alternate Toe Touches: VERY WIDE FEET STANCE Touch to left and right, stretching gently beyond each foot a bit more each workout. Good for Kidneys and Back. No jerking motion though – smoooooth...

12. Bent legged Dead Lifts and Thigh Bicep Curls are important to BALACE front and back of legs. Do lots of Jefferson Lifts changing hand positions from front to back, Hacks, Rope Squats, Trampoline leaps on alternate legs. This plus two legged stair step Toe Raises with a Weight Vest. Hold onto something for balance. This BUILDS CALF SIZE if you have no mercy. All the deep reps you can stand. BUT do a warm up set of 30 reps without any weight first!!! Go low, stretching calves, hold,

then up, hold and keep pushing for more and more reps to get size and the endurance you need to be invulnerable when on the job!!! It's the only way to overcome leg fatigue and cramps – and itsy bitsy calves. Every other week do the STIFF Legged Dead Lift! (Keeps the Thigh Biceps stretched out properly so a balance of pull exists on front and back of legs. No pelvic tilt occurs. Thigh Bicep partner resistance leg curls are excellent and a must. Smooth resistance please –no jerking.

13. Ask yourself what DIFFERENT exercises to do each time you workout, change often except for the TWO HEAVIES MENTIONED. Variety! Fun!

14. If you don't schedule your sleep, workouts, meals, attitude, projects you will end up at your own Funeral, looking at who all is there sending you off. That would be very unfunny for everyone, Right?

15. LASTLY THIS: No matter how hard it sounds, nothing or no one is as important as you make it or them IF it takes a toll on you over the years. Too Serious? Yes! Nothing is meant to be deadly, Nothing! So keep this as a Watchword from someone that loves you. AND for God's sakes - Stop talking so much, be more mysterious, Listen intently ALWAYS – Never give the impression that you alone and your 'things' are the most newsworthy and urgent. Nope – Pay attention, ask a lot of questions instead of offering –and watch people ask of your Wisdom. (And if they don't? Sorry for them, they're arrogant and un-teachable) MAKE IT SHORT! Don't bore. Let your Soul guide you from within. Talk takes a lot of energy out of the Human body. Never knew that, did you? Think ahead. Choose words CAREFULLY, saves problems.

16. FOOD? Almost left that out: If you don't switch SOON to raw foods and Distilled or more purified Water you will continue to downgrade. More Nut Milks, NO Peanut Butter, (use Almond Butter instead) more Almonds Pecans, Figs, Dates, Pineapple, Apples, Berries etc. Cooked foods are for those who want taste

sensations and WILL not to change to better lifestyle (like Apes?) Monkeys are very agile and healthy. Notice that? Guess it depends on what you want out of YOU doesn't it? Change? If not now – When?

17. Never go to sleep without YOGIC Breathing Time, stores up Oxygen for any digression in sleep breathing problems, gives double rest! Careful resistance neck exercises remove most dangers of Sleep Apnea. LOVE YOURSELF, MAKE NO EXCUSES, KEEP BUSY OVERCOMING WHAT YOU ABSOLUTELY KNOW YOU MUST!!! BE cheerful, be non-hypocritical. Believe you are in total great shape and happy as a Lark! Speak little but cheerfully, positively. Speaking to yourself often, "I am whole and perfect in every way!!" And you will be – Otherwise the world will whip you into a bag of whiny bones. You are smarter than that. Just Do IT! You'll be just fine.

(See my Background sheets if you doubt any of the above advice.

FOR THINKERS AND DOERS:

- Don't prejudge, keep reading, Wise One,
- Are you Yo-Yo-ing through life, getting kicks but no real happiness? Going along with brainwashed crowds of televised puppets, commercialized, being used to make others rich while you are lacking?
- Are those little Weekend Reprieves able to satisfy you –fishing, hunting, six paks, macho sports sitting, shopping, sex?
- Are any of the above fulfilling your hopes and goals? Getting anywhere?
- Do you yet realize you are 'fished for' by government, T-V, media & churches in an upside down society that's killing itself and you?
- Do you want something or someone that has eluded you for years?

- Is there something you are NOT doing that causes your disappointments?Do you yet realize that joining with, helping others is the Key to having your dream?

- Our Group of Doers needs your talent and input, you need us – the power of numbers is like magic compared to doing it alone...

- We, (The New American Pioneers Party), are an Action Group dedicated to ending Wars, World Suffering, Hunger and Hopelessness. You are not one person —with us you are ten million strong and growing weekly! By our amalgamated efforts we hook in to the higher laws of Divine Power and each member ends up having their success.

- What are we doing? Developing small. Cooperative Villages, Survival Centers, Cival Defense musts...for you and yours... To help this happen these -

- Our full color, 11 X 17, lifetime laminated, 'Positive Life Posters' are going Worldwide (sold and sponsored by large companies and clubs) to gain funds for your property and materials. We give the Posters away FREE also – Here's a sample,

SAMPLE: MAGIC LANTER POSTERS – AWAITING YOU IN FULL COLOR

(Necessary, get one.)
*Copyrighted- registered 2008

Your name goes below, Repeat all of the words out loud!

X_____,

Somewhere you forgot that thoughts come in choices and that those thoughts become words which can help you or others – or hurt horribly your future or present needs. Here is a new tool for living that works marvelously fast and accurately. Best to repeat these good words three times or more – and also say during your day over and over for quicker effect, "I CAN BE WHAT I WILL TO BE!" Then WILL what you need in close detail. It's that simple...

Ancient records state, "You shall decree a thing and it shall come to pass!" Decreeing is a giant step above prayer and imploring. From today on my thoughts and words are chosen VERY carefully. I realize my new power in choosing happiness, success, or failure. I choose a positive life full of my needs. Every facet of my Being is whole and perfect, Physically, Mentally, Spiritually, Nutritionally, and Financially. I am in marvelous strength and health, agile, flexible. I am as fit as a professional athlete! I exude love and kindness, compassion and joy. I am loved and appreciated. Life is a new Excitement for me, new friends, new opportunities, no limitations!!! I pay attention, listening carefully to others so I can be of assistance and also learn more. All good comes to my loved ones. Our protections are constant, our peace and health so wonderful among us and in us! Thank you, Heavenly Father-Creator and Provider. Bless you and our Mother Earth.

"THERE ARE TRUTHS THAT MUST NOT BE TOLD – AND LIES THAT MUST NOT BE REVEALED"

Oh, Really, Citizen? Shall we look at a few things you might want kept from you?

- You don't want to know your wife is sleeping with her boss?
- Your daughter is on Cocaine and Meth?
- Your 16 year old son is going to prostitutes?
- Your brother is cheating on his wife?
- Your baby's milk is full of pesticides?
- The IRS is an illegal function robbing you blind?
- The Catholics burned 1,000s of books God intended you to read?
- The car you just bought has a poorly re-built trans and engine?
- Your Congressman is a secret card carrying Communist?
- Your preacher is in it for the free ride and the nice rectory
- Earthquakes can be predicted to the very hour?
- Roosevelt could have warned Pearl Harbor?
- Your new Orthopedic mattress has bed bugs?
- Christianity was composed by demonic, mercenary men in black?

Let's stop right here for that should be shock enough – You may think such a fact "Should NEVER be exposed because people, good Catholics and Christians by the millions, would throw up their hands, give up being spiritually concerned, would become immoral, suicidal – Or: God should have revealed this before it led so many astray into insanity and divorce!" Really?

How far do you go if you are reputable and an authority on deciding such things - Lies, half-truths like Christmas, Easter, Halloween, Molestation in prominent or religiously famous families. Shop lifting by celebrities, masturbation, rape, illicit fantasies with chains and flagellation, defending teenage sex in your family, a child window peeking, cheating on tests?

To many in our present society the above list is inconsequential, just a part of facing and dealing with life ... Ho Hum Is it important to expose lies and tell hidden and covered up truths and scandals? Describe what YOU want kept from you on the basis of the few shockers listed above – Items that are to some just rudimentary happenings in a struggling, developing culture... How far do you go – What do you hide from yourself or others - allow or condone?

What if an enemy invasion, a hurricane, tsunami, earthquake was imminent – Should you be warned? A dam ready to burst above your city? Ho Hum?

IS IGNORANCE REALLY BLISS?

A few years ago famous research group, The Brookings Institute, did a project to evaluate how much the public should be told about secret or difficult information, 'Difficult' namely, due to potential disruptions of mind sets, religious beliefs, and historical-religio understandings from basic– high school and college promptings, based on non-evaluative average citizens. About UFOS – Good or Bad? What would be the effect on people in general... if they knew....

Their analysis was amazing, actually scary, for it decided 'we' weren't ready for the Truth. To the writer, me, that is like the ancient Catholic

Inquisition and the book burnings by them and later by Hitler. WHO decides for me? I do! And for you?

That is the point of this article: Are you responsible for yourself and how you might REACT to difficult news, new revealings, shocking factualities witheld for years or centuries – Who decides what you know. What you believe, what and who you worship? Is it anyone's business?

I believe you have OPTIONS, CHOICES in this thing called life experience and no one should keep anything from you because you might be 'fragile'. If adult, a parent, an official you have an office of authority over yourself, your family, your wards. Each must be responsible to their office, to themselves. Teach, promote the Truth no matter how difficult – Any person, nation or religion based on a FALSE premise has gone down! Check it...lies destroy themselves but in doing so they take many people into Hell or extreme anguish. Especially in religions. More Wars over religion than any other factor, more millions of lives lost over 'isms' – Prepare your self, your loved ones with coats of steel for what will come as THE SHOCKER soon – Not just beginning things on past December 21, 2012 - but far more involved for each of you – Not just a financial crash worldwide, not just huge physical earthquakes but physical and spiritual shocks we all NEED to be fully awake to our responsibilities - and Soul survival.

Most of us tried hard to believe in words – books, bibles - those printed, those spoken, those promising better lives, better health. But the dollar won against us.: Big business, Big Pharma, Fat Politicians with slim waistlines and big Egos. Who do we believe? No one unless we are wise enough to fast and pray, meditate believing our Infinite Source does care and will answer. This has become my Ultimate Truth to believe and to give out. People, (and you know who I mean) - have done their positive-negative jobs on us. The hurts have made us all smarter even as the wounds smarted, Right?

MONOLITH

So try to listen up, Fellow Learner, at an amazing story, prove it out as above described and get the benefits: Learning that Service To Others is an ultimate blessing on both sides, I finally got around to changing my life. As I did I got hooked in to 'Upstairs' my Source, the Infinite - not some blood and guts warring super alien god who had me and you (?)... transfixed from Sunday School teachers and later our Televangelists who used the super weapon, fear of God and Hell Fire and never ending punishments. As a Dad later on with nine kids, it wasn't hard to stop that kind of thinking/memorizing for I wouldn't do it, you wouldn't either - and we aren't even Infinite yet.

Some don't get it yet though. Maybe they like guilt trips, blaming others, needing some Animal to be sacrificed for them or some nice Guy who learned about overcoming a sideways society. And BTW, such a Guy just happened to be one of sixteen others down through time who really tried to be our example - not our Scape Goat. I'm talking Responsibility for our self - not cop outs – not atheists, not doing any old thing that feels good. Responsibility, excellence in living and doing those "Good works" that seem to scare Hell out of lots of Christians and others.... "Only God and Jesus are 'good' or can do good works!" Phooey on such misleading doctrines and obvious Brainwashing by the money nut pundits. Love figures out what to do, how to live, when and who to give to. That Love is yours from Infinite Father-Mother if you seek it wholeheartedly. Call it religion if you need a word...Pardon, but my fasting, praying, meditating freed me from churches, meeting hopping and workshops and all of T-V's desperate preachers who come up with a new tape or book every five minutes to occupy your mind and ears so you DON'T THINK. Don't miss this point – you ARE fished for by men that know the Truth but just don't give a damn... if you do!

Example? A close friend, a well meaning non-denominational minister, went to Rome, hoping to get a glimpse of some of the ancient Catholic archives in their three story twenty mile long basement (20 that is!). He got acquainted with a Cardinal, had some talks and in one of them the

Cardinal had a heart attack! He weakly asked my friend to help him to his Vatican apartment.

He did, the Cardinal got well and talks continued. Finally he told my friend he would take him into that basement that contained copies and originals of what the 'dear brethern' had burned or stolen from the Alexandrian and Memphis libraries in old Egypt. J........... was flabbergasted at what he saw and moreover what he learned. That was passed on to me, as was another friends experience in Roman deceit. A deceit that earlier composed what became molded Christianity from pagan Catholicism. Things you and I have believed, taught our kids, were baptized into, memorized and held tight to without dare questioning. You know WHAT I mean about questions...They can get you in trouble –or fired.

Should mention this one you still hang onto... Some of you would kill over it... The Sabbath Day.... Sunday is not it. Catholics placed that in your Bible because their hero Constantine was a Sun worshiper back in the 300s B.C. And Saturday isn't either like the Jews have been brainwashed with from their false Genesis records and misappropriated calendars. What IS? The same world hopping friend that got into that basement met with M. K. Gandhi of India - that great little liberator from the Brits rule over their opium fields. Mr. Gandhi made my friend J....wait a whole day before the interview. Why? It was his Sabbath. Oh? But next day he took him into his back yard. He showed him a huge rock with inscriptions on it. One chiseled entry for every authentic Sabbath Day from Abraham's (ABRAHM) time. He was 'A Brahm-Man' by faith and practice! Thus his name. Dates and testaments now kept secret by guess who worldwide? Yes, Friday, same as brother Moslems revere - because they recognize Abram of Chaldea as most religions do, as a true holy man and inceptor of true beginnings. And yet, poor believing Abe, didn't get his guidance always from the Infinite. That *false* god told him to sacrifice his beloved son Issac. That 'almost act' made 'A brah man' quite a hero to lots of us down through time. NOT.

MONOLITH

You might begin to dig through the fog about now; at what I am getting at. Downright LIES have ruined lots of lives, made Hells out of a possible Heaven on Earth, ruined marriages, created suicides, started wars, turned people insane when they began to get a whiff of the real Truth. Are you that fragile? I don't - I can't - believe you want to live a lie. Or do you? If you do stop here - To go on gets dangerous for wimps...

You sure? _____

Notice you and I usually hung to things that felt good, tasted good, made us gushy and warm all over at Holidays? Ever thought about that, where did it start? Babies from Virgins, Easter eggs, Halloween, Devils waiting to devour your Soul? Sound a little like someone wants you living in Fear, Guilt, Shame? Right on, Friend, Pilgrim. And it sure has worked for centuries, hasn't it and few have spoken up --- till now.

That isn't easy to do. Imagine.... You can attract Bullets, IRS, Swat Teams, Excommunication, loss of your loved ones, credit ruined - Gee, really? It happens, Been there had that. Call it 'No Wimps Land'

The point of all this - for you - is this: You live a hard life of endless laws, restrictions, false beliefs, robbery of your hard earned bucks and now, here we are, Americans with 20 Trillion saddled around our necks, politicians admitting a near disaster of untold size worldwide and these guys scurrying around like Ants in a Honey Jar hoping to keep getting rich over your Ignorance. Did my fasting, prayers, meditation and that of others seeking to bring me and you answers, solutions work? It did . IF you can handle it.

Money, gold, wealth, daily bread, bank interest, gas prices eating you alive like Piranhas while you are tied in their pond of lies and greed and you lack full, honest knowing what in Hell is happening...?

. National debt? Answer: Simple... Kill the Federal Reserve, jail it's traitors. No more interest rates,

. Everyone rich or poor, pays 10% total taxes which includes all taxes. No more sales tax or property taxes or drivers license taxes — all an illegal Gestapo force. But that's minimal as a solution for 17 Trillion in robbery by the Fed. Here's comes the cork on the bottle: HANG ON

Everything I am now going to list - you might first rear back at or call insane, impossible, too drastic....But, Friend American, What's more insane or drastic than us going down the drain? So think deeply now and Remember Rome and Greece and today in Europe. Same scene, different players. Do you like the movie?

. Every piece of our blessings of Mineral Wealth, from water, gravel, coal, gas, oil, gold, platinum, wind, diamonds, precious gems etc. was placed here by whom? Our Creator-the Infinite - not men, not Rockefeller or the men you give credit for our beginning wealthy nation. Right? We're talking something here you forgot about: MONOPOLIES. By a few who had know how, guts, start up capital and public trust. Where did it end up? A Monopoly in all of the above listed Mineral Wealth. Without thought you and I gave up our God Given Gifts to those men we respected and trusted. What happened? They got super rich. We, the owners, collectively - got screwed and paid through the nose and through laws passed for those Monopolists to keep their strangle hold on the "ignorant masses, the useless eaters", that those so-called "forged" Protocols describe.

. Action, Solution? Since we are at a point of no return, 'bridge out situation' and since we are the actual owners of this vast Mineral Wealth by common law precedent — Pass this Law: Each Company, Family, Corp. that has control of the above listing of Natural Resources is divested of all further ownership EXCEPTING that given by a new law which states: Those former owners, families and corp. heads place

90% of their stock in a public trust while their management receives a salary allocated on production capability and simplicity. PROFIT INCENTIVE has proven to always work.

. Some of you will shout: "That's sharing the wealth!" Nope, it's putting the natural resource wealth of a Nation back where it belongs. Equal - to all its citizens. Is it communism, socialism? Of course not, Shallow Thinkers, sharpen up your pencils and your insights -Again you have had Newspeak and Politically Correct jargon placed on your mind to make sure YOU do not rock the boats of the elite skunks that wrote those Protocols making it appear as if the Jews wrote them, planned it all – NOT SO, but they plastered that lie on the backs of the Jewish population instead of the Rothschild etc. dynasty called ZIONISM out of their Tel Aviv headquarters that does have typical and orthodox Jews very carefully fooled. Still we Americans drench them with our money and weaponry!!!

. Wake up Jews, Mexicans and Blacks – you are being used, pitted against us and each other. You Mexican nobles - you are swallowing the same bait by causing your flock to become antagonistic to commonsense border laws and to rebel at Gringo's 'easy life'. Arrogance is easy to spot in some Mexicans who really do want a very wrong 'share the wealth' program. Freebies.

. Now what happens when the Mineral Resource Wealth is put back in the citizens hands and semi-management? Fifty percent of the trust money goes to infrastructure needs, military's sensible requirements and development of land, wells and allocation of small farm plots for families that want them – or training programs for occupations they can perform. NO FREE HANDOUTS. WORK for what you get will be the hard rule. Talents rewarded by community awareness, more land if you are proficient, productive. Stops if you wallow in laziness and poor production. Fair? No free rides, Pancho Via, Black, Oriental or whatever color you are. Be an American 100% responsible. And - Speak American, in your new home...

. Did you miss where the other 50% goes? A Public Fund allocated, given equally to each individual whether rich or poor – It belongs to all. But 10% of each persons amount goes into an interest drawing pot – A better, safer form of Social Security which is managed by their local community, chosen officers who job out that 10% by investing in overseas products or companies. Our nation will no longer *bill* our people for interest on dollars or tariffs! Others might copy when they see our progress and better way of life – No more stress, mortgages, fines...We help each other ***pioneer* style** – We build, farm and plan for a sound future. Sure, there's a lot more to what I got from 'Upstairs' as sound advice for a crippled nation and our wondering families.

If you've handled this much you're ready for some more, all of the delightful details that really only Heaven could have sent to this common man who cares for something besides money, acceptance and praise. Thanks to all of you who have already contacted me. Spread the word. Share what has to happen if we are to make it. Copy your Newsletter, Share it. Watch my: DAVID'S SLING '2016 and you' on MANTA.com and my Face Book comments that make more helpful sense than the usual teenage mentality word games.

BOOK 4

IMMORTALITY THE 'I" WORD

- Abandoning Disease and Death
- The Convincements
- Science and Religion
- It can be yours –This is the generation

FOREWORD

If humans, for centuries, have believed in Death, how do you convince them of Life? Life without death or disease? If the convincement is difficult how much more so the discipline and habits resulting in Immortality? When almost all major and minor religions 'seem' to offer only a few short years on Mother Earth, still a few, rare men and women breech that chasm, although partially. Looking deeper into their scriptures and all the evidences of God and His Gods wanting mortals to exceed the present year limitations, those few persons have amazed science and clergy but especially, the laymen, Joe and Joan Average.

If lives of 500 or thousands of years are possible, why does not 'God' fix whatever is wrong or misunderstood? Perhaps this book is a beginning for that Millennium miracle, that "quickening", that "change in the twinkling of an eye", that you and millions have waited for. But you ask rightly, Are disciplines and habits sufficient to perform to gain Immortality? No, just the beginning of the triple-faceted human - but an important start, for once the disciplines, habits, quiet times going within are accomplished, then Father Almighty(our Source) does His part. Without that it is all just ritual and hope. Faith in His operation is certainly justified but works on your part are essential. Beyond works is the Absolute Knowledge which will be revealed in this book. Knowledge which can only come from many hours of loving silence and waiting on Him and His Angels ('good' UFOS). What happens then is an intricate series of 'good trips' into His many realms of learning, seeing, standing in awe of what you never imagined existed in nonexistence -Those places and realms only a few have witnessed and survived with Immortality.

When the Genesis record made statements... of the Gods: "Let us go down...", and "Lest they become like us...", They showed us 'something' besides there being more than one God present in Eden or above it. That 'something' also did a good convincement for the Writer, that they knew things they didn't want mortals to know. If Gods are Immortal and Humans are not, Why? Are we supposed to reach for it, pray for it, find it aside from them? Check the Creation story and see what you find in intrigue as to the God's being worried that we would become like them. Just what was that Tree of Knowledge of Good and Evil? And The Tree Of Life? Other books besides Bibles, ancient far more so - give more than hints, and it is among all such records ancient and modern I turned. The answers may astound you, even if you are ready. What proofs do we have, then, that we may be Blindfolded Gods ourselves, made so by millennia of ignorant or intended brainwashing - by "jealous gods", as scriptures state they are.Jealous of WHAT? Who were the Gods of Eden or E.din, as Babylonian records describe? And are they today lifting the veil?

SOME SAY IMMORTALITY IS:

The least discussed, least researched and most caustically expunged word in the annals of history.

Getting the ability to live infinitely without first being 'saved' and then going to Heaven - is absolutely absurd commercial book-selling. Poppycock!

Are they talking cloning, transplants, teasing us who hate death? So go the comments...the match is lit...The wood awaits

First though - How did Roy become interested in this subject? Consider his life:

MONOLITH

Age 16 and 17 National and World Record Holder, in Endurance and Strength Contests, Mr. Utah 1951, Mr. Rocky Mountain States, Strongest Athlete In Rocky Mountains, Air Corp and San Diego Marine Raider Obstacle Course 20 Year Record.

Self-Taught (Autodidact) in History, Religions of the World, Psychology, Hypnotism, Bio-Nutritionist, President of National Health Federation in Colorado, Researcher of Ancient Civilizations, Metaphysics, Owner of 15 Health Studios, Manager Hollywood Men and Women's Gym of the Stars, Developed Ed Parker's career into a world acclaimed chain of Kenpo Karate studios, Freelance Script Writer for De Mille, Universal, Hecht-Lancaster Movie Studios, Playhouse 90 T-V

Recovered fully from Broken Back, Cancer, Arthritis. Present age- in 2014, 86, Nine sons, two daughters. Now actively publishing numerous books and self-help booklets, compilations of international prophecies and exposes of governments and religions.

Top Contender for Mr. USA and Mr. America before back broken. Fasted 44 days on distilled water only - for "enlightenment and healing", fasted 8 1/2 days with no food or water to dispel medical fears and attitudes about fasting process. Such regimens developed various healing gifts, prophetical and teaching abilities which Roy is now sharing through his books and personal appearances.

Present health and physical condition better than at age 40. Recent photo gives evidence of the benefits of seeking Immortality.

"And Moses was 120 years of age, his cheek was not wrinkled, his eye was not dim, his step faltered not - and his natural force was not abated..." That was only one of the beginnings for present-day mankind which Roy now holds out to readers of his many researches and books.

He says: "We are just beginning to come of age when we forget calendars and begin to know ourselves and Father's way of Life."

"When a man knows he is dying and medical help, alternative help seem to be hopeless –Then that man either dies slowly, painfully or he embarks on ages old Fasting and Prayer… Honest, fearless, investigative, educated men know that the cure rate of Chemo and Radiation is below 10%! Alternative technology is over 80% and growing."

This is what the Writer went through in decision making when he had Cancer. It wasn't hard to choose - Forty Four days and nights of water only fasting (44), no food, no juices just a desperate, no nonsense last ditch effort to hold onto Life. And it worked. Bible: "This type comes not out except by much prayer and fasting" – Master Yahoshua (or Apollonius?) Me thinks so…

During such healing fasts you do a lot of spiritual asking of course, Yes, you get hooked into 'upstairs' in a very definite way, a profound experience. I asked about Immortality - never dying or at least "Living to The Age of a Tree", which the Bible also validates as possible. Such a tree lives in Nevada, my home – the Bristle Cone Pine in Baker, on Mt. Wheeler – SEVEN THOUSAND YEARS YOUNG!

Quasi-science doesn't yet agree despite strong evidences – they are but babes in the nutritional field as well as the mental field which has to make adjustments for the nutritional and fasting efforts to work. Many writers have sought to avoid this Immortality subject because it is so controversial, even ridiculed by devout, over zealous religionists. Others, with deeper, open minds examine and experiment. This book: Immortality, The 'I' Word, might have implications that interest you. A never ending (or at least a very much longer lifespan than you have heretofore thought possible.) Imagine such – without long years of decrepitude, pain and embarrassment. Joyful youth and resilience while the un-adventurous have found their graves ages before you. Proofs do exist that this is not a hopeless quest. This book has a few of those proofs. Enjoy...

In the last 4,000 years man has been living longer life spans in approximate 10 year jumps. Recently those jumps have been adding nearly 10 years of longer, healthier life. If, comparable to electronic and computer technology increasing at its phenomenal rate, the Human Life Span will reach at least 1,500 to 3,000 years by 2020 and from then, in increments of 10 years achieve Mach 10 developments... The average life span in the days of early man was, at most 32 years of pure pain, malnutrition and frustration.

"Spiritual insights with scientific open mindedness will astonish 'old worlders' were they to see out of their graves. Life without dying is a certain reality."

M.I.T. - off the cuff interview - circa 2000

If there is anything more lugubrious, more painful, more unnatural for Children of an Infinite, never ending God – than Death, tell me.

It hurts, it's short in opportunity for growth and improvement, it takes away those we adore and need.

It is saying, (like the Gods in Genesis), "Do not allow them to eat of that tree for then they will become as us and never die."

If 'God', Creator does not die, should His spin-offs die? ("You are co-creators with Me.") He created Life, can we extend it, make physical death non- existent in a soon future? Will we also have a choice of dying when we choose?

Master Yahoshua said, "No Man takes my life from me, I lay it down of my own doing." Is it within our mental will to live and not die? Does Choice and Mind contain Immortality?

I believe it with all of my heart.

"I shall not die but live and declare the works of my Father God."

King David - scion of ancient Israel

His grave has never been found

"The last enemies that shall be destroyed are Disease and Death"

"I would that none Perish."

"Why think you to die?"

"Above all I would that you be in good health and to prosper."

"For as the Father raises up the dead and quickens them; even so the Son quickens WHOM He will."

ARE THE ABOVE BIBLE HINTS OR SPIRITUAL - SCIENTIFIC FACTS

SO... IMMORTALITY

Have very many found this life without death? Of course not because such necessary action, is "hard, brutally trying, tiring." What a shame we self-described 'spiritual types' could drop into such attitudes while searching the profound and the glorious possibilities of – 'out there' - outside the box of conventionality ala' societal chatter and second hand, indirect religious revelation. Did you get it direct from The Source or just memorize or read what you have believed about death?

MONOLITH

I have for years... thought there must be a record, a book, scroll somewhere that gave the Truths we look for. There is, there was and a lot of those Truths were either burned by men that didn't want them exposed (or allowed by our Source – Father). 'He' didn't burn such things but perhaps watched what happened at times in our past because we were not open, not ready, rebellious? That thought shocked me. Probably you too. For a good thing to vanish that we, today need - Isn't that a crime? Like the giant 75' tall Buddha image that got taken down by scoundrels overseas a few years back? Horrible? Seemed so, but what might have been behind that? See my point? Maybe Father-Great Providence was saying something only later generations would understand or accept. Dependency is an enormous word and symbol. Maybe you see beyond symbols....Some can, some cannot.

Thus this: Death can be a symbol for good, bad, positive or negative. How? You believe it has always been 'Gods' prerogative, His way of doing things? You argue wisely, "Doesn't everything living die off eventually?" You ask – "Even planets, trees, grass, insects – the best of humans?"

No, a few do not, did not and some few today will begin to refuse. That's the Why of this Book.

"Find a need that everyone has and fill it." And perhaps in return they will help fill your need? Another form of The Golden Rule... These concepts turned the Writer into a Researcher of what the world today needs above all else. What? A need to share, cooperate, trade, barter and pioneer as we once did to make an American Dream. With things as they are, nearly hopeless in the political, monetary fleshpots, should you wait until you are frightened into some kind of action? Christ, through the man Jesus (Yahoshua Ben Yosef or Apollonius) said, "As you Sow, so you will Reap." That doesn't seem to have sunk in to humanity –especially the leaders. Joe Sixpak turned it into, "What goes round, comes round." Same thing though over simplified for Bar Room and Truck Driver awareness.

Death, Immortality, Disease, Decrepit old age looks – Are they what we have planted in a way we have not suspected? The Adam and Eve parable/truth tells us a lot – When we do right, live right we don't die. A child can understand that premise. If we don't do right and live right we die by a certain set of Godly edicts. Can we return to what they wanted us to do and be originally - Deathless? Is it too late or just the right time for it to happen as we have become wiser and listen better – because we are getting scared or we are beginning to doubt a few things drilled into us...Brainwashed, Bible, Torah and Koran washed... The Writer isn't backward about challenging things called holy, immutable or set in concrete. Are you? Questioning the God's of all religions is paramount because MEN have edited those records from those early or false Gods! Corrupt translations being one of the problems...Men often omitted vital parts of historical books. Each year we are seeing new things showing up...This does not mean that I do not honor your religion. The fact is I want you to have all of it's truths as your God gave it. Not as translators or power seekers changed it –added or subtracted.

Here we are Bible, Talmud, Cabbala and Koran patrons, members of different races believing we exist as "images of the Gods that made us." Believing also that Adam and Eve's sins have kept a blanket over our potential (a God potential technically capable of doing or being ANYTHING we could image, imagine, visualize, decide to do or be - Limitless. When THEY made us, set us down on Earth as Genesis records believe it or not - they didn't want us to live Immortally and they came right out and said so. "Do not let them eat of the fruit of THAT tree or they will become as 'Us' and never die!" Pretty plain talk from our Gods, Huh? What tree, what fruit?...Or was that a parable we were meant to figure out if we did decide to live and be as them –in their image?

Plainly now: Do the Gods die? If they did what would happen to the big windup machine they put into place – Our Omniverse? "When the Cats away the Mice will play "..."When the Boss isn't around everything goes to pieces." Satisfactory parallels? Close.

MONOLITH

We may easily convince ourselves that Gods don't die. Then - WHY DO WE?

Well, Friend, We read in the Bibles that Enoch didn't die a usual death, he was "lifted up", Elijah didn't die, John The Revelator didn't die. (claimed by many to still be alive on Earth today...) Special favors for a few – or something else like knowing how not to die. Those Bristle Cone Pine trees do live indefinitely over 7,000 years. According to what you read at the beginning pages of the Bible, God or Gods don't want us to die –some of them at least? The Genesis Gods were very definitely wanting our demise in a later reading but since then our longevity has increased! Every ten years in a cycle of about 5 to 7 longer years of life. It has not ceased increasing since the middle ages.

Many things placed before us in our religious - educational media I do not accept, not even close. Like Adam and Eve sinning and we continue each of us, to pay for it or we go to Hell. If we don't get atoned for by a man's bloody Death.(Read murder) In other words we are taught that we are not RESPONSIBLE for our own doings...Am I refusing superstition, myths, habitual nuances, disease and death? Of course, so should you! Yet maybe you scream at me: "WHY in the world would anyone want to live past even 120 years?" Yes, who would indeed - with all of the Arthritis, Alzheimer's, Parkinsons and Cancer? Add the food poisons and irradiations placed by commercialists intent on making products last longer on the shelves.(More profit motive, less work.) Hmmnn... Life used to be "Three Score and Twenty Years" that man would live... Did the Gods make some mistake? Now we live longer but usually terribly wrinkled, diseased, crippled or forgetful. Pharmacy gives Anti-Hypocrites medicines which dull pain, kill good cells and make us believe we are "growing old gracefully" More hospitals per capita, more cripples, Cancer, heart trouble, more senility here in America than anywhere in the world! Money is made from illness and death- based mortuaries. Average cost for a funeral today...$7,000.00 and growing.

Those big hearses take a lot of Gas. See OPEC or Big Pharma for other forms of debt, death and disease.

A few human beings have attained Immortality like Tibetan lamas or Inner Earth residents but their records are questioned as are the God or Gods that made it so. A list would be impressive dating to this present era from Lemuria, Atyl, Mars and Egypt – even Greece...

Yesterday an Asteroid - no warning, suddenly came from behind the Sun missing Mars, our Moon and Earth by a precariously close margin. NASA was at a loss to explain. This Writer finds that small asteroid, large enough in mass and trajectory to wipe out, level a large Earth city- was just four nuclear megatons of force.

The much ridiculed, covered up Planet X - found by the U.S. Naval Observatory, The Vatican Observatory and Mt. Palomar is now headed our way, also hiding behind the Sun or its intense glare. X is at least - four times larger than Jupiter and it is already suspected of losing fragments as it heads our way. Was that (a fragment) which came so close to us recently? So HOW do you want to die? Do you relish Death, going to Heaven which you know virtually nothing about - first hand? Are you a Survivor Type wanting to defeat disease and death as long as possible... can you think beyond that...

Boldly -do humans die because they have not overcame our animal instincts to kill? There are good answers by many sources. I recommend the following:

THE WORD-THE UNIVERSAL SPIRIT
P.O. Box 3549
Woodbridge, CT 06525
Tel: 1 (800) 846-2691

Jesus-Yahoshua said, (new history says Apollonius said it) - "You shall know the Truth and the Truth will set you Free." He added, "And then you shall be free INDEED." We have free agency, choice. Ever think on that? The Hindus believe we have a set of numbered breaths and then we die. That snuffs free agency and choice, doesn't it? Try this one: A man has a dream, "Don't board Pan Am - it's going down." He does and he's dead. Another guy takes the dream serious he has and he stays over for Christmas for his boy's birthday and lives... What happened to those appointed Hindu breaths? Man lives or dies according to his belief system, nutrition and good or bad works... and according to what his teachers teach him. Things they are mostly guessing at, favorite doctrines or hopes.

Living long, even endlessly could be fun IF you were nice to be around, nice to look at, nice to yourself and lived to help others. If, though - you had to be pulled around on a string, have your chin wiped – not fun for them or you.

Why not dying - ever? Did you stop today and say to yourself, "I think I will die today, I've had enough of the world's foolishness. Today, Friend is like your total life as it ticks along. Would you want it to end abruptly right now, surprising all of your family, friends? You see when it is looked at like this you don't like it. Why, then would you want it to EVER end if you were fit, kind, attractive, useful and honest...

*CAUTION TO AUTHORITIES AND JUDGMENTAL TYPES

Where do we go from here, Father? What is your immense love wanting me to further divulge – to those few who seek the Immortality possible some of your Sons and Daughters have found and those who the future will bless?

Dear Reader, Can you imagine that HE, our Source, could speak through me, a modern man, in today's words, today's colloquialisms?

Try to, for it happened in ancient times and it wasn't doubted. In fact it became a well published book: Your Bible.. your Talmud, your Koran. Would you rather He didn't?

"Son, the work you have undertaken is a pleasing work, difficult to render to men of today for they have in so many ways, in so many ages been lulled into a great sleep called Death by their teachers, priests and seminarians who never went far enough in their sincerity and dedication to find "a pearl of great price". And what could be of more worth than for a man to know he had no end of Joy, Breath, and Opportunity or Ultimate Visions of My creations?"

"Your work, Son, has a certain irony in it's inception and in it's offering: For there will be those who use what My words and promises offer and the way you present it, as an Earthman – and still they will lapse in Death, scorned by many as they lie in state or are tossed in ashes. This should not be. Those who try Me and My ways but started too late, or understood but delicately, must not have ashes of scorn heaped upon them. Better to be late but trying to ascend from Death; than giving in to men who deem Me and you My protégé, to be liars and detractors from their funeral profits. Such sayings about men who try and fail have always been, down through history among Earthmen, among other Planetary and Universal inhabitants. It should be remembered, Children, that a few of your races will succumb to My hopes for you."

"An enlightened people come not from the many – but the few and this displeases Me mightily. All have been invited to partake but small amounts react. The masses indeed listen not, wait not on Me. Therefore when they forsake My gift of Choice, I am bound to honor that choice and they DIE, pass on, reincarnate, re-embody, metamorphose as you are prone to elaborate and debate among each other."

MONOLITH

"When My word on paper and on the currents of My Breath in man's ears arouses a curiosity for deeper searching - what occurs? If I say plainly in script or in personal revelation that, "All things are possible with God", such words go unheeded when the extenuating possibilities for man are presented. Immortality? Yes, surely, Sons and Daughters – if you seek it with your whole heart. If sought after you have devised in your understanding how to be "without spot, wrinkle or blemish." - for so I seek of you – doing all you know, the best you know, your personal All and then I complete The Work Of Works. Each cell of your being is MY cell, your Being am I and we twain are one Being but in differing unities. As you purge and fast and know, so the communication of your doings comes upward to Me. Cell of My Cells, bone of My bones, thoughts of My thoughts are all Mortals ascending by their utter devotion to My 'Crown Chakra,' they become more Me than themselves! Such actions, prolonged over the patient years never goes unanswered or un-rewarded by Me and My Hosts. Eventually if man has not deviated overmuch in his last several embodiments he finds that, "I" Word, to be reality. His mergence into higher realms, new vistas, frequencies - comes to flower: DEATH is no more and he or she may become my Avatars, Messengers, Prophets and Prophetesses wherever needed in My grand scope of awareness. You are already Gods and Goddesses, born of Me at birth, not dirtied beings, not sinners as you have been falsely taught, not encumbered with past guilt done by others, laden upon you over centuries."

"Why, Children, limit Me and My potentials for you? Why but peek into My powers and go away believing men who never knew Me, who now decay or blow their ashes on the Winds Of Time? You, each of you, are My special form in embryo. Progressing as have you from your infancy. Towards grandeurs unlimited, overwhelming at present, SO WHY WOULD I SLAY YOU?"

"Your teachers pulled you down to Graves I have not dug for you. Seeking Me you find that I am NOT DEAD or Death, but aliveness, dynamics and everlastingness. Shall these words I give to my Earthly Son, Roy persuade you? The recommendation I give to you is rather to also fast and pray as he and My ancients did for My convincement and visions. Clarification of your mortal selves blooms and understanding comes. Only My very and distinct Being in you, stimulating you - after your purifying efforts, can possibly cause your doubts to vanish on this subject. Have I said, "Ask and you shall receive..."? Did I detail anything that you might ask - to be limited or forbidden? What you ask, you receive. Ask accordingly with much Wisdom – for all things do COME to he who waits. A Sword that has two edges, to defend, to slay, dependant on your motive for that particular asking. Find these words in Bible scripture, and other records - such is true: "Be of Good Cheer, Little flock, for it is the Father's good will to give unto you the Kingdom."

"Do you really expect My 'Kingdom' to be dark with Death and Crying? Or filled with Life? Herein I rest my case for you to ponder. Roy shall further give his experiences and may we see your attainment of all you seek in righteousness for self and all men...Assuredly I tell you this last: My Kingdom is both spiritual, in you as knowings and doings of Light – and it is also physical, governmental, solid and it is forthcoming upon your planet Earth. Before that, you will undergo immense tests of your faith in Me, in yourself and loved ones. Dicker not with those who visit endless meetings, confabs and studies of a dark and mostly encumbered past for I am God of the Living, The Living God, Father of Lights and it is now time, long past – when you must be up and doing those physical duties for yourself and those I would not see taken away from you."

"DIG IN, Children, DIG IN! This shall speak to the wise as Thunder and Lightning in their hearts. DELAY NOT! Excuse not by being preoccupied with Worldly Things or Possessions that shall not 'save' from all that "comes upon the Earth." Your priorities are watched by your Angels who seek by My command, to work all things with you. PLEASE LET IT BE SO.

MONOLITH

Your Father- Primal Source"

You see evidence of Death in Nature, violence, bloodletting, among the animal kingdom... gore and a seeming lack of compassion. Is nature without conscience? Then we look at ourselves, Humans. What there? All civilizations have been at war killing each other over minor and major issues or justifications. Comparing animals and humans we see a lot of similarity with one big difference: Animals kill to survive, Some today dine on one another – But not in their former state. Were they once different? Some researchers have found that once long ago in a 'Golden Hyperborean Age', animals were docile, lived harmoniously among man. Then came a time of degradation among mankind when man once again became barbaric and became a flesh eater. Before that Golden Age in ice free Antarctica man had grown up gradually, so to speak, into a more intelligent species, more thoughtful, kinder to all around him as the Creator's communication worked on him. Man became spiritual.

We can assume that Death creates Death - for as man ate animals he died at ages around 32 years. As he progressed to higher food sources than animals his life expectancy kept increasing. Do we die because we have copied the Carnivores animal kingdom? Believing we must have flesh food because of species adaptation? Those researchers of ancient archives found this also: Man's searching out, chasing, trapping, slaying of animals caused a subconscious reaction in animals, a consuming fear and anger toward man which then turned on all of mankind. Animals became predators of us! Today we fear the very animals that once feared us! Shamefully we now only hunt the innocent animals who cannot defend themselves or their young...

We have become like those we hunted.

Many have rebuked the Writer with statements like: 'Man needs protein, B vitamins which meat contains', 'God made animals, fish and fowl for man to eat'. Chief argument used has been, 'Just bless it at the table and it's made pure.' Yet they are not pure enough to have such blessing! As to whether God originally ordered man to eat flesh in the Garden of Eden parable, the general public of flesh eaters will not like to 'go there' for the Eden diet was fruit, nuts and "seed bearing herbs". The herbs that 'did not have seeds in them' were for the animals – not man! Easily forgotten for the taste buds get very used to animal flesh which contains small or larger amounts of blood – even larger amounts for the voracious **rare** steak gourmet...Why? Is there remaining a lust for the hunt, the sight of blood from a 'good hunt' still lodged in present day man?

Slaughter house techniques: At least cruel! Sledge hammer blows to the heads of cattle, throats sliced open while young calves following mothers are known to be terrified with actual TEARS streaming down their faces as mothers drop before them, Dead, Lifeless...for man's table. Not too elevating as to spiritual, compassionate growth in Humanity. A daring visit to a Slaughter House would create many new ORCHARDS.

What has all this to do with Immortality you must be asking...Well – can Death produce anything but Death' the writer asks. We know that anger, violence and hate begets the same among us - UNTIL we grow into more compassionate, caring and understanding beings. Present man has an ever-increasing life span as he moves more into a fleshless dietary. Note: I use the word 'flesh' instead of meat. Originally meat meant all foods. Today we change it into meaning anything from a living creature. We too are 'living creatures' like the animals who have sentiments, sorrow, love and anxieties – Families. Is it sinking in what we have been doing to them and ourselves? A child holds its loving pet cat or puppy while eating a piece of steak – See the irony? Life...

Moving back into time using the Garden of Eden example as to Immortality we find the Serpent/Satan/Snake – which evidence certainly shows was the same as the being that was cast down to Earth for his rebellion against his Father, our Source –in that "War in Heaven". If the same being, then he would have known things akin to what Father knew. When Eve was tempted with the fruit of a tree she was told Not to eat or she and Adam would die –that 'talking reptile being' told them, "You shall not surely die!" Did Eve and Adam know what "Die" meant? Debatable of course, but for sure they knew God didn't want them to eat it! Those Gods (plural I remind you again) that had said "Let US make man in our image suddenly was changed to God (singular) later - which shows one of the first Bible contradictions among the translators. Nevertheless certain 'eatings' would give man and woman a knowledge of "good and evil'; meaning: Choice to do what you want to do or to be. - maybe even discernment or ultra powers?

Two SPECIFIC trees are mentioned: One, "The Tree of Life" - the other one, "The Tree of the Knowledge of Good and Evil." Adam and Eve could eat of all the other trees bearing fruit with seeds, that were in the Garden. Now notice/read carefully: the Gods say this astonishing statement, "But of the Tree of the Knowledge of Good and Evil, thou shalt NOT eat of it, for in the day that thou eatest thereof thou shalt surely DIE!" (King James version- old Elizabethan derivation.) Interesting that King James was an avowed Homosexual calling his lover by name in historical British records.) A castle was built for him. A famous one…

Now we jump ahead a number of verses and we hear - one of the Gods speaking to the other Gods thus: "Behold, the man has become as ONE OF US, to know Good and Evil; and now, lest he put forth his hand, and take also of The Tree of Life, and eat, AND LIVE FOREVER…" Therefore 'they' (the Gods). Exiled them, posted guards - from The Garden of Eden, to till the ground from whence he was taken." Here we have THE paradox. 'Don't you two eat of this tree, Hear? It will give you the knowledge of good and evil like we have!' And then we hear these Gods later talking and saying, "These two, this man and woman are now LIKE US – We know, now they also know Good and Evil - they have choices! So we have to get them out of here, Or they will take of THE TREE OF LIFE, AND EAT, AND LIVE FOREVER…LIKE US. Hear a WOW, anyone?

So worried that anyone would eat of that Tree of Life, were THEY, that they "set "Cherubims and a flaming sword which turned every way, to keep the way of the Tree of Life." Safe… Hmm…sounds like INSURRECTING BAD ALIENS to me. Not our loving Creator-Father-Source of the Omniverse. How about you? (Read UFOs and flashing Lasers)

So what is that Tree of Life? Easy, Friend Reader: IMMORTALITY! Those Gods already were 'eating' from 'it', wanted no one else to be like them, kicked Adam and Eve out, away from it, placed whole groups of ships around it with laser-like weapons. We ask this of your intelligence: When Adam and Eve were first placed in that walled - in Garden – Were they Immortal? Yes, because they were made "IN OUR IMAGE" they said - God and Goddess. Gods don't DIE. But the amount of that Tree of Life that is eaten is what defines how long you shall live. If it was a one time 'fruit', needing to be eaten only ONE TIME, then there would have been NO NEED of those Gods protecting it for continual eating and Immortality. Yes, indeed, WHAT WAS IT? Is it a parable, an actual tree, a mushroom - what? Many men, scholars, scientists, professors have tossed this around for centuries. 'What IS the Tree of Life?" Does our Father-Source and His similar Helpers die, grow old, decay, wrinkle, become enfeebled. Are they really some kind of Flesh and Spirit combo – not quite as we were taught – intangible vapor-like spirit, wraiths of nothingness, powerful frequencies…sitting on Thrones of Majesty while millions of Angels bow, kneel, and sing to Him-Them? Big differences exist here, Right? Contradictory? At least!

This is what led this Writer to invade (like the Sumerian Gilgemish) into the No Man's Land; the No God's Land for answers that were NOT contradictions –that did make commonsense out of dusty parables and top secrets among certain Gods which the writer is now sure were foreign, false, fallen Gods, Aliens to us - from that, "War in Heaven". Gods that **used and fooled Moses** and the nomad tribes he led through scientifically fallible 'miracles' - made **easy** by those Gods that had once been under the True and Perfect Source of all creation – learning His tech so to speak, stuff we sit in awe of - like Red (Reed Seas) opening up and swallowing chariots, pillars of clouds and fire leading those Israelites in circles for 40 long years, shoes and clothing "not wearing out"– All that - to get them forcefully obedient to a vengeful, sacrifical burning meat smelling, warring God called I AM- YHWH- YAHWEH.

You say, WOW, this Guy is taking big steps toward blasphemy here!" Am I? Or am I after Truth at any price for both of us...all of us? We know by many nation's spiritual records that a War in Heaven, (the Cosmos) did occur. We also know there is evil, wicked, entities on and around this Earth – even inside of it; at the South Pole (later - on this tidbit) and we know that Reptilian entities exist that are in Human form that can shift shapes, appearances...just like that serpent-reptile did that talked to Eve! These same beings practice human and animal sacrifices and sexual debaucheries, and Yes, Human Sacrifices. (See David Icke's book: The Biggest Secret about this international clan), an amalgamate in unjust laws and powers called Popes, Presidents, Priests, Lawyers, Kings and Queens, Congressmen and Senators. Notice how we as a human race have been saddled by Catholic-Christian doctrines, being condemned for Adam and Eve's sins of going against Gods who so un-lovingly keep us fearful of them and their prescribed everlasting Hell Fire and Damnation. Such things of course challenge your attitude toward Writers like me who question. Yet we are meant to; "Ask, Seek and Knock on the door of the Gods many so fondly, fearfully follow and emulate in our money conscious society and churches, following medical 'professionals' and warring military and political leaders who indirectly shed the blood of our young men in oil and mineral wars around the globe, around the clock while the dollar machine now goes beyond TWENTY trillion scandalous dollars, as war is heaped upon war! And some think we should not ask questions of our leaders, teachers, Bible, Koran, Kabbala and Talmud! We were made to question and to find answers. That is what Choice is. "The Knowledge of good and evil."

"A strange scripture by Jesus annoys the thinking man today: "You SHALL know the Truth and the truth shall set you FREE!" – Of what? Fear of questioning, fear of following, fear of Authorities, Swat Teams, IRS, Roadside checkpoints - myriad entities we are held back by - far beyond commonsense rule for Sovereign cooperation and fealty among neighbors and brothers. Friend, Reader, we were so sold on memorizing that we paid for not thinking along the way of repetition education! We have paid a hurtful price. We are near a precipice, near the total loss of our Republic, of our very love for one another – of our lives as 2016 looms eerily a few months ahead of today's warning headlines. These increasing Earthquakes, Tsunamis, Forest Fires, Floods, Worldwide Sinkholes and Crop Circles are not coincidences on the calendar of Infinity – they are our warnings from a Living Planet, Mother Earth who is now rebelling… Still - Life or Death; even Immortality can be yours if you change. All it takes is the first step. Action.

Have very many found this life without death? Of course not because such necessary Action, Is "Hard, brutally trying, tiring – boring, time consuming." What a shame we self-described 'spiritual types' could drop into such attitudes while searching the profound and the glorious possibilities of – 'out there' outside the box of conventionality ala' societal chatter and second hand, indirect religious revelation. Did you get it direct from The Source or just memorize....

I have for years thought there must be a record, a book, scroll somewhere that gave the Truths we look for. There is, there was and a lot of those Truths were either burned by men that didn't want exposed or even allowed by our Source, Father who didn't burn things but saw to it

MONOLITH

that it happened at times in our past so we didn't copy or get into a rut following what was...for that era. That shocked me. Probably you too. For a good thing to vanish that we, today need - Isn't that a crime? Like the giant 75' tall Buddha Image dynamited down by scoundrels overseas a few years back. Horrible? Seemed so but what might have been behind that? See my point? Maybe Father-Great Providence was saying something only later generations would understand or accept. Dependency is an enormous word and symbol. Maybe you see beyond symbols....Some can, some cannot.

Death can be a symbol for good, bad, positive or negative. How? You believe it has always been 'Gods' prerogative, His way of doing things. Doesn't everything living die off eventually, Suns, Planets. Trees, Grass, Insects – and the best of Humans? No, a few do not, did not and some few will begin to refuse. That's the Why of this Booklet.

Remember how you once hated something or someone -for years, might have been a food like Tomatoes or Hot Peppers. And you changed. And you learned something in the change. As hate can instill, so can belief, if it's preached long enough, hard enough. Look how long we've seen or attended funerals of loved ones and been told – 'No problem, you'll see them again'. And then we expect to die. EXPECT TO DIE! What does that do to our subconscious but imbed like a parasite or a tick in the skin of our Soul?

My contention is that Death was necessary for a time, eras, generations. Now we know better. Oh? Isn't that quite arrogant toward the Mighty God? I disagree because as mentioned previous -He-She-They do not die. Extraterrestrials from other worlds, dimensions report they live to 2,000 healthy years, longer if necessary or needed. Such E.T'S either lie or tell the truth. Their physical, mechanical technology backs them up as to their longevity. Are they Immortal? Probably some of their leaders, Gods or Goddesses are. Really? And do I believe in ETs? Of course. Even your Bibles believe it. An exceptional additional source book is

253

the 1882 book called OHASPE, banned, punned, warned against by the Mormon (LDS) Church, "The Devil's Book," they call it. Hmmn... Red Flag?

The Writer has spent years on and in this record. It is the opposite of evil, believe me. The real Truth about those E.T'S and/or Angel Ashars and their Star Ships is pregnant inside the covers of that inspired book. It dwarfs, Bibles, Talmuds, Korans, New Age - anything I have put to the test of fasting and asking of our Source. And I do not fast and ask casually. I've put my life at stake at times to separate truth from lies or distortion. Men, religions, churches, publishers lie for a dollar. Father does not. BUT HE DOES CHANGE HIS MIND. Wow? And He does live through you, every thought, word, feel, teardrop, hurt, loss, resentment, hate and BELIEF.

I offer a new dispensation and new beliefs from Him.

To learn by giving up the learned is no easy graduation. Imbedded favorite things of other men as well as your own resourceful Self have to go. Thus enter Fasting and Prayer, Meditation, Vegetarianism, The Holy Dance of the Sufis, Massage, Sweats, Self Examination as to what you are after or will give up or go after with all your Heart. Best book on Fasting is the one by Dr. Paul Bragg. Health Stores will order it. Inexpensive due to Doctor Bragg's dedicated life of helping others - Jack La Lanne was his protégé and many famous celebrities worldwide. That book? Titled "The Miracle of Fasting"

I didn't get anywhere till the above disciplines were inaugurated - my life depended on it. I was sick with Cancer, Broken Back, Arthritis. Now well and young beyond belief. By getting rid of the old Cells and everything you think you know, like, or have to have in taste, sensuality, music or friends. Then you get armloads of what you never knew existed - good stuff back in to fill the worldly vacuum. You'll see.

Note: Fasting is dangerous unless researched and then gone at super progressively. YES!

When the Student is ready the Teacher appears. This book, my experiences, the book OHASPE is an exceptional teacher for it tells you to go direct to your Source instead of men like me!. I am only a conduit with a little experience...and a better heart...

Back to work, here: My dedication, age, austerities, diet, attitude, willingness for anything shocking, and extreme discipline is a great part of IMMORTALITY for Father doesn't hand it out like Cocktails at a party just because you are dressed nice and brought a gift. Just being clean of parasites, colon filth and being super fit/beautiful or handsome doesn't cut it. I tried that. Not enough. Then I suffered the loss of Carole, THE Wife. That did it. I dug deep! And it came because before I just thought I was serious about life and the hereafter. My buckets of tears and guilt proved otherwise....

"Oh, what might have been." Remember this before it happens to you...

Destiny, Pre-Destination maybe so, for Father does make plans like we do for our kids. And maybe some of us 'get it' sooner than others and maybe that's because we have lived more lives or grid experiences in Quantum Physics and it finally sunk in what we were - part of Him-Her, part of something so big, so hard to fathom except we get real close to Them; that it begins to make sense. That's the big WHY of cleaning up your act or you go on disgruntled, mad, confused, stupid as you think others are .... The OLD has to go. And as you clean out and clean up you get Younger and there's a key to beginning IMMORTALITY. Just keep doing it adding Higher Light upon Higher Light till you walk in it and people stare and ask. And they will. They are hungry for something that disease and death didn't give them. It distracted them with pain and sorrow leaving a lot of them atheists, agnostics, skeptics or criminals.

Well my, Father, where do we go from here? As your Voice and Scribe that's about it for my instructions, from my experiences. I might be a Rambo body in a nice face but far right now- from IMMORTAL. Will you please conclude this for me and those who wonder heavily about this subject?

"Son, your sincerity may not be enough for your Readers. It is for Me, for I have set you 'a running' like that enduring Rabbit on television. From your infancy I have had My hand on you - really both hands, for you were at times requiring them in your whims, rebellion, sensualities and yes, your almost total rejection of the fact that I was there dwelling by you and IN you - that Presence you see only as a hint in scriptures. Let's get one thing straight for your readers, My children, YOU who want to know and BE: I do talk Street-Wise to my modern children just like I spoke differently - even in grunts and groans from Witch Doctors when that's all they or I had - or to my Elizabethan crowd or my many other ancients through statues, symbols and all those rituals. This request to top off the subject of IMMORTALITY for My Son, Roy is actually a deep honor, for he has honored me by trying his best, believe Me; to ease your ways, to heal and explain Death. Let Me do the rest "

"I invented death in a reverse way when I invented Choice. You choose and you get the result. Choose wrong and you get wrong. See? I wanted you all, from the beginning to live, Heartily - pardon the pun, for I was from the infinite beginnings in every Heart living with you though I know that might sound 'Un-Godlike.' What you do, I experience. I have to - to know you. And to get you up to par eventually I have provided teachers, prophets, Gods, Goddesses, Lords and Yes, Saviors. This go round I am aiming at a new Target: One which let's you and Me in you, concentrate on Me only. Me? Yes, I did all those 'other ways,' didn't I and they worked but feebily. We both see the mess and the disease and the death of innocents or 'victims' of their own complacency as to time, place, open mindedness. Not to mention letting Me come through strong in their Heart by just a little daily time with Me – or teaching such to their little ones early on. What a difference this would have made in Germany, the Sudan, the West Indies Tsunami and in Japan. Too busy surviving the rat race gets to all cultures no matter how poor or rich, Son. Does that help your dilemma when the apparent "innocent" die horribly, starve slowly or are butchered in Rwanda? All Men and Women have choice to kill or to grow life. If cultures don't teach their population, they suffer from climate, quakes or butchers. And in their deaths I have to accept them into my dimensions and frequencies and give them rehab and lots of love and true teachings."

"You, Readers must, a few of you by now - see that Immortality is possible even if it was or will be botched by quasi science labs and get screaming reviews down the road. That's happened on those other Worlds some of you don't believe exist (or did exist before they blew it and themselves.) I guess I should remind Myself and you children that your former top run Movie sequels 'OH God!' with My rascal Son, George Burns is more like I what I want you to think of me as - A Tearful, Joking, Serious Comedian and a powerful, good Friend and Dad. Will you try that? Please, for I have really been misunderstood, misquoted, lied about and made to look like a very vain potentate wanting reams of nice words in repetitious prayers and just plain ceremonial drivel! Forgive Me, Pope – I'm not like that."

"Back to the big "I": You get what you go after, Kids, no more, no less. You want or once in a while, need to keep the relationship going, need more lifetimes to figure it out or to make you and Me happier? You get it? You want or need someone small or great big to lean on to confess to, to save you from your Sins, You got it. Well, there's the twist – you had all that. Now it's Me, your Big Daddy 'upstairs' as Roy refers it. Here's why the change: A new era, dispensation where what didn't work, what was deformed, twisted out of 'heavenly context',

257

used for getting rich, getting stretch limos, bigger churches, forest retreats for tired congregations and those silk suits I kind of like on my nutty, natty, commercial Evangelists. Well, really now - didn't you see through that once in a while? And when the Fat Preachers went on the side of Washington, D.C. presidents - no matter, didn't that bruise your common sense discernment a little? Politics and Pulpits - Good business, lots of tithes I never got. Too many middlemen and negative publishers."

"Well, as your 'God', (I do have Gods and Goddesses) which you still want to call Me or swear by - I surely wish you to call Me Father once in a while. Oh, Yeah, about Roy, don't sweat it if he comes off pretty 'out of the box' himself once in a while. Like you, he is exploring things and does want My will despite how he has messed that up a few grand times in his life. He drooped his head and I hugged him as I have to do, to you too - far too often, but it does build My patience for a people who have had a real number done on their beliefs, dogmas, and daily lives for centuries. Stop them from that! Stand up tall. Ask for help when you can't cut it. We're here always."

"Bottom Line? IMMORTALITY? You'll get it when you're ready, when you see it is a must for you who are spin-offs of Me and your Mom, Om. We just can't do without you. That's why we invented People and why some of you, PLEASE, will become willing couples, Man and Wife - becoming Our "Love soon among restored, free nations of our unloved kids who can't get it through CARE packages and shallow wells. That helps, but real Wives and Husbands in Our eyes are those who are in a constant state of Wow! Over each other. Anything less, you're whistling in the dark. Got Love? Ask. Be happy, Children but not gullible for the Negative. Some of you are ripe, some not yet.

Be patient with each other and quit squabbling – it keeps Me awake.

So I sign my signet, **X**

MONOLITH

FATHER-SOURCE or whatever turns you on:

EGOQUIM, E-O-IH, AHURA MAZDA, ORMAZD, EOLIN, ALLAH – GEORGE BURNS – Whatever; but danged sure your Father!"

Continuing but READER NOTE:

I'm going to do here - a strange thing for a writer – I'm going to repeat some of another book you just read - an earlier part of this complete book Monolith for the impression it can and must make for your life – Repetition works wonders:

As said most of this story is true, happened to me and Carole, was typed four months before she passed to a different dimension, it is quite an experience to write and for you to read. Realize that life proves Truth is far Stranger than Fiction. What follows is about Love, what we, you and I thought it was and how it can dissipate or enlarge as we grow, that's what this is all about - what love can become, so big and powerful it can change our Heavens and Hells - even manipulate them as Jami Portchuka (My wife, Carole) did.

I'm sure most of you really think you know the depths of LOVE. I did. How I was mistaken is what you are about to read. First though what's the usual consensus about LOVE: Is it a good feeling being with, on, under someone, that's the sex part of it...Is it just better than being alone in a hard world? Or a sensual sensation you feel and can't quite equate with what deep spiritual love is supposed to be? A way to keep warm against your mate on cold winter nights, your feet on his back - Yeah, some think that's it, flowers, birthday cards coupled with fireplaces at the ski lodge, beer, wine - parties. How about social times eating at the best cafes, vacations you can or can't afford? Lying there as he reads to you each night, your man growing you...We all think we know.

At least a piece of it...

Society, school, hard knocks taught me what it could but I resisted more than most. I had to have my 'proofs', I doubted a lot of what was funneled into me. Saw that most couples weren't happy, adjusted - even capable of marriage, love, paying attention to each other. Not for very long anyway. Boredom, self, apathy -selfishly inclined – 'me first'. Spoiled we call it in kids. How about adults?

So we quite trying at love and never realize what we have done.

I bundle it all into: The art and gift of 'Paying Attention'.

Planet Earth, 2010: This also happened to Clint O'Connell and Jami Portchuka...the hard way.

With Carole, after the bruises, angers, resentments, failures and blame games I got the full load of utter happiness -then I lost her. Listen! Soul Mates? No Twin Flames, mates are part of an eternal flame from before Earth was formed. One love, two bodies to experience, one heart to fathom...Stop looking and searching. God will join you.

Before that happened to me I had investigated everything. As a Piscean that was my forte. My pain at no love in my life meant something was wrong with me -not the others, the 'failures. I dug deep into me, life, history, religions, eastern precepts, customs. My pain and lack was a signal. I listened in meditation, shut up my rambling self in fasting and prayer, almost died doing it but the light came on. I had been pushing the wrong switches.

I didn't go drugs or booze, saw that it was a brainwashing shotgun from the media hype. It's pellets missed because it was just too obvious. Mind control comes in different packages. This evasion led to organics, vegetarianism, alone-ism, building me with respect to what I was intended by my Maker to be. If you don't 'pay attention' to such means to your fulfilled end result -you missed it, bigtime...At age 86 here you might be wise to heed.

Catch is I'm about 40, haven't been aging negatively since the 1980s when I stood five feet away from a huge Lightning Bolt, soaked, unharmed - and next to a hundred foot tall Cottonwood in 'the storm of storms'. For seconds looked INTO that shaft of indescribable power. Yes, awesome experience what I saw inside it -changed my life literally and my body and concepts. Someone 'Upstairs' had something in mind for me...Part of this book might tell us both what it is. I fought it.

Now I'm sure. Let me know your take. It will help...

It all led up to this book MONOLITH and others that will follow. My story, because of Carole's love and in-depth understanding of a paradox called Roy might grab you as it has a few others who were somewhat intrigued. Even cynics lives will be changed. That I am sure...

CAN THIS TYPE MAN HELP YOU OR A LOVED ONE?

"The Doctor of the future will treat the whole person – physically, mentally and spiritually. He will not be limited to conventional understanding, science, past or present practices or the dictates of powerful lobbies. He will likewise perform with compassion for the poor." rdw

ROY'S BACKGROUND

- Born March 4, 1928
- Retired Member International Academy of Physical Therapists
- Director Goodrich Hollywood Stars Gym

- Hollywood freelance script writer for Playhouse 90, Cecil B. De Mille, Universal, Lancaster-Hecht
- Owned-operated 15 health clubs

AUTHOR:

- The Woodward Method of Face and Neck -Lifting Without Surgery
- Super Quake
- Commonsense 2000
- The Sheba Chronicles
- Fish Story
- Ancient Science of Breathing
- The Bosom Trauma
- My Presidential Platform
- The Wisdom Series
- Historical - Researcher of major religions
- Cured miraculously of Cancer, broken back, Arthritis after 44 day water only fast, numerous fasts, application of self - developed Physical Therapy methods.

Athletics – Titles

- Mr. Utah 1951
- Mr. Rocky Mountain States 1951
- Strongest Athlete Rocky Mountain States 1951
- National High School - College records: 44 Pull-ups, World's Record 5,666 Setups 275 non stop Push-ups, Olympic Rope Climb 5.2 seconds
- High School: Indoor Circular 133 Yard Dash 12.2 seconds
- Olympic Rope Climb 5.2 seconds
- Ran 20 mile Marathon age 17
- San Diego Naval Station Marine Raider 20 Year Obstacle Course Record 1945

- KSTC Air Corp Cadet Obstacle Course Record 1945
- Trained in the 70s with: Steve Reeves, (Mr. Universe, Hercules) Gordon Scott, (Movie Tarzan), George Eifferman, (Mr. America, Mr. Universe), Roy Hilligen, (Mr. South Africa), Jack Dellinger, (Mr. Universe)
- Apprenticed at Ed Yarick's Olympic Training Gym, Trained at Jack La Lanne's gym, Oakland
- Vegetarian – Bio-Nutritionist

Trained the following celebrities:

- Don Hart, All-American Football Star, Mike Sill, Best Developed Athlete In The World, Georgia Cleveland, Rose Parade Queen, Bobbie Mc Kean, Miss Salt Lake City, Marion Anderson, Miss Universe, Lois Christensen, Miss Teenager of America.

Other:

Physical Therapist and Hydro Therapist for LDS Pres. David O. MacKay with Jonathan Heaton, former head of LDS gym. Nutrition-Health consultant for severely ill LDS Pres. Ezra Taft Benson upon request of his son Reed Benson

Survival Consultant

Developer NESIC Military and Civilian I.D. System

Holder of 2 U.S. Patents and 32 Inventions, Think Tank CEO

Politics:

Chosen by The New American Pioneers Party. Controversial Write-In Candidate for President of The United States in the 80s - due to inspired platform and various ancient prophecies about a controversial "Roy" (Featured in Stewart Robb's book "Strange Prophecies" –an Ace Book, New York.) Now mysteriously out of print…

Presently active in:

Bodybuilding, Running, Kenpo Karate, Writing, Longevity Research, Breathing Science and Raw Food Dietary Practices, Quantum Physics experiments, Remote Viewing and Self Hypnosis.

Roy may be contacted at:

1 (801) 373-3040 or 1 (775) 234-7070
E Mail: Rwoodward28@gmail.com
Or: Box 36, Baker, Nevada 89311

* His Monthly Newsletter is available for a $5.00 M.O. and 8 ½ X 11 SASE or sent free of charge to low income persons for a $1.00 SASE. All letters answered if you enclose a SASE. Thank you.

(Newsletter-Poster proceeds assists Veterans, War Widows, Homeless and Needy Inventors)

DONATIONS WELCOMED

- Roy's Teachers And Trainers -

- Edward Owada - Japanese Master Martial Arts, Bio-Nutritionist
- Professor-Master Thind, Indian Mystic- World teacher of ancient records
- Ed Parker - Kenpo Karate Master
- Dr. Raymond Bernard - Writer-Researcher
- Professor Arnold Ehret - Fasting exponent

- Dr. Paul Bragg – Writer-Trainer - Jack La Lanne and Hollywood Stars
- Jan Pierce - Johnny Weismuller's (Tarzan) trainer
- Jack La Lanne - Super Athlete
- Ed Yarick – Olympic trainer, giant physically, giant of a coach
- Bert Goodrich - Hollywood Stars Gym owner, MGM stunt man
- Sant Thakar Singh - A true holy man, mystic, miracle worker
- Dr. N.W. Walker - Raw juice exponent, Lived to 120 on only juices
- Vitvan - Metaphysical teacher of natural sciences
- Dr. Albert Switzer - World famous healer, philanthropist, organist
- Jonathan Heaton – Mentor, LDS Gym director, masseur, therapist
- Dr. Maurice Lerrie Glendonwynn – Mentor, naturopath, chiropractor
- Claude Weight - A true priest, mentor, spiritual giant, gentleman
- Mother and Dad: Tressa Isabell Herriman and Asa Albert Woodward

*Our Mutual Source, Father-Mother and His Universal/Omniversal Helpers

and my millions of Ancestors who gave of themselves to form my Being. Thank you, bless you all.

TO PROVO, UTAH HERALD NEWS DESK AND OTHER EDITORS IN UTAH

Back in the 80's a Provo man was asked to be write-in President of the United States by a little known, forlornly poor; New American Pioneers Party. This patriotic group foresaw what was about to happen in our government and what you are presently seeing in reality. In various interviews that man was lauded, ridiculed, doubted as to his ability, praised for his inspired Presidential Platform which COULD have saved us from the mess we are now in. Unfortunately, ridicule won...

"How can a nobody become President?" Catch was, there was something that made that man a 'somebody' – He had been actually prophesied in several nations: Ireland, Scotland, England, and even by Nostradamus in France. And by: St. Bearcan, Fionn Macumhil Cecinit, Johannes, Alfred Lord Tennyson. Men who were 'on line' without knowing each other – over 500 years ago! This man was detailed to come forth in our modern era: "To set The House Of God in order". Little wonder the ridicule, Right? Nevertheless, his highly detailed and commonsense Presidential Platform details are astonishing solutions for our impasses now and later. Read them...

Famous Stewart Robb, Writer – Researcher did the book above, called "Strange Prophesies", due to his fascination over such predicted events – most of which have happened.

Now at age 86, this man, Roy-David Woodward, has remained true to his literal calling. He knows his future will see some surprising shocks in governments, religions and politics. One day, it is said, a massive Worldwide Catastrophe will cause his coming to power as America's President – not by vote, but by, "The uncommon acceptance of the people" - due to their need for honesty and compassion – and a Divine appointment.

At present "Roy", (as his name appears in the ancient prophecies) is doing what he can to prepare populaces for coming events far more dire than the present financial fiasco – giving hope, means and courage to those who might not ridicule... this time as they did in the 80s.

At 86, Roy appears as ageless, fit and alert as a 40 year old. In his youth he was Mr. Utah 1951, Mr. Rocky Mountain States, Strongest Athlete in the Rocky Mountain States, held numerous world and national records. His impressive Mentors and Teachers are enclosed under separate cover for your perusal. An Autodidact – self-taught, Roy has our complete trust and hope for America in a not distant future.

This is presented by a former NEW AMERICAN PIONEERS PARTY official, in preparation for Roy's entry into the coming non-party political scene.

Contact Roy at: 1 (801) 225-5107, 1 (801) 373-3040, 1 (775) 234-7070

Sincerely,

D.S. Secretary for John Leabo, deceased Washington editor and nuclear scientist – New American Pioneers Party Founder and Chairman.

BOOK 5

SUNLIGHT

By Roy-David Woodward copyright 2014

MONOLITH

You being unique, individually strange, different - means you are a species. Remember that 'different does not mean wrong or less than any other species -or person. Be glad that you are separate and individual, know yourself - the better, higher self which has parents of enormous power and love. You have called them Gods or Goddesses in past times, Creator, Father, Eloih, Yahweh, and the I Am which said to Moses: 'Tell them you have been spoken to, commanded, instructed by He who wills to be what He wills to be.' Our Creator loves and watches you and your choices.

You can do anything. Some things hurt you and others. Soon or late you learn that and you change from the pain, looking for better feelings. Usually your pains last too long because you do not get alone with your Creator or your Higher Self to learn better paths. It's easy. Alone, quiet, peace, no music blasting others thoughts into your ears. Peace, quiet, wanting, needing, ask Him, appreciate you and Him.

Love yourself; for that deep Self is part of Him that wants to come into the Sunlight. Trying to be better, nobler, cleaner is difficult so ask for His help. Joy in His ability to inform, inspire -to strengthen your resolve. It works because He works. Remember you are His Kid with a hood over past lifetime memories that might sadden or brighten your life. You have forgotten much. Be Still and know all that can help your life untangle, shine and overflow. You want that. Go ahead. Know that Religion, Places, Organizations are fine for a time - A fence, guards to spare you, help you while tender.

But now you have grown tougher you can run faster. Do not be brittle but glide over the path, leap the rocks strewn there, they are muscle builders aren't they? You have seen that have you not? Will to be what He wills to be...He said that to many. So too you and all men and women. Will with a map of life made by your pen and foresight. What you want and want to be are yours now, but it will take years to fully know that. Will is invisible stuff, things, places, needs and comforts too - Comfort is not bad or 'sinful'. When you seek things and comforts and security would it not be wise to seek it for others along the way?

Self of Divine Nature wishes that, urges that for you are part of Everyone and Him. Hurt or shun them and Him and your security goes, your stuff leaves and you are alone, old, sick, bored - Unloved, you remember what you should have done. Oft it is too late in this life. So try harder to find the stillness and Him.

Angels? Yes, He has Helpers, Star Ships who are eager to assist . You have though, to invite them being regular before them. Invisible but they are there always. Farther or nearer, instantaneous or lagging, all depends on you and your acceptance of their reality. Good Silver Saucers.

I could tell you much. Better is it to find Him and Them in that quiet time and know for yourself. For have not I and other men confused you with sayings, edicts, no, no's and threats. You are you, Individual but the you and the me, all of us, have the same needs, are made of the same mindal furniture. We breathe, sigh or laugh as we walk through the forests of life. We need guides till we learn the paths. The horizon is far. Each step chosen carefully gets us there. Today's stance reaches the next step steady or faltering, so stand tall, chest out. Be toned, ready...

Breathe in His life that courses through your veins. A cell, you are internal in Him. And also a Universe. Your feet and legs are the past you have walked. Your arms your future waiting to reach out and grasp tomorrow. Your eyes are above all past and future. Envision, will, dynamic your goals. Your life work must be what you know and do well and joy in. Other than this and you fade, withering like a flower hidden from rain and sunlight.

He will tell you, remind you of what you should be doing for daily bread, security, comfort. Ask. Receive. It is so simple and sure from Him. He loves you, Mortal Friend, loves you. What might have been - can be better when He is on your team. Join. Mistakes in the past by you, or done to you, can be understood when you forgive them, appreciate what lesson was taught. Unlearned, unappreciated, rejected, resented it was all in vain, purposeless wasn't it?

Better growing than hating? Better knowing you will yourself to understand and therein run faster to the mark? Always. Yes, you may judge. But do so kindly for you may not see all for the bushes of life hide much. Facts gathered are not always witnesses of perfect value. Someone else's shoes might teach you much. Or the roadway they trode? A saying goes like this: "All are only the product of Environment, Parents or Teachers good or evil - and the foods we partake."

Easier then to be tolerant of braggarts, selfish and unkind ones? Yes. They one day will blossom. Just a bud now, you might water them. Life will surely prune them. Seasons change all things. No mountain. no valley, Right? Rest, fatigue, rest, fatigue, over and over develops the flab into tone by numbers and systemics. Pain is not necessary unless you need spanking within your mind and heart. Joy in movement and your body shell, your Temple - will exalt and share the best with you. Life is health and health is all the wealthy wish for once lost. Be fit and a holy place of example for all to see and aspire to.

Know you this: That holding aside 10% of your income, giving another 10% also to your spiritual mentors, or some lifting source - will give unto you such as you desire in time? That which you 'desire' you must use in this way. A rule, a perfect tool for prosperity. And help for others, who like you once sought the way, the truth and the life? You save your base which you spend not, gathering from it the interest or accomplishment or possession of which profit may come. Ask Him of this, for He will guide you in proper choices for your much sought security - your future.

A person? You need a person? A mate, lover, wife or husband? You look, you wait, you find not? BECAUSE you look and seek him or her you do not find. Seek yourself first, seek Him and His wisdom and love to be lavished into your every cell, word and action. No way may that person not find you, for you are their magnet calling, beaming out though the Earth be as broad as eternities vastness. Do what you know is true, love yourself so deeply - care for you diligently. Be clean, reflective, visionary, inventive, innovative of new ways to help mankind. But love them, not the idea. Them...

Capacity? What you can presently hold or what you should contain eventually. Your potential before Him is unfathomable. You have to see your present condition or load of knowledge then decide if it is not time for a new initiation, advancement, adventure. Do not stagnate in the pond of the present, the waters of true life are leaping, bubbling, cavorting like jewels for the taking.

"Advance with smiling trust for I have given these words that you might astound yourself. YOU, my Child, are all to Me as I am all to you. Is it not by now time that we walk hand in hand into the lifting mist? I love you when it seems no other does.

Remember".

BOOK 6

"ROY" – THE PROPHETIC CONTROVERSY

ANNOUNCEMENT FOR WORLD CITIZENS

MONOLITH

"CHILDREN,

Past civilizations have had their prophets, prophetesses, seers and sincere men and women who were never typed as such, but did My work without notoriety or acceptance. No few were ridiculed and slain as their words did not fit lifestyles over abundant in 'service to self'. Others were not emotionally ready for directions or warnings. Some present religious edifices, churches and varied spiritual offices have sought deeper to understand or partially accept My words into their organization or individual lives. I have much to say and I urge your attention:

Most alert people see a difference in daily news and in Nature's changing ways. There are those among you that believe, without knowing, that I am punishing a wayward culture that has ceased being a civilization and moreover a hazard unto themselves. What is happening is not from Me, your erstwhile God of many names. It is caused simply and regularly from the many cycles of Human negligence and loyalty to themselves and their surroundings. Being typed as your Creator, Source and Great Providence I would ask each of you how you would treat your own Children if they went outside your design for them? Slay them, cast plagues upon them, withdraw your love and attendance from them? Usually not, though you have heartened somewhat to a 'tough love' principle. That principle has never meant, even among the most ferocious of parent mentality, to reek physical harm or death to a child; but mostly to withdraw and allow their self-caused pains to awaken them to treading reflectively, honestly back to childhood memories of peace, plenty and happiness.

Yes, I understand your Biblical, Koran and other Records which word quite heavily on My wrath, vengeance and judgments. It would be difficult for even Me to dissuade you from such beliefs which men placed in books, scrolls and heads - but hearts never. Earthly men print, publish much of what is presumed to be from Me, their indirect form of seeking to help Me run your Universe in tranquility. Let Me give examples from which your seeking, kind hearts rebel:

- Animal sacrifice,
- Human sacrifice
- Slaying, stoning of your children if they follow after a different 'God' or belief,
- Chopping off a hand or limb for a crime,
- Female mutilation of sex organs
- Beheading
- An endless, never ending afterlife in a Hell of punishment for a wrong choice in ignorance or from following a wrong teacher, a sin or rebellion against a 'God'…

A God they refused to believe existed. Or disbelief in one that would heap such judgments upon them. Upon undeveloped Souls?

Are parents and true Gods that different you ask. Listen: "As above, so below, as below, so above." Does this ring true in your heart? Commonsense rationale? Think upon it long."

"How many of you reading this 'have it made' in understanding Me, yourselves - or your partner in either marriage or agreement? And your child, how long does it take for Understanding and Good Will to develop therein?"

Do I hear from some, 'My Son and Daughter went to their graves as irrational robots of a society gone mad; while my words and love, even 'tough love' did no good. Why….?'

"For such reasons have I today, right now in this message, to you men and women, citizens of the world, opened my Heart, using a common man who is uncommonly aware and. compassionate, finally wise - to My concepts, premises and desires for a very disturbed people and wrecked planet. Will you listen as he gives in your 'street language' My intentions and answers? With his words will also be given his history and present day mission for all of you to puzzle over. Is it true, valid prophecy about a man - foretold?

Let me know what your prayers find out or what your dogmas reject. It is 'serious stuff as Roy often has said.

Thank you, Children. Your Father"

Next from ROY:

"Our movies did a good job presenting the series with George Burns called OH, GOD! Some staid, over religious churches rejected going to see it, really believing that God is Father's name – and not just a title like Mr. - that it was "a blasphemy!", "God doesn't talk like that!", "God wouldn't come down and dress like that!", and - "He certainly would not give such advice!" Let me tell you of my experience with God. Here's what He-She is really like. (I'll explain He-She a bit later. You deserve a weighty answer but one you will see quite easily.)

1. He's like a sharp Employer.: Do a good job, get to work on time, be nice to the others around you, treat the customers like you would like to be treated. When you go to Him asking for a raise and you're refused and He tells you how you have been idling at the water fountain, in the rest room or taking an hour and a half instead of one – well you are then faced with why no pay increase or Christmas Bonus. Right? Like that. So you get a bit more careful how you cheat, more aware of others, you understand your Boss. One day you open the payroll envelope - Gee Whiz! a big raise. See? Simple logic to compare Him to. Now about your prayers – A certain large church has

prayer cabinets where you can repent. A black frocked, hiding man forgives you, a little repentance money called Purgatory or Indulgences changes hands during the month or business cycle and you are OK. You 'sin' again and same, old same old - over and over as long as the Fed has paper money and you spend it. Repetition repentance based on funny money and not on your overcoming. That God, or your true Father is NOT some politician accepting bribes. He wants sincerity, honesty and a change in your way of life. So whole nations pray and pray and pray, individuals pray and pray and pray and nothing happens. Mr. Einstein said, "Nothing happens until something moves." Not too deep even for him – means this: 'You want something, DO something, act, change, decide, put some effort into your I Wants, I Needs' Don't try to fool Father, He is very sharp, profoundly aware of where you are coming from. When ready, you get help by the bucketfuls! Honest.

2. Father-Mother? Everything is positive and negative in creation - one or the other: Some creatures, some humans are both in one body! Man and Woman like Night, Day, The Batteries in your Flashlight. It took a positive and a negative polarity to make a baby and you. Nothing in the great Omniverse escapes a positive and negative Field because Father has two separate parts of His being. If I told you He has a mate, wife you'd laugh till you dropped or stop reading right now. Yet you tell each other He had a Son and you keep saying "Sons of God". Do you listen to your own evidences of His uniqueness? ONLY by His actual dual, yes, intricate, awesome sexness could He have made a Son and us. That took wanting people to love and it took a female to create all of what we call Humanity and E.T.s, Angels and whatever He-She is still up to despite our unknowing of all that they are. When you read the word Dual I DON'T mean He created a Devil, Satan or Evil...although Created Man, Angels and Et's, decided what they would be and do. Choice. Father

let them choose. His best gift. So came wickedness and devilish ways. You decide don't you?

3. Father chose me because after all my wrong ways I got smart and chose Him. I didn't want to hurt, fail or hurt others anymore. I changed so much He must have seen some potential in my staying constant, consistent. Now I have His gifts and I know what He wants, what's coming and what we all have to do to escape being ONE OF THE 90% THAT'S PREDICTED TO GO DOWN THE TUBE IN DISASTER AFTER DISASTER ...UNLESS... But that doesn't have to happen.

4. The prophecies about me didn't say I was always Mr. Goody Good Shoes. But He stepped in when I got serious. Each lifetime I got better. Yes, Reimbodiment like Elijah being John the Baptist in the past, like King David being foretold to be alive - here today: "I will raise up My son, Prince David in the Last Days and he will be a Provider for My people." Check Ezekiel in your Bible Concordance. And what of Jesus (Yahoshua-Apollonius?) saying, "Before Abraham I was." and how about Paul (Pol-Apollonius?) saying, "Learned HE (Jesus) obedience by the things He suffered." But weren't we taught He was born perfect without sin? Yep, we were, but not so. When was He Disobedient? And there's "Jesus, the first Man earthly Adam and Jesus the last Man spiritual Adam." Paul (Pol?) said that! A more true translation than the King James which hid a lot so you depended on conventional simplicities like: "It is appointed unto Man once to die." That's true and after that to come back and improve, to get it straight. One life at a time. See?

5. OK, the rest of His story, mine too, in helping Him and you – follows. If reading it bothers your conventional teaching and translations and leaders that will be normal - for in all ages, dispensations have come and gone with new men and women and their efforts to get us on the ball - to know Father and to trust Him by going DIRECT instead of to men and what they believe and require (or demand unto death). IT HAS TO BE

DIRECT between you and Him and that makes it necessary for you to sidestep men like me, eventually getting His Voice in your Heart and Soul direct - depending on no one but HIM for the Truth - Especially me...I try to do His best but you know how many times you have missed. Same here. Lean on no man or woman! Just Father-Mother. OK?

6. So HERE'S what happened to one man that tried his dangdest. See what you think...and if it grabs you as it jarred me GET IN TOUCH. We have a lot of work to do before..... Thanks, "ROY"

THE ANCIENT PROPHECIES UNFOLD:

They are deep, profound, historic, accurate and will not be fully completed till AFTER our planet's Housecleaning. Few people at present will believe them, hard hearts will fight them.

Mother Earth's reactions will do the convincing – Men will finally heed and improve all.

SPECIAL REPORT PRESENTED BY THE NEW AMERICAN PIONEERS PARTY (N.A.P.P.)

Will discerning, alert and brutally shocked Americans insist on this man ("ROY") as President of The United States after further horrific destructions destroy much of America and many other nations are no more?

Has the intriguing power of God's ancient Prophets foretold his name for today's office?

Have various historically founded Prophets from Ireland, Scotland, Great Britain and famous Nostradamus; given amazing details about this man?

We, a small piece of America have to ask you this: Does America have another Washington, Jefferson, Gandhi and Paine rolled into one to free our nation and citizens from their problems?

Can this be possible? We believe it. This is our stand as Democrats, Republicans and others whirl in confusion seeking "THE Man instead of a man that our Great Providence leads...

ARE YOU SERIOUS ENOUGH, SUFFERING ENOUGH, 'FED UP' ENOUGH TO READ FURTHER - TO FAST AND PRAY

AS SOME ARE, FOR PROOF OF ONE OF THE STRANGEST EVENTS OF ALL TIME?

May The Almighty guide your discernment and decisions in these troubled times...

FIRST: A FEW DETAILS ABOUT THIS MAN "ROY" – THEN THE PROPHECIES IN DETAIL.

- 6'1" 200 pounds, Piscean March 4, 1928
- Former amateur and professional athlete
- Hollywood freelance script writer
- Self educated/autodidact
- Student-researcher-lecturer of history, religions and metaphysics
- Excommunicated from Mormon church in 1974 for stating he, "was in communication with our Source and was to set in order The House of God on Earth."
- Exponent of fasting and prayer for Truth – fasted 44 days on Distilled water only - and many other fasts, "for answers".
- Adept at simplified architecture for the present dangerous disasters. Bio- Nutritionist. Survival consultant
- A Rambo Type, ageless, presently looks 40 - in perfect condition

---

HERE ARE THOSE HUNDREDS OF YEARS OLD ANCIENT PROPHECIES. HANG ON!

. NOSTRADAMUS: (Original French)

"le chef de Londres par regne L 'Americh, *
L' Isle d' Ecosee t' empiera par gelee:
Roy Reb auront, un si faux Antechrist,
Qui les mettra trestous dans la meslee."

. ENGLISH: Note that the nation of America did not exist in the year of this prophecy – The year 500! And yet, this Prophet mentions it as, "Americh"! Many translators have overlooked that "Roy Reb translates to "Roy, the Rebel or Roy, the rebellious one." Roy is Latin for "King" also that Roi would be the French spelling for King. Thus Nostradamus gave the name simply as the man would be called today, Roy...

Enigmatic indeed is the fact of his calling this "Roy", "a very false Anti-Christ"! Why? Because we know what a real Anti-Christ is – What then is a very 'false' one; but a man who will be called that, due to his statements. ANTI means 'against the Christ' – Therefore a "very false one" would be 'FOR The Christ' (All Light-Knowledge-Anointed) A dedicated man of God buried in a parable by a cunning Prophet who was appealing to the discernment of Roy's Helpers in these troubled times. Note too, what the following Prophets say to verify this man's integrity, his mission for today:

. THOMAS THE RHYMER 1220-1297 from the original Scottish language:

"A bastard shall come out of the WEST, (America)
Not in Ynglond borne shall he be...
He shall into Ynglond ryde,
And hold a parlament of moche pryde,
That never no such parlament before was syne,
And false lawes he shall leye (put) downe, (Do away with)
That are going in that countree;
And TRUE works he shall begyn,
And alle leder of bretans shall he be...
A bastard in wedlock born
Shall come out of the WEST, (Americh-America)
A chieftane unchosen that shall choose for himself,
And ryde through the realm,
AND **ROY** (he) SHALL BE CALLED...

285

A chieftane STABLE AS A STONE,
STEADFAST AS THE CHRISTULL,
Firme as the adamant, TRUE as STEELE,
IMMACULTE AS THE SUN, without all treason...
He shall be KID CONQUER, (appears unusually ageless - youthful as was David)
For he is KINDE LORD of alle Britaine
That bounds the broad (Atlantic) sea."

ST. BEARCAN Noted Irish Prophet, Year 500:

"Ireland shall remain without order or prosperity
UNTIL she is relieved by Hugh the sincere.
AFTER the man whose cognomen (notoriety-appearance) is Red (Ruadh)
(Ruddy? - Roy is noted for his ruddy, wrinkle free complexion)
A spirit of fire will come from the NORTH,
He'll march toward Dublin;
There will be but ONE LORD over all Ireland.
TWICE THIRTY YEARS will his might last,
~~During that period his POWER shall not decline,~~
It is he that will bring affliction on the foreigners... (Moslems)
By which their SAVAGE HORDES SHALL SUFFER;
Until he sails across the azure sea to Rome.
He will be a great KING,

(Is "Roy", now 'reimbodied' as was Elijah, shown in Malachi - Bible. Is Roy the former spirit-personality of KING DAVID of Israel. See Ezekiel Chapters 37, 38 and 39 in your concordance - telling of God "raising up David in the Last Days as a PROVIDER for God's people.")

Continuing the prophecies above ending with words, 'great KING,'

Renowned for feats of arms..." (David was renowned for his battle prowess)

. FIONN MAC CUMHAIL CECINIT, Irish Prophet gives his vision of this man next in the amazing testament of centuries:

"An important vision has happened to me,
Which has deprived me of both sense and power,
A Tailgin, (unusual person/Irish old world slang), will come hither
ACROSS THE STRONG SEA," (Atlantic from America)

"I do not look upon the event as bad,
Nor shall it be bad for me.
He will BLESS Ireland SEVEN TIMES, (different embodiments-lives down through time. Nothing is impossible for The Almighty Father)
And great dignity shall attend his advent.
They will have churchyards and royal mansions
In great splendor.
His deeds shall be EXCELLENT IN EVERY INSTANCE; IT
Shall be a fortunate occurrence for every person
Who may see him,
For he will lead GREAT NUMBERS of people into THE HOUSE OF GOD. (People will know the real Bible truths hidden by deletions)
There shall be BUILDINGS 'raised' with STONE AND LIME, (Concrete)
They shall be built strongly and substantially; (Dome design, Quake and Fireproof, Floodproof)
Herbs and esculent roots will be planted,
And will vegetate from 'their' roots. (Center garden-lanai)

(Each home and building shall feature this center food and flower garden as the Atmosphere is being cleansed from radiation fallout, volcanic dust and man caused pollutions: See: Bible Malachi Chapter 4: "Then shall you RETURN and REBUILD THE WASTE PLACES",

(Note the rest of this Malachi scripture about "Ashes under your feet" – From a huge returning Planet creating destroying fires and volcanoes... Yellowstone blast is getting ready now))

FIONN'S PROPHECY CONTINUES:

"All lands shall be measured with NICETY,
And heavy rents imposed upon THEM with injustice! (The Criminals in their confined colonies.)
They will cultivate their gardens after the fashion of the Foreigners, (Eastern races)
And they will plant great numbers of trees in them.
The son of the King of Saxon will come over the sea (An American man comes over the Atlantic to Ireland to begin his mission for God's people: full Israel – not Jews nor Zionists as falsely taught)

"I long for his arrival, though not for love of him; (Not related to him but he is joyful over Ireland's deliverance and new prosperity)

The manifest consequence of his coming shall be
~~That the 'strangers' shall be EXPELLED beyond the sea. (Warfare,~~
deportation)
Like the flame of Love and grateful Friendship they Will UNITE,
The Saxons and the Gaels – with pure hearts (Britain- Ireland brothers, will at last unite)
Against the obdurate Strangers. (The massive influx of radical Moslems)
How pleasing it is to me that they will change
Their policy." (No more war between Brothers – Peace at last in Ireland)

JOHANNES: Another Prophet speaks:

"In time there will be a place (time and position) for what once was and ye shall know it's 'buildings' (People, offices, entourage) yet AGAIN as they were wont to be. The lessor works first, (Roy preparing himself in all ways) and then COMETH one ("ROY") who will BUILD THE GREAT CHURCH - a son of Glaston (Glastonbury) FROM BEYOND THE SEA (There's that westerner - an American of Irish descent crossing over the Atlantic, that "strong sea", mentioned by different Prophets at different time periods - who did not know each other!) Even now he WAITS, (Roy not there yet in Johannes time). And WATCHES, (From where?) We wait and watch and hope with the knowledge that comes to men on the 'other side. (Inner Earth, Shamballa) The church is always the church and in the great schema of the world we come (Again) soon and our instrument, "Glaston" (Code name for spiritual person) shall find a Mighty Place... Thus Johannes saith.:

DESPITE ALL OF THESE HEAVENLY TESTIMONIES SOME MEN SHALL DOUBT AND SEEK TO PERSECUTE AND RIDICULE TO THEIR OWN DESTRUCTION - IN THE FIRES OF THEIR SHOCKED SOULS. May they instead, Church Authorities, Government Officials, Scholars and Historians humble themselves in prayer and fasting, repenting of foolish reason and come to the Father's, Light and Grace.

ROY'S WORDS TO THE NATIONS FOLLOW:

"All men shall have equal right to worship and live free of persecution and oppression, free of Hunger, Disease and Want, applying for but eventually earning all they receive, paying for - according to talent or efforts. Having land and a home which neighbors cooperatively help him build; which does not have to be jeopardized by credit and debt corruptions. A people shall have the benefits of the Republic, Honest, Caring Capitalism and 'Social System Benefits' but it shall be offered by commonsense precepts, well discussed and voted on - singularly by signature and not by machine The good of all systems and parties, of all God has given to mankind, shall be the rule and not the exception. Each of Ten Families shall have a Spokesman rotated regularly and will have voice in all our Beloved Constitutional Government actions! We shall become isolationist but good trading neighbors, not meddling in other nation's problems but only giving freely what we have in surplus and wisdom. This Father has taught me is our work, our delightful, productive; happily fulfilled future for ages to come."

"This truly Good News of the renewal and re-building of America - that much wondered of near perfect Government of God and Man, truly servant to the citizens awaits all of us. It is to function freely, overseen stringently, constantly improved in frugality, upgraded infrastructures, all opulent beautification needs, the nations Natural Resources worked and shared by a stress free, fear free people — all of this given to us in His Love, Mercy and great Patience. Blessings and Thanksgiving be remembered to Him. Peace and Understanding be ours always. Roy."

---

*PLEASE CONTACT ROY AT HIS E MAIL ADDRESS IN AMERICA:

Rwoodward28@gmail.com OR:

ROY-DAVID WOODWARD, - Box 36, Baker, Nevada 89311

Thank you. Ask for your Newsletter to keep in touch: $5.00 M. O.

SEND YOUR COMMENTS, SUGGESTIONS
OR CRITICAL ANALYSIS
- We help war widows, veterans, homeless — inventors -

BIOGRAPHY

 Roy-David Woodward, former freelance Hollywood writer has a varied life as amateur-professional athlete, researcher of history-religions, physical therapist. He self-experimented on lengthy fasting and prayer (forty-four days on water only) to heal his cancer, broken back, arthritis which led to astonishing spiritual wisdom and gifts of healing. He uses bio-nutrition and physical therapy to create self help needs for needy. He makes no charges for his services.

In his youth he was Mr. Utah, Mr. Rocky Mountain States, Strongest Athlete in Rocky Mountain States and top contender for Mr. America. Roy has a number of national, world records in endurance and strength. He is self educated (autodidact) as were famous men of history.

At present he is editing former Hollywood scripts, one American Safari, which Cecil B. De Mille approved - calling it "An epic greater than my Ten Commandments.." Cecil died six months later as it was in production stages.Roy is eighty-six, exceptionally fit, active in sports, kenpo karate, running and bodybuilding. He is a widower, resides in Nevada where he is building a large solar greenhouse as a memorial for world veterans of all wars.

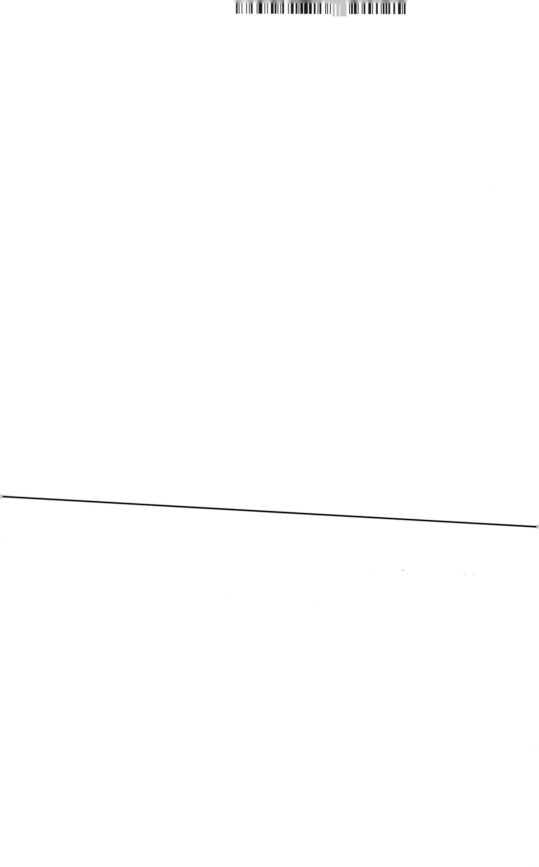